P9-AQC-718

By Loren D. Estleman from Tom Doherty Associates

City of Widows
The High Rocks
Billy Gashade
Stamping Ground
Aces & Eights
Journey of the Dead
Jitterbug
The Rocky Mountain Moving Picture Association
Thunder City
White Desert

The Rocky Mountain Moving Picture Association

LOREN D. ESTLEMAN

A TOM DOHERTY ASSOCIATES BOOK
NEW YORK

This is a work of fiction. All the characters and events portrayed in this book are either products of the author's imagination or are used fictitiously.

ROCKY MOUNTAIN MOVING PICTURE ASSOCIATION

A Forge Book
Published by Tom Doherty Associates, LLC
175 Fifth Avenue
New York, NY 10010

www.tor.com

Forge® is a registered trademark of Tom Doherty Associates, LLC.

ISBN 0-812-54154-5
Library of Congress Catalog Card Number: 98-47238

First edition: April 1999
First mass market edition: July 2000

Printed in the United States of America

0 9 8 7 6 5 4 3 2 1

For Betty and Dean Morgan

Acknowledgment

I owe thanks to my wife, author Deborah Morgan, for many things, the most recent of which is the title of this book.

1926

A Death in Season

Buck would have loved it: the throngs in fedoras, straw boaters, and cloches compressed into squares by Jimmy Walker's Finest, the best cops money could buy, in their shining rubber ponchos and cap shields; the ropes and barricades erected to funnel the mourners from four abreast to two, forming a line eleven blocks long; the rain sizzling off the awning of Frank E. Campbell's Funeral Chapel and making the sea of black umbrellas glisten. That last was a bit of cooperation from the weather Buck had never managed to achieve, which was why he refused to make up a shooting schedule, preferring to hold off the cemetery procession until the rain decided to fall. Plugging in the desert chase when the sun insisted on shining. Buck, who never believed in chance good fortune, would have scanned the rooftops looking for men with hoses. Airborne cloud seeders weren't out of the question, provided Adolph Zukor agreed to a quid pro quo with George M. Cohan in return for permission to rain on Broadway. No one understood the territorial imperative better than an old pirate.

He shook his head, missing Buck, and handed five dollars to a fellow who had stood in line two hours for the express purpose of selling his position. He was in no great personal hurry, but the price would only go up, and he'd heard a rumor that Harry Klemfuss would soon seal the casket to prevent the taking of souvenirs. It was the kind of rumor that could spark another riot—the mounted patrolmen were already in place, prepared to charge—and in any case he hadn't come all this way and stood in the rain all this time to look at a silver-bronze box.

Klemfuss didn't care who took souvenirs. Another riot would actually help ensure the box office for the two unreleased films in the can. Hell, Hollywood would say, Harry will do anything to get you ink, even after you're dead. Buck and Klemfuss would have gotten along. Until their interests conflicted.

The crowd was orderly. Not like earlier in the day, when gangs of young women armed with umbrellas had laid siege to the entrance and had to be beaten back with billy clubs. Many wore black veils and armbands, although here and there he spotted a fancy boy in droopy balloon pants and a sodden bolero vest; even at the height of the "pink powder-puff" controversy the press had ignored the man's vast homosexual following. The woman to his right, a plump chatterbox clutching a framed studio print to her breasts, said she had seen *A Sainted Devil* seventeen times. Her makeup was streaming, but he suspected it was more from the rain than from tears. She was as animated as if she were on her way to a personal appearance.

Inside the entrance he stood aside to let the woman start up the stairs ahead of him. The deep red runner was striped down the center with brown mud tracked in from the street. From here on it was step up, wait, step up, wait. The wait was seldom longer than a second. He'd heard that a woman who had fainted from anxiety and the August heat had been allowed a three-second visitation to compensate her for her ordeal.

He was on the landing now, close enough to see through the open door into the small room where the body lay in state, where it had been moved from the larger and more prestigious Gold Room after the ornaments and fixtures had been sacked by rioters. He saw the tall candles, the marble statuary, the wall of ferns behind the bier. He couldn't see the casket or its occupant for the Hollywood *fascisti* surrounding it. Another Klemfuss coup, although Mussolini had sent a cable denying ownership of these particular Black Shirts, or of an ostentatious wreath bearing the legend FROM BENITO.

Hellinger and Winchell were back in their offices banging black-box Remingtons to commemorate the spectacle, and of course Jimmy, the Night Mayor of New York, had had words to say. Grogin of the *Evening Graphic* had faked up a cadaver shot before the genuine corpse had even arrived at the parlor and composited a cordial meeting with Caruso in the Afterlife. No confirmation yet that Capone men would board the funeral train in Chicago to accompany the body across the continent with tommy guns in their laps; that one had Runyon all over it.

Anyway, it was a woman's event. Pola Negri, they said, had paid her respects in three-thousand-dollar widow's weeds, with the help of an army airmail plane to whisk her there from the West Coast. Ziegfeld beauty Marion Kay Brenda, a floradora in search of a surname, had taken umbrage, claiming that she, not

the Polish actress, had been the deceased's future intended: Mary Pickford was expected to show up at
the services later at St. Malachy's. No suicides there,
that was reserved for those who didn't know him. In
London an Apache dancer had poisoned herself. In
New York a housewife had swallowed iodine and shot
herself twice, sprawling poetically on a pile of eight-
by-ten glossies. In Santa Monica a woman had put
on her wedding dress and walked into the ocean; but
that was California. He wondered if any of them
thought they had a better chance of meeting the object of their passion in a crowded heaven than they'd
had on earth.

He was in the room now. The air smelled woozily
of flowers—thousands of flowers, sent from as far
away as Bolshevik Russia, bouquets and baskets and
pots and gondolas of roses, carnations, hibiscus, peonies, buttercups, tulips, lady's slippers, lilies, poppies,
geraniums, chrysanthemums, primrose, orchids, bluebells, African violets—all the obnoxious and dazzling
bounty of a death in season. The room had not been
sufficient to contain them and they had been spread
out throughout both floors. Farther in, in the aftermath of olfactory overload, he noticed the more prosaic odors of melted wax, rubber galoshes, and wet
wool. These smells reminded him of a field trip to a
museum.

He took his turn at the bookstand, where he was
forced to wait while yet another guestbook was borne
away, heavy with the weight of its signatures, and its
replacement brought. The spine cracked when it was
opened by a young attendant in a black cutaway and
white cotton gloves. He accepted the feather quill and
without thinking signed a name he hadn't used in ten
years. He'd been ruminating too deeply on the past.

He made no attempt to correct the mistake, but surrendered the quill and shuffled forward with the line, his hat now in his hand. Now he heard sobbing (genuine, probably, Klemfuss's hired female mourners having wept their bit shortly after the doors opened), a whispered snatch of the Twenty-third Psalm, the toneless chant of the Black Shirts' selected spokesman to "Keep it moving, keep it moving." And now he was at the opening in the ropes, and now he was there before the casket.

They had him propped against a white satin pillow in a black tuxedo with extravagant lapels and a silk bow tie, under a dome of shatterproof glass; so much for souvenir hunting. They'd wound a rosary around his folded hands, the white fingers with their waxy nails, and turned his head three-quarters so he could share a slight conspiratorial smile with his visitors, amused by the ludicrous turnout, far better than any of his premieres. Especially the most recent.

Peritonitis. It seemed a drastic thing to have to do to win back one's audience. Jerry Jarette would have found a way to fake it.

He looked down at the marble-white features, the obvious paint. Where was the powder puff now? There was the lacquered black hair, no gray in it or dye, as why should there be at thirty-one, showing the marks of the comblike grooves in a new record. There were the razored sideburns, the dimpled upper lip and long swooping lashes. It couldn't be real. He looked too much like his movies.

And then his second was over. He turned away, descended a homely set of stairs with a rubber runner, and passed out through a side door where he suspected the corpses entered, wrapped in rubber sheets and without music; out into the snotlike rain, among the klaxons and electric signs and the stink of horseshit, the last so reminiscent of a Rocky shoot. Putting on his hat thinking, Rodolpho Alfonzo Raffaele Pierre Philibert Guglielmi Valentina d'Antonguolla, Great Lover, Mighty Sheik, O Immortal Valentino, in what unlabeled pauper's ditch would you be lying had not Arthur Bensinger, Jr., tripped over a bucket of washers in the Bensinger & Rausch Hardware and Electrical Supply of Union City in 1909?

1913

———

Chapter 1

———

The name came to him the way everything did that he trusted, when he was reading Jack London.

He had just opened the semimonthly magazine of *The San Francisco Call*, the December 1, 1912, number containing the story "The Captain of the Susan Drew." The provocative pen-and-ink illustration, and the electrifying byline, warmed him in a way the wood-burning stove at his elbow could not. But the lead paragraph might have been written in Balinese for all he comprehended it.

Suddenly he put aside the magazine, touched the blunt point of the whittled yellow pencil to his tongue, and wrote the name on the sheet of coarse paper he'd been using for his figures. He looked at it, holding the sheet out at arm's length, the way his father tried to read things when he'd misplaced his glasses, then put it down and copied out the legend again and again, now printing, now in cursive, upper case, lower case, upper and lower; stacking it down the sheet like a bride-to-be trying out her new name.

He had to see it in type. He reached across the

rickety worktable, slid over the Blickensderfer No. 7 on its wooden pallet—good, loyal Blick, fellow veteran of a hundred thousand unpublished words—rolled another sheet into the platen and pecked out the letters.

"Who's Tom Boston?"

He jumped. He'd been so engrossed he hadn't heard the door opening behind him or even felt the rush of razor-cold air that came in with Yuri. The big half Tartar was wearing his bearskin coat and hat, and at a glance he appeared to be covered with coarse hair from his head to the tops of his lace-up boots. Only his Rasputin eyes and wind-chapped condor's beak of a nose showed between the long whiskers and thatched brows. His moist breath had frozen the hairs about his mouth into stalactites. He was staring at the sheet in the machine.

"I am," said the young man, calmed now by the Ukrainian's presence, which was like a huge enveloping muffler. "If it works. Does it work?"

"What's wrong with the name your father gave you?"

"Nothing, except that I was ten years old before I could spell it. Would you buy a story from someone named Dmitri Andreivitch Pulski?"

"Why should I buy one? You read them to me all the time for free."

"I mean if you were an editor. Jack London got a hundred and sixty rejections before he made his first sale. That's twelve less than me. I'm just as good a writer as he was when he started. It must be the name."

"Why Tom Boston?"

"It just came to me. Forget you've known me as Dmitri all my life. How does it sound?"

"I guess it's okay. I don't read anything but signs. If I was to start, it wouldn't be because of a name."

"Not everyone's like you." He looked at the sheet. "Tom Boston." It was the first time he'd said it aloud. He tore out the sheet, folded it, and put it in the breast pocket of his heavy woolen shirt. It would be a valuable artifact. Then he lifted the typewriter's cover from the plank floor and snapped and latched it into place. The curved wooden case looked like it belonged to a sewing machine. "Anything wrong?"

"I just came in to tell you we're ready to start cutting."

"I'll be out in a minute."

When Yuri left, the young man put on his mackinaw and fleece-lined cap, buckling the strap under his chin so his ears would stay covered, and found his mittens. He gave himself the indulgence of an affectionate look around before he turned out the lantern. The six-by-eight shack, built of corrugated iron with a tar paper lining, was the only private place he knew. Although it was intended for the workers to escape the weather and warm up over coffee, they seldom entered it when he was inside. Everyone who worked for the Sierra Nevada Ice Company knew that the owner's son was going to be a great writer like Pushkin, and that writers required privacy the way ice cutters needed strong backs and vodka. Guilt for his selfish acceptance of this favor kept him from personalizing the shack beyond the occasional copy of *Century* and *The Overland Monthly* and a picture of Jack London using a boulder for a desk, clipped from *Cosmopolitan* and tacked to the wall above the work table. He did most of his writing and reading there and stuffed his manuscripts into brown ten-by-twelve envelopes for mailing. He thought of the place as his study, but never referred to it as anything but the shack.

He remembered to smear lampblack under his eyes before stepping outside, and he was glad he had. Although Yuri and his crew had thoroughly planed the snow from the lake's surface, the ice beneath remained white enough to dazzle in the bright sun, and if one failed to take precautions against the glare, to blind. To the east, Mount Shasta below its frozen peak was the precise deep blue of the sky, and might have broken away from it in a jagged shard, as if the sky were a pane of glass and something had struck it from the other side.

As he watched, a wind fourteen thousand feet up skinned a slice of dry snow from the peak and scrolled it outward like smoke. The curl would measure a mile. It confounded all his senses to think that that distant puff was a dozen times more powerful than the gust that now came at him from the opposite direction, pushing a solid volume of air that boxed his ears and shook the side of the shack, making tinny thunder. He turned his back to keep the ice crystals from cutting his face. It was just the kind of scene he'd labored hours over the Blick trying to get right and hadn't yet, not to his own satisfaction. But he would.

Once the lake was cleared of snow, activity had continued with all haste before it drifted back. The ice plow, built heavily of elm and cast iron, required a six-horse team to pull it. The driver, an elderly Cossack named Esaul, labored to haul himself into the iron seat and groped for the lines, at which point the years fell away like the halves of a dried pod. With a series of barks and whistles through his remaining teeth, he coaxed the brutes forward, cutting twin furrows as straight as piano wire from east to west. At the end he turned the team and repeated the procedure from west to east, and when the entire lake had been scored in this way he drove to the north shore and began cutting from north to south, carving the surface neatly into three-foot squares. Then the sawyers moved in.

This was where Dmitri took his turn. As the son of the owner, he was there to oversee the operation, but as he began to spend more and more time while on site in the shack, reading and typing, Yuri had assumed most of his responsibilities as foreman. The young man insisted on carrying his weight, however, and had surprised and impressed the others by selecting the most arduous of all the chores involved in harvesting ice.

The work commenced with chipping a hole in one corner of the first square with a pick or chisel. When an opening had been created that was large enough to insert the end of a long, square-toothed sawblade, the cutting began in earnest, each man sawing along the lines scored by the plow. Showers of ice shavings like sawdust stung faces and made eyes water. Once a brisk rhythm was established, the friction did much of the work, slicing through the ice like a heated knife through lard; but on bitter days when temperatures neared zero, as they did today, merely pausing for breath allowed the ice to refreeze around the blade, locking it in place. A series of huffing, two-handed lunges was then required to break it free. Very soon Dmitri was sweating in spite of the cold. He paused after cutting his third block to strip off his coat and mittens.

At the end of a section, he and the others traded saws for crowbars and cant dogs, prying loose the section and heaving it aside with the hooks, hinged like

the jaws of a mastiff, to form a canal of open black
water. Men then moved in with poles and pushed the
floating cakes along the canal or heaved them up onto
the uncut ice and slued them to shore, where the rest
of the crew waited with cant dogs to hoist them onto
chain-driven belts operated by hand cranks. The
cranks were seized and turned. The chains clankety-
clanked, caught up the slack, and carried the great
silver-blue blocks up to the icehouse on the hill, where
they plunged through a loftlike opening onto a plank
floor covered with sawdust. As architecture, the stor-
age building was considerably more substantial than
the shack, which had been thrown together as an af-
terthought with sheets of corrugated roofing left over
from the larger construction. It was as big as a ware-
house, with triple walls built of native pine, the spaces
between packed tightly with sawdust and wood shavings as insulation against the heat of summer, when
the lake was open blue water and even the white cap
of Shasta had dwindled to half its present size. By then
the great stack of ice would be nearly as valuable as
bullion.

The harvest complete, Dmitri climbed the slope to
the shack, foundering a little in the deep drifts, as
much from exhaustion as from the awkwardness of
the footing. He carried his coat slung over one shoulder with the mittens in the pockets. His own sweat
had begun to chill him beneath the flannel lining of
his shirt; he hoped the ashes in the stove were still hot.
He didn't look forward to starting a new fire from
scratch, shivering in the dank interior cold.

A puff of warm air surprised him when he opened
the door. Then he realized the lantern was lit. His
father was seated at the worktable, holding the sheet
Dmitri had been scribbling on earlier.

"Who's Tom Boston?"

Andrei Ivanovitch Pulski was a compact man, small for a Russian, who looked more like a St. Petersburg haberdasher than a man who had spent most of his life laboring with his hands. He wore suits everywhere, even up here, where he had on heavy tweeds with the trousers neatly tucked into the tops of knee-high stove-pipes. His overcoat with its astrakhan collar and cuffs hung over the back of the chair. He brushed his thick brown hair straight back and had his goatee trimmed by a barber twice a week.

Dmitri hung up his mackinaw and cap and went over to warm himself by the stove. The woodbox was nearly empty. All those years of cutting and carrying ice had left the elder Pulski with a chronic chill that even in summer forced him to lay a fire and spread a blanket over his knees when he studied the company ledgers in the evening. Dmitri had never seen him read a book or give more than passing attention to a newspaper.

"Just a character." He didn't want to get into it just then. "I didn't see the Ford."

"Your Uncle Paul dropped me off. He's in town picking up the mail. Is this what you do when I send you up here to work?" He brushed the sheet with his fingertips.

"I just finished cutting a ton of ice."

"That's not your job."

"I'm better at it than I am at giving orders. Half these men watched me grow up. They've seen me in knickers."

"Then there shouldn't be any confusion about whose son you are."

He made no answer. His father was slow to anger, but once he began there was nothing to do but wait until his passion had run its course. Andrei's own grandfather had cut ice in Alaska to fill the demand created by the Gold Rush, then when the demand subsided had come to California to hunt sea otters for the Russian-American Company. When the otters played out, San Francisco was still in need of ice, and so Andrei's father and a partner had formed the Sierra Nevada Ice Company to harvest the northern lakes. He was the grandson of a mountain man and trapper, the descendant of an officer in the czar's army, and stubborn traces of the career soldier and hearty pioneer remained beneath the executive exterior, like the tough sierra grass under two feet of snow. He had spent his youth working side by side with his own father's employees until the business was sound; now he took it as a personal affront that his son should do the same, as if the years of toil had made no progress. Dmitri couldn't tell if his father was more upset by that or by his own ambition to be a writer instead of an iceman.

Andrei surprised him, for the second time that day, by letting the matter drop along with the scratch sheet. "How much ice do we have in inventory?"

The young man hesitated. "About eight tons, including today's."

"I've received an order for all we have."

"Who from, the City of San Francisco?"

"Some company in Los Angeles." He pronounced it with a hard *G*, as did everyone Dmitri knew. Only the occasional Mexican who came up to work with them for a winter softened the consonant. As he said it, Andrei drew a folded sheet of paper from an inside breast pocket, snapped it open, and hooked on his gold-rimmed spectacles to look at it. "The Rocky

Mountain Moving Picture Association. Have you heard of it?"

He said he hadn't. Moving pictures. He'd seen two or three flicker shows at the end of the vaudeville bill at the opera house in San Francisco—crude, jerky images of firefighters in action and young women undressing—but it had never occurred to him that anyone made a living making and showing the things.

"We don't sell that much by August," Dmitri said. "It's only January."

"See for yourself."

Dmitri accepted the sheet and turned it toward the lantern. The name his father had read was professionally printed across the top, along with an address on Yucca Avenue.

Dear Sir:

An exhaustive survey conducted among suppliers of ice throughout the Pacific Northwest has led us to the conclusion that the Sierra Nevada Ice Company offers the highest quality product at the most reasonable rates.

Kindly accept our order for ten tons of quality ice, or if you have not that much on hand, as much ice of the highest grade as you can supply us at this time, provided the amount is not less than six tons. Delivery to be arranged pending your positive response on or before 15 January 1913.

> Yours very sincerely,
> Arthur Bensinger, Jr.
> President

"I didn't know there were different qualities of ice." Dmitri gave back the letter.

"There are two: thin and thick." His father glanced again at the typewritten words, then laid down the sheet and returned his glasses to his pocket. "I think we ought to check out this Rocky Mountain company. No one I've asked has heard of it or Arthur Bensinger."

"It's good stationery."

"Anyone can manage that. It doesn't mean they can pay for eight tons of ice."

"What do you suppose they plan to do with it?"

"That's one of the things I want you to find out."

"Me?"

"I want you to drive down and take a look at their operation and report back to me. I'll lend you the Ford. Don't wreck it. I'd send you on the train, but how would you get around once you got there? Los Angeles is a desert town, strung out across ten miles of dust."

"Why me?"

"I can't spare the time, especially if it turns out to be a wild goose chase. Sooner or later every crook and four-flusher in the country winds up in southern California. Moving pictures." He stood and put on his coat. "Learning how to separate the charlatans from the solid customers will help you run this business. I have nothing against your wanting to write, Dmitri. But when times get hard, entertainment is the first thing people find they can live without. Meanwhile they'll always need ice."

Chapter 2

Dmitri left his father supervising the stacking of the blocks in the icehouse and rode back to Ingot in the back of the delivery wagon. He'd brought his typewriter and dilapidated briefcase containing the manuscripts of some stories he was working on; he'd been told to pack his things and leave straight from the house in the morning. Yuri, the big Ukrainian, rode beside him with his long legs dangling over the open tailgate, smoking his short blob of charred pipe. He was the only employee under the age of fifty who had not been born in California as a descendant of the founders of the original Russian colony. The rumor persisted that he had caved in a hetman's skull with a bung starter during an argument in a tavern in Vladivostok when he was seventeen and fled by way of Siberia to escape the wrath of the man's Cossack friends. Dmitri thought him capable of the act but not the argument. He considered Yuri a big powerful dog that didn't need to be belligerent in order to get its point across.

They were nearly in town before he took his pipe

out of his mouth to speak. "I hear you're going down to Los Angeles."

"You must have heard it from my father. I haven't told anyone."

"They say you can see whales from the beach."

"I wouldn't know."

"I've never seen whales. Sea lions, yes. Whales, no."

"Did my father tell you to come along and hold my hand?"

"I wouldn't hold a man's hand unless he was going to hit me with it." Yuri had a literal mind. "They say they're like islands that swim."

"I'm twenty years old. I can find the place without a nanny. If I miss it I'll just turn back when I get to Mexico."

"I'd like to see those whales."

"You don't drive, so you can't spell me at the wheel. You don't know how to patch a tire or change the brake bands or stop the radiator from leaking. What good could you do me if I brought you along?"

"I've got a tent."

All his life Dmitri had heard that the steppe dwellers could read men's minds. He'd been wondering where he would stay nights. It was a three-day drive down the coast, longer if one figured in the inevitable puncture and breakdown—hotels, he had heard, were inconveniently located and much too expensive; the three hundred dollars his father had proposed to advance him had to be made to cover his expenses while in Los Angeles as well as those incurred during the journey south. The prospect of camping out along the way nearly eliminated the latter. On the other hand, the cost of supporting two men far from home was exactly twice that of supporting one. And he had no illusions about the fact that his father had instructed Yuri to go along because he had no faith in his son's ability to carry off the mission on his own.

"What will you live on when we get there?" he asked.

Yuri looked around. Night was falling, the smoke from the chimneys of the houses on the edge of town said that most of Ingot was inside sitting down to supper. He unfastened the top button of his heavy woolen shirt and pulled out the end of a necklace fashioned of gold coins the size of nickels. Dmitri couldn't read the Cyrillic characters stamped on them, but he knew enough about Russian history to recognize the likeness of Czar Alexander II.

"My mother's dowry," he said, slipping the necklace back inside the shirt. "It hung down to her knees when she married my father. There's a coin missing for every slump, and a slump for every war."

"Are you sure you want to spend your mother's dowry on a trip to Los Angeles?"

"It was getting heavy anyway."

Whatever argument Dmitri might have introduced lost its opportunity as they slowed for a hill. With a Tartar's athletic grace the big man sprang off the back of the wagon.

"Where are you going?"

"To dig out the tent. I'll be at your house at dawn." He was already a disembodied voice in the shadows.

The Pulski house was a Queen Anne, the largest in its neighborhood, with gables and turrets sufficient for a structure six times its size. It replaced the saltbox Dmitri's parents had moved into shortly after their wedding, three rooms without electricity or plumbing that Dmitri's mother still spoke of with nostalgia. Andrei had demolished it, hired an architect from San

Francisco, and begun construction on the new place the first year the company showed a profit. Bad weather had prolonged the project an additional six months, and between the extra cost and the Panic of '93, the black figures disappeared from the ledgers and Andrei had been forced to offer a partnership in the company to his brother-in-law Paul in return for funds to avoid bankruptcy. Dmitri's father and uncle barely spoke except to argue about how the firm should be run, and although the fact was never mentioned, it was no secret that Andrei loathed the house and blamed it for the loss of his autonomy.

Dmitri kissed his mother, a tiny woman with black hair and eyes, and went up to pack his things. Her grave expression told him she knew of his father's decision. She had married Andrei by proxy in 1890 and had been his wife two years when she left Siberia and came to America to make his acquaintance. Her father had died in the salt mines for his friendship with a man who had been executed after the assassination of the second Alexander, and her mother had taught her always to be grateful to Andrei for having delivered her from poverty and shame. She was by and large silent.

The door to Dmitri's turret room stood open. This was by his father's decree, that he might summon the other members of the household without having to stir himself from the hearth in the parlor. Because the noise of the Blick disturbed him, and because Dmitri required a sense of isolation to concentrate, he wrote very little at home. Only in the shack could he be prolific.

His suitcase, brown leather with brass corners, still smelled new after two years. It was a graduation present, requested by him, but his youthful plans of world travel after the example of Jack London aboard the *Snark* had been shelved when he went to work at the company full time. On top of socks and underwear he placed a stack of cotton shirts for the gentler climate down south, two pairs of flannel trousers, a wool pullover for the transition, and for entertainment his copy of *Burning Daylight*. After tucking his shaving things into a corner there was just room for the briefcase and a ream of paper. If his idol could produce a thousand words a day even on a round-the-world cruise, he had no excuse not to work, although he hoped it wouldn't come to his having to use a boulder for a desk.

His father was on time for supper, as always. The three ate in silence, conversation having been banished from the table as harmful to digestion. Afterward they sat in the parlor. Dmitri read "The Captain of the Susan Drew" while his mother sewed buttons on shirts and his father went over the ledgers. Not a word was spoken until the eight-day clock on the narrow mantel struck ten. Andrei confirmed the time upon his pocket winder and looked at his son. "Early day tomorrow."

Dmitri nodded and stood.

"I had that Mexican fellow at the garage fill the Ford with water and gasoline, the cans as well. The atlas is on the seat. Keep the ocean on your right below Salinas and you won't get lost. You have the letter with the address." It wasn't a question, but Dmitri affirmed he had Arthur Bensinger's letter. His father produced an envelope from the side pocket of his smoking jacket. "Three hundred should cover any emergency. I expect half of it back. Keep a record, and save receipts. If it's a loss we'll have a hard winter making it up."

He accepted the envelope. He had never held that much cash at one time. The elder Pulski handled all the collections and payments personally. Good nights were said and Dmitri went upstairs.

The prospect of the trip excited him. He had never been that far from home and parents. As a writer, he was troubled by his lack of experience. At his age, Jack London had been an oyster pirate, sailed the northern seas, ridden the rods across the country, and begun preparations to prospect for gold in the Yukon. Dmitri had spent that time cutting ice and reading. The stories he wrote were products of imagination, with liberal borrowings from London, Joseph Conrad, and Rudyard Kipling. They were set in places he had never been and described actions he had never seen. Even his account of the San Francisco earthquake had been inspired by descriptions he had read in the *Call*. He was in school in Ingot, memorizing his times table, when the city shook apart. If there was still adventure to be had in twentieth-century California, he meant to take it in between here and the offices of the Rocky Mountain Moving Picture Association. On that thought he dropped off, dreaming of earthquakes and pirates.

He was up before dawn, but not ahead of his mother, who when he sat down at the dining room table placed before him a plate of eggs and sausages and a mug of scalding coffee. His father appeared, suited and collared for the office, as he was finishing. Dmitri rose to accept his lecture of paternal wisdom. Andrei looked at his watch, returned it to his vest pocket, and said, "I will expect you back on the twelfth. Use the telegraph if you run into trouble."

Dmitri's mother had prepared sandwiches from last night's ham. She presented them to him in a paper sack along with a vacuum bottle filled with milk. He kissed her on the cheek, put on his mackinaw and cap, and carried his suitcase, typewriter, and provisions outside. Yuri was seated on the running board of the black tin-box Model T parked in front of the house. He wore his bearskin. A roll of faded green canvas lay across the rear bumper, secured to it with rope. The Ukrainian's breath smoked in the flinty dawn cold.

No greetings were exchanged. The young man strapped his suitcase to the running board on the driver's side, found a place for the milk and sandwiches in the toolbox mounted behind it, and stood the Blick on the floorboards against the seat. There was an anticlimax to his farewells when the crank failed to turn the motor over and he had to go back inside and heat a teakettle. With steaming water in the radiator, the motor responded reluctantly. Another trip inside and a second dose of hot water were required before it coughed, bucked, and settled into the *pocketa-pocketa* of its delicate idle. The pair climbed in, Dmitri released the brake, engaged the clutch, and the odyssey began—with a thirty-minute interruption two miles south of town while Dmitri pulled the left rear wheel off the rim, patched up a fresh puncture from the vulcanizing kit in the toolbox, pumped up the tire, and bolted the wheel back into place. Yuri lit his pipe and watched.

Past Chico they drove out of the snow, although it could still be seen topping the Coast Range to the west and the Sierras to the east. They shrugged out of their coats.

At noon they were still ten miles north of Yuba

City, an hour behind schedule, but they pulled off the road to refill the tank beneath the seat from the five-gallon can on the running board and to allow the overheated motor to cool. Dmitri and Yuri split up the ham sandwiches and passed the cup from the vacuum bottle back and forth, washing down the salty meat with milk.

"Big state," Yuri said.

"I didn't know the roads would be this bad."

"I was sure we broke an axle on that hole up by Los Molinas."

"When we get back I'm going to write a thank-you letter to Henry Ford."

Dmitri replenished the water in the radiator and they resumed their journey. Outside Sacramento the brakes went out and they rolled to a stop against a tree, bending the front bumper. Dmitri's father, who knew nothing about automobile mechanics and trusted too much to the people who did, had neglected to have the brake bands changed and they had worn clean through. Dmitri crawled underneath, removed the canvas scraps, and put on new bands from the toolbox. They were always wearing out; in the course of a year he had whittled down the time required to change them from two hours to forty-five minutes, purely from practice. Still, the operation put them further behind schedule.

The state capital made Ingot look like the wide spot in the road it was. The residential streets were lined with colonials and Queen Annes, the smallest of them as large as the house Andrei Ivanovitch Pulski had nearly bankrupted himself building. The business district alone was larger than Dmitri's hometown. Model Ts, Oldsmobiles, and one elongated Thomas Flyer were parked on the main street beside brewers' drays and saddle horses. A cardboard sign erected before the entrance to the Sacramento Theater advertised that a moving picture would be shown there that evening, entitled *The Squaw Man*.

They had hoped to make San Jose before nightfall, but as the sun was going down the radiator boiled over and Dmitri sent Yuri into Stockton on foot to refill the water can. By the time he came back, dusk was settling. They pitched the tent on the roadside. The Ukrainian had brought a duffel containing tins of meat and oysters and assorted utensils. They gathered wood, built a small fire, and made oyster stew, which they ate from mismatched bowls with battered spoons.

"Hard to believe we're eating outside with our coats unbuttoned," Dmitri said.

"They're having a January thaw here."

"No, I've heard it's like this all winter."

"Where do they get their ice?"

"From us." He tilted his bowl. "What's Stockton like?"

"I didn't see much of it. I don't think it's as big as Sacramento."

"Nothing's as big as Sacramento, except San Francisco."

Yuri put down his spoon and lifted his bowl to his lips to empty it. "They got those moving pictures. I saw a sign."

"What's this one called?"

"I don't remember."

Dmitri set aside his bowl and rubbed his hands over the fire. "What time is it?"

"I don't have a watch. Early, I guess. Seven maybe."

"I'm not even a little bit sleepy, are you?"

Yuri used his sleeve to wipe oyster stew from his beard. "I can't sleep much more than four hours."

"I wonder what time they start showing those pictures."

"Half-past seven." When Dmitri looked at him: "I remember numbers."

"We can't leave the tent, can we?"

The Ukrainian looked at it. It was patched in several places and spotted with mildew like white buckshot. "Who'd steal it?"

Stockton was bigger than Ingot; but then, considered Dmitri in the light of his newfound worldliness, almost every place was. Beyond that it was a miniature version of Sacramento, right down to the theater, a plain building with a shallow entryway decorated only by an old poster of Anna Held, corseted literally to within an inch of her life. Dmitri handed a quarter to a bald man in handlebars behind a counter and got back two tickets and fifteen cents. He gave the tickets to a stout woman with her hair dyed black and pince-nez glasses on her nose, and she pulled back a curtain so he and Yuri could pass through. Now they were in a narrow auditorium lit by bowl fixtures, with Ionic columns painted on either side of the proscenium. Most of the seats were occupied for the first showing of a feature called *The Musketeers of Pig Alley*.

They passed a projector on a table bolted to the floor. Dmitri had seen one of the contraptions in the San Francisco opera house, but this time he paused to study its two big reels, operated by a hand crank with a wooden handle, and the way the glistening strip of film traveled over rubber pulleys and between plates of glass on its way from one reel to the other, like spring runoff spilling down the uneven surface of

Mount Shasta. The machine was built of pebbled black sheet metal with a cast-iron base and probably weighed fifty pounds.

They found two seats together halfway down the aisle, where they had an unobstructed view of a taut canvas screen erected behind the footlights. An upright piano stood against the wall to the left of the stage with a landscape painted on its front panel. Dmitri, craning his neck to see everything with a writer's eye, watched the stout woman waddle down the aisle and hoist herself onto the stool in front of the piano. She switched on a green-shaded lamp, arranged a sheaf of music on the tiltboard, adjusted her pince-nez, and cracked her knuckles. The sound, like a string of firecrackers going off, sent a chuckle rippling through the audience.

At that moment the bald man came in and took up his station behind the projector. He flipped a switch, releasing a shaft of light from the lens that shot over the heads of the audience and splashed onto the screen. When he stepped over to the wall and pushed the button that extinguished the overhead fixtures, the bright screen dominated the room. Tobacco smoke—for the room reeked of cigars—curled in the powerful beam.

The crank was engaged. As it turned, ratcheting gently, the film whizzed through the projector, then slowed as the first images appeared; fuzzy at first, then coming into sharp focus. Numerals, jerking in and out of center as they counted down from ten to one. There were several blank frames, transparent but for spots and bits of thread crawling through them, then the title card came on.

For the next twenty minutes, Yuri was no longer in Stockton, California, but in the slums of New York

City, trapped with the smooth-faced hero and unbearably pretty heroine between two bands of thugs at war over the profits of vice. Some people—Yuri was one—actually jumped in their seats when gunfire exploded onscreen, punctuated by the stout woman's fingers banging the bass end of the keyboard. During the chase she tickled the high notes, imitating running feet, then switched to a pastorale when the young man put his arms around his big-eyed girlfriend. A triumphant arpeggio accompanied the appearance of THE END. As the lights came on, the audience applauded.

"What did you think?" asked Dmitri when they were back out on the sidewalk.

The Ukrainian rubbed his eyes. "I think you better get the money up front."

Chapter 3

Los Angeles—hard *G*, soft *G*, pronounce it how you would or abbreviate it to the "Ellay" preferred by those who lived nearby—was an enormous letdown.

As far south as San Jose, it had occurred to Dmitri that civilization, in California at least, increased in proportion to the nearness of the equator. Although San Jose was no larger than Stockton, and both were not as large as Sacramento, the presence of light and telephone poles was more obvious in the smaller communities, the roads were in better condition, and the streets filled with motorcars, grumbling and backfiring in an atmosphere of silver-blue exhaust, with here and there the high square profile of an Edison electric ghosting along in eerie silence. Streetcars whizzed along polished iron rails, connected to overhead wires by poles that sprayed blue sparks as they slid their length. The horizontal, mission-style buildings of the Spanish occupation stood in the shadow of newer constructions ten and twelve stories high, with more going up. It all looked very like the new century to a young man whose neighbors lived by kerosene light and the backs of horses.

From Salinas on down everything changed. The valley, deep green and banded with rich black soil where the earth had been freshly turned, grew lettuce in city-size patches of startling chartreuse and rubber in long straight orchards blue-black with shade. Migrant workers bent over rows of sugar beets, and trucks with weathered sideboards and radiator grilles like iron cages grunted along gravel roads bearing the turnip-shaped harvest up to a sprawling refinery on a hill, whose chimneys flew black streamers against the painful blue of the sky.

The coast road was harrowing, a gravel track atop high cliffs overlooking the Pacific, smashing itself against the shore as if infuriated to find a continent in its path. Yuri kept his eye out for whales and twice asked Dmitri to stop when he thought he spotted one, but each time it turned out to be just another sea lion, undulating through the waves and flopping onto a rock to sun itself at low tide. The towns they drove through along this stretch were mere strings of board shacks and fruit and vegetable stands offering the week's bounty of lettuce, artichokes, and garlic. At dusk the orange light of oil lamps glowed greasily in windows, and there were no fueling stations. They were coasting on an empty tank when they stopped in San Luis Obispo, where wooden oil derricks stood against the sky, and filled up. By that time Dmitri had patched two more punctures, mended the radiator hose with a red bandanna, and gotten a shock reattaching a headlight wire. It seemed they'd stopped at every stream and tidepool south of Monterey to refill the radiator. If this was adventure, he would take his little six-by-eight shack on the western slope of Shasta.

Los Angeles was twenty miles in from the coast. Their first glimpse of habitation was a scatter of low buildings of adobe and stucco across a flat patch of desert, with a thread of river running through it like a child's finger track on a dusty sill. A number of church steeples, some of them very old by northern California standards, were the tallest structures in sight, and the tallest had not much height on the palm trees that grew in untidy clumps and obviously wild. On a closer look, as they ticked along through a business section of general and dry goods stores and real estate offices, they became aware of an elaborate street railway system of intersecting tracks and crisscross wires dividing the sky into grids. Boxy red cars shuttled high up into the foothills of the San Gabriels to the north. But as the settlement in that direction appeared to confine itself to small clusters of houses separated like barren seeds cast away by an impatient planter, the system seemed overambitious at best. Most of the real estate agents stood in their open doorways, thumbs hooked inside the armholes of their vests, staring morosely out at the plume of dust trailing behind the Ford.

A sign identified the street they were on as Cahuenga. Spotting a group of men lounging in front of a corner saloon, Dmitri wheeled into the curb and asked one of them where he could find Yucca Avenue.

The man, long-faced with a sandpapery complexion, wore ranch clothes: shapeless hat, tall-crowned and broad-brimmed, faded flannel shirt, striped trousers, and hook-heeled boots. He planted one of them on the running board and shifted a plug of tobacco from one cheek to the other. "What you looking for there?"

"The office of the Rocky Mountain Moving Picture Association."

"You an actor?" The man's faded gray eyes roamed over the dusty automobile.

"No."

"Director?"

Dmitri shook his head. He didn't see any reason to discuss the nature of his business.

"I can ride upside-down and fire a Winchester under the horse's belly at full gallop."

He didn't know how to respond to that.

They had attracted the attention of the rest of the group, which had moved in close. All the men were dressed similarly, although their hats were blocked and pinched in a variety of ways, some quite elaborate for such a homely item of ranch gear. Their faces were brown and sun-cracked. One moved off a little from the others to twirl a stiff rope looped into a circle, then leap nimbly in and out of the loop. Dmitri, who had grown up among laborers, detected the distinctive aroma of sour mash.

"Anybody can do that," one of the others said. "I can roll a horse and not break so much as a rib."

"Whose, yours or the horse's?" came a voice from the crowd. Several men laughed.

Dmitri said, "I just want to find Yucca Avenue."

The first man leaned away from the Ford and spat a brown stream that splattered on the sidewalk. "Just keep headed the way you're headed. It's two blocks up. Make a right to Rocky. Tell 'em what I said? The name's Chickamaw."

"I'll try to work it in." Dmitri thanked him and put the car in gear.

Yuri rested an arm on the back of the seat and watched the crowd receding behind the rear window.

"I never saw so many men dressed for work doing nothing in the middle of the day."

"Maybe it's a local holiday."

"Why would you *want* to roll a horse?"

"I'm still wondering why anybody would want to shoot under one's belly."

The address belonged to a store building with THE ROCKY MOUNTAIN MOVING PICTURE ASSOCIATION lettered in yellow block capitals across the false front. A painted poster standing in a display window showed the head and torso in profile of a man wearing a big hat like those worn by the men on the corner. His elbows were bent to reveal a shiny pistol in each hand. The legend BANDIT CANYON blazed across the bottom in fiery orange.

A bell mounted on a spring clip above the door jangled as the two men stepped over the threshold. The room took up the entire storefront, but the clutter inside made it resemble a cramped and ill-kept junk shop. There were more garish posters, some on the walls, others leaning against them in stacks; eight-by-four-foot rectangles of stretched canvas with doors and windows painted on them—false walls erected in front of real ones—and numerous odd items, including a six-foot section of weathered picket fence and a massive and apparently solid millstone that slid six inches when Yuri bumped against it accidentally; it was made of plaster and hollow. A saddle with a tattered fleece lining lay at a crazy angle inside a baby carriage.

Opposite the door, where a counter belonged, stood a yellow oak desk with a sheet of poster board thumbtacked on the front in place of a modesty panel. Behind it sat a woman reading *The Saturday Evening Post* with George M. Cohan on the cover dressed as

George Washington. She looked up as they approached. She was in her early twenties, with a dusky complexion and a mass of blue-black hair in lacquered waves. She had large eyes with blue-shadowed lids, high cheekbones, a straight nose, and lips painted red. Dmitri's mother had told him often enough to beware of women who made up their faces to fascinate him with the breed. She wore a starched white blouse with puffed sleeves. The top two buttons of the collar were unfastened, exposing the smooth brown line of her throat.

Her eyes moved over them both boldly from top to bottom. She said nothing, waiting.

Dmitri said, "Arthur Bensinger?"

"I'm not him." She pronounced the *h* huskily, like the Mexicans with whom he'd worked. "We can use your friend when we rob the bank. I don't know about you. You're kind of bland-looking. Can you die?"

"What?"

"Everyone thinks it's easy until he tries to do it. There's a lot more to it than just falling down. Raymond Hatton's the best. Did you see *The Squaw Man*?"

"No." He was beginning to understand. "We saw *The Musketeers of Pig Alley* in Stockton."

She was silent long enough to convince him he'd committed a social error. "Griffith. He keeps piping on about going beyond two reels. Buck says no one can sit through a picture show much past thirty minutes without getting a headache."

"Buck?"

"Bensinger. No one in the business calls him Arthur, except De Mille." She looked him over again, curious, then opened a sandalwood box on the desk, took out a foil pouch and a small rectangle of paper, and poured a quantity of tobacco onto the paper from the pouch. She wet one edge of the rectangle with the tip of a pointed pink tongue, rolled it into a tube, twisted the ends, and struck a match on the edge of the desk. Dmitri watched her light the cigarette, mesmerized. He had never seen a woman smoke, much less roll her own. She shook out the match, took an egg of smoke into her mouth, and blew it out her nostrils, watching him back. "Who are you?"

"We represent the Sierra Nevada Ice Company. You ordered ten tons of ice."

She nodded then. "I wrote the letter. We're not ready for it yet. You were supposed to let us know if you could fill the order."

"We didn't bring it with us. We came down to see what you wanted with it."

"Is that usual? I never knew a business to concern itself with what happens to its merchandise once it's paid for."

"Not once it's paid for."

"Ah." She tapped ash into a brass canister that looked like the base of an artillery shell. "I can't show you the books unless Buck says so. He's shooting up on the ranch."

"The ranch?"

"He's leasing a thousand acres outside Santa Monica from Tom Ince for the Fetterman massacre. He wanted to do Custer, but Francis Ford beat him to it last year."

"A thousand acres?"

"Ince has thirteen thousand more. He wants Wild Bill Latimer to play Wyatt Earp. It's a cheap enough trade." She tilted her lacquered head in the direction of the poster in the window. Then she glanced at the clock on the wall behind the desk, a big electric one with a medieval-looking punch mechanism under-neath. "I can take you there if you've got a car."

"I don't want to put you out."

"I'm expected anyway. It will save Buck sending a car." She dropped the cigarette into the canister, still smoking, took a wicker-and-leather purse from the file drawer of the desk, and stood. She was barely five feet tall. A slender hand came out and grasped his firmly. "Adele Varga."

Dmitri made a lightning decision. "Tom Boston. This is Yuri."

She smiled at the Ukrainian. Her teeth were blue-white against her dark skin. "Just Yuri?"

"I don't use the rest much," he said after a moment.

She came around the desk then, fishing a big ring of keys from the purse, and went to the door. She wore a long gray suede skirt split for riding and high-heeled black boots. She opened the door and held it.

Standing on the sidewalk while she locked the door behind them, Dmitri glimpsed the man in the big hat on the poster—Wild Bill Latimer, he now knew—and remembered something. "I'm to tell you a man named Chickamaw can ride upside-down and shoot under a horse's belly."

She laughed throatily. "Who can't? You must have stopped at the Watering Hole. That's where every saddle bum goes who wants to be the next Broncho Billy, or just to cover his poker losses. Buck only goes there when he needs to get up a posse."

The Ford was parked out front. Dmitri opened the front door on the passenger's side and held it while she stepped up on the running board. "Oh, you forgot to punch out."

"I'm still on the clock. In addition to answering the phone and typing letters and balancing the books, I'm the female lead in *Sioux Massacre*." She gathered her skirts and sat down.

Chapter 4

Driving back up the coast road north of Santa Monica, the young man felt the Model T leaning over on its springs and knew Yuri was straining to spot whales from the backseat. He himself pretended to look at scenery while stealing glimpses of Adele Varga's profile against the window on the passenger's side. Her high forehead, long straight nose, and round chin reminded him of the illustrations of Latin beauties that accompanied Richard Harding Davis's memoirs of the war in Cuba in *Scribner's Magazine*. She spent much of the ride with her eyes closed, enjoying the sea air coming between the louvered panes in the windshield and speaking only to give directions. He thought he was more to blame for the lack of conversation than she; his work at the ice company seldom put him in contact with women, and he was at a loss for a subject to introduce that he thought would interest her. She smelled of some kind of exotic blossoms of which his mother would no doubt disapprove.

He was not sure what he thought of this part of California. When he directed his gaze toward the coastal ranges he thought of home, but a slight change of angle gave him a view of a desert. Twenty short minutes on the road took him past verdant valleys, rounded bald hills, and foaming ocean inlets, as if the region itself could not make up its mind whether to charm or to awe or to frighten or to soothe. The soil was black loam; red clay; porous sand. From it grew tall evergreens, exotic palms, flowering bushes, and cactus. A herd of fifteen deer grazed on the far edge of a field, not bothering to raise their heads to look at the gas-burning contrivance rattling by. Turning a corner, he swerved to miss a gaunt coyote; it scampered away fifty feet, then slunk back to its feathered kill as the Model T rolled on. The wild animals he had glimpsed in the Sierras were shy, furtive things, wary of man, while their cousins to the south seemed merely to tolerate him.

It was all very distracting, and so foreign to the things he knew, that it had seemed natural to introduce himself not as Dmitri Andreivitch Pulski, but as Tom Boston, the name by which he intended one day to become famous. And the longer he drove through the shifting landscape, the more he began to think of himself as Tom Boston. By the time Adele pointed out the outbuildings of the ranch in the distance, were anyone to address him as Dmitri, he would not have answered to it right away.

They turned off the road onto a sandy trail deeply imprinted with the chevron tread of tractor tires. Little attempt had been made to grade it, and they bucked and jarred over as bad a series of bumps and holes as he and Yuri had encountered during the drive from Ingot. He slowed to five miles per hour to avoid a puncture. After twenty minutes he rolled to a stop in front of a whitewashed board gate in a barbed wire fence stretching to the horizon in both directions. A man in overalls and a stained fedora rose from a wooden bench and approached the car carrying a double-barreled shotgun. He was a charcoal-skinned Negro, and when he scowled at the unfamiliar face behind the steering wheel, his features resembled a carved African mask. The scowl softened when he saw the woman.

"Good day to you, Miss Varga. They didn't tell me you was shooting today." His voice was a gentle rumble.

"I'm not, Lester. I'm bringing someone to see Buck. Where is he?"

"The big barn, I think. These fellows all right?"

"True blue."

He let the shotgun drop to the end of his arm and went over to unhook the gate. She waved at him as they drove through.

"Do you really need an armed guard?" asked Tom Boston.

"You never know with the Trust."

"Trust?"

She waved him off with the flick of a scarlet-nailed hand. "The password's true blue. That's all you need to know if you make a deal with Buck over the ice. If you don't we'll have to change it."

"Why true blue?"

"Opposite of pink. Turn right. Toward the big barn."

He turned, putting aside the question of what was wrong with pink. This path was even more deeply rutted than the other, and led up to a building at least two hundred feet long and sixty feet wide, with a hip roof and the leaden-colored boards showing through its last coat of whitewash. But Tom was less interested in the condition of the barn than he was in the object in front of the wide double doors at the near end. In the box of a board-sided truck like the ones he'd seen carrying sugar beets up to the refinery outside Salinas, lashed with rope, crouched a brass cannon on spoke wheels as tall as the man who was standing next to it. Another man stood on the ground, leaning on his hands on the open tailgate. Both wore overalls and heavy white cotton work gloves, well soiled.

"We need a ramp if we're going to unload it here," said the man in the box. "Oak planks, not pine. It weighs half a ton."

"Why'n't you bring along the ones you used to load it on?" asked the man on the ground.

"Didn't use any. We pushed it straight on from the loading dock behind the army museum in Monterey. Son of a bitch's been taking up space there for twenty years. Before that it was at Fort Humboldt since '64."

"When's the last time anyone fired it?"

"Beats me. I think the barrel's plugged."

"Well, unplug it. Buck didn't shell out two hundred bucks for a thousand-pound paperweight."

"Can't he fake it for the camera?"

"He ain't using it in a picture."

The man in the box grinned. "Who's he expecting, Stonewall Jackson?"

"No, just detectives."

"Well, where's he want it?"

The man on the ground pointed. "Up on that hill, where it can be seen from the road. What's its range?"

"How the hell should I know? Couple of hundred yards, I guess."

"Shit."

"He wanted more, he should of bought a newer

one. They got a shitload of Spanish-American War artillery in Tijuana."

"Too modern. It might get into a shot. Well, hello there, Senorita Varg-ass. How's business?" The man on the ground aimed an expression at Adele that Tom Boston, the writer, would have had to describe as a leer.

"I wouldn't know, Morrie. I'm in pictures. Grand Vizier inside?"

He nodded. "Been monkeying around with lights since breakfast. What do you think of my big gun?" The leer stayed in place.

"Nice. Too bad about the short range."

The doors were latched on the inside. She surprised Tom by stepping back and kicking them repeatedly with one of her boots. They shook and rumbled. After two minutes something grated on the other side and one of the doors opened outward the width of a face. The face belonged to an Indian, complete with feathered headband and stripes of white warpaint like cat's whiskers on his face. He had blue eyes, and Tom suspected his features had been artificially darkened with some kind of stain. The blue eyes lingered on the woman for a moment, then moved to take in the young man and the bearded Ukrainian.

"Closed set," he told all of them.

Adele inserted a foot into the space between the doors. "Tell Buck it's Adele. Heap fast, Geronimo. I've only got a year's lease on my house."

"Keep your bloomers on." He withdrew his head.

She pulled the door open the rest of the way and stood aside for the others to enter. "Supers," she said. "Extras, Buck calls them. They come and go and never stay around long enough to find out what's what."

Yuri started inside, but Tom put out his arm, stopping him, and motioned for the woman to go in first. She lifted her eyebrows—they were black and thick, tapering to plucked points at the apexes—then preceded them. Yuri went in last and drew the door shut.

A lingering sweet smell of grain was the only thing inside to remind them that the building had ever been used as a barn. A floor had been laid of broad white planks, with coils and tangles of thick electric cable everywhere, some of them winding up the four-by-four posts that supported the roof, where black canisters attached to the rafters shed harsh white light at various angles, illuminating every corner, as bright as the sun. It seemed to Tom that actual particles of light swirled and swam in the beams like swarms of fireflies. He could feel the heat on his face and on the top of his head. Warmth was everywhere in southern California. He could scarcely believe that only a few days previously he had been content to wear an overcoat and fleece-lined cap.

Under that burning light labored a small army of men, carrying tripods and boxes, unreeling yet more cable, lugging double armloads of flat round tins, scaling stepladders. Tom was forced to change positions several times to avoid a collision, and Yuri actually made physical contact with a fellow half his size, who bounded off him, nearly dropping the two rustic chairs he was carrying, but kept going, slinging only a single dark look back over his shoulder to acknowledge the near catastrophe. He wore a fringed tan jacket and matching leggings. It seemed half the crew had on some kind of costume, with thick pancake makeup on their faces and kohl around their eyes. Tom was reminded of an amateur theatrical production he had once been part of in Ingot, where actors doubled as stagehands in the absence of personnel. He himself had been both the set dresser and a mute soldier in the service of Catherine the Great.

Adele alone navigated her way through and around the many obstacles with grace, steering between crates and upended barrels and sidestepping a Royal Canadian Mountie and a laborer in dusty twill carrying a carved totem pole on their shoulders like a battering ram. Tom and Yuri followed her to the far end of the building. There two log walls had been joined in an L, one containing a window that looked out onto an unconvincing landscape painted on canvas. A bearskin lay on the floor and a barrel stove stood in the corner where the walls met. The fellow in fringes was there already, unburdening himself of his chairs: one next to the stove, the other in the center of the bearskin.

"Not on the skin, for chrissake. It's on loan from Essanay."

The man who had issued the command stood with his back to the three newcomers. He was stocky in a baggy white shirt, brown whipcord breeches reinforced with leather for riding, and mahogany-colored boots to his knees. The Indian with whom Adele had spoken saw them coming, touched the man's shoulder, and pointed. He turned his head their direction, giving Tom a glimpse of a shock of thick red hair falling over his forehead, then came around the rest of the way and closed the distance between him and Adele in two strides, taking her hands in both of his and kissing her cheek.

"Pepita, you got your days mixed up. You're not shooting till tomorrow." His voice was a reedy tenor, out of place considering his build.

"I know that, darling. I've brought someone to meet you."

He looked at the others then. Tom decided that this couldn't be Buck Bensinger, president of the Rocky Mountain Moving Picture Association, with authority and funds to order a city-size supply of ice in one load. His broad, open face was unlined, and smooth enough at that hour of the afternoon to suggest that he had difficulty growing whiskers. He had clear gray eyes, a pug nose that added to the overall impression of youth, and a riot of freckles from hairline to shirt collar.

"The big one might do," he said. "I haven't cast all the mountain men. I don't have anything for the other one. He's got no mileage."

"Buck, dear, they're not actors. They're with the Sierra Nevada Ice Company." When he showed no reaction she said, "You wanted ten tons, remember?"

"Jesus, you didn't bring it already? *The Trail of '98* isn't on the schedule for two weeks. I've got no place to put it." He was looking at Tom.

Adele said, "They're not deliverymen either. This is Tom Boston and his associate, Boris. They—"

"Yuri," said Yuri.

"Yuri. They've been sent to find out what kind of rubber your checks are made of."

Buck Bensinger flushed bright orange under his freckles. "Fuck 'em. We'll go someplace else."

Tom said, "It's a big order. It's more than our entire inventory. If you tell us why you want it—"

"What are you, the fucking Bank of Sierra fucking Nevada? I want it to put on my piles, how's that? Del, you know better than to bring in these fucking foggers when I'm working. They shit all over the creative spirit."

"I'm a writer."

Bensinger looked at Tom again. He ran a hand through his shock of hair, but it fell right back over his forehead. "What?"

"I'm a writer. I understand the creative spirit."

"I thought you were an iceman."

"My father owns the company. I'm only helping him out until he finds a replacement. I write for magazines."

"No shit. Your father owns the company?"

"Darling, you're not listening. This young man is telling you he's a fellow artist."

The moving picture maker's smile was bright. The flush had disappeared. Tom had never seen a man's moods change so completely so quickly. "Buck Bensinger. Tim, is it?" He held out his hand.

"Tom."

Bensinger's grip was bone-crushing. He wore a ring on his little finger with a yellow stone and a thick silver band. "What magazines do you write for, Tom?"

"Oh, *Collier's, Century, The Saturday Evening Post, Scribner's.*" As he recited the names, he saw the logos on their letters of rejection.

"How much do you know about moving pictures?"

Adele spoke up. "He's a student of D. W. Griffith."

"Good man. Got some crazy ideas about how long the human bladder can hold out in a theater seat. If you can't say it all in two reels, preferably one, you should be writing a novel." He put his arm across Tom's shoulders and turned him away from the others. "Let me tell you what we're going to do with your old man's ice. How big would you say this building is?"

"About two hundred—"

"Half a million cubic feet. I'm going to fill it up with ice, right up to the rafters. It could be the middle of July, you come in here and freeze your pecker off in thirty seconds. Why would I want to do that?"

"I can't think."

"I'm going to rebuild the Klondike right here in this barn. Skagway, Dawson, the Chilkoot Pass—every last detail, right down to the spittoons in Soapy Smith's saloon. Why am I going to do that?"

"You're making a moving picture about the Alaska gold rush."

"Right! Say, you're wasting your time at the ice company. Wait till you hear the story. This drifter stumbles into a gold camp cabin in the middle of a blizzard. He tells the other miners his tale of woe, full of bad luck and bad weather, and when he's finished the others drink him a toast and give him gear and provisions and send him back on his way. A little later a Mountie shows up asking after a gent who answers the drifter's description and saying he's wanted for this and that. The miners give him a cock-and-bull story and send him off in the wrong direction, because miners stick together and there are no scoundrels who can stand up to the rigors of the trail the way the drifter did. What do you think?"

"It sounds like 'To the Man on the Trail,' by Jack London."

"Well—superficially. We do a lot more with it than he did. The scenario's a corker. So it's no longer his story."

"Did you buy it from him?"

"He's too hard to reach. He's always off on some cruise around the world, or lecturing in New York, or covering some war. I doubt he even has time to look at a moving picture."

"But won't he sue you or something?"

"I told you, he won't even see it. Anyway, he's a Socialist. They don't trust the courts. What is it?"

The man dressed as an Indian had left them, then returned to touch Bensinger's shoulder. He leaned close to the moving picture maker's ear and whispered. Tom's hearing was excellent. He heard the word "sheriff."

Chapter 5

Bensinger said, "Shit. Peavey, or just a deputy?"

"Peavey *and* a deputy," said the Indian.

Bensinger said "Shit" again and left the others, moving at a lope. The Indian trotted to catch up.

Adele touched Tom's sleeve. "Come meet Jerry Jarette, Buck's favorite cameraman. He photographed the Chinese revolution."

He ignored her, caught Yuri's eye, and followed the moving picture maker. The big Ukrainian accompanied him.

The door at the far end was already closed when they got to it. Tom opened it and they stepped outside, where Bensinger was engaged in animated conversation with a tall, stoop-shouldered man in a buff-colored twill uniform with a sheriff's star pinned to his left breast pocket. His Stetson was pushed back from a low forehead with a tuft of dark feathery hair on top. Tiny black eyes glittered on either side of a straight beak of nose and a brush moustache drew a straight line across an upper lip that never moved, even when he was talking, although he wasn't doing much of that. His mournful expression and the long, sad S of his posture as he stood before the gale of the much shorter Bensinger's wrath, one hand on the polished wooden butt of the revolver in his sagging holster—not threatening, just resting there—made Tom think of a character in a comic strip. The others present, the man in Indian dress and a younger, powerfully built, Mexican-looking fellow wearing a uniform identical to the sheriff's, were only background features in the cartoon landscape.

The sheriff waited until Bensinger's mouth stopped moving before he spoke. "There's no call to bring a man's parents into this." His drawl was so much in keeping with his general appearance that Tom smiled.

"There is if they didn't teach you how to read a calendar," Bensinger said. "I've got a paper with Judge Mortenson's signature on it giving me till the first of February. That's three weeks away."

"I ain't here to foreclose yet. I'm on my way up to Sacramento to talk to the governor about the new reservoir and I thought I'd stop in to see if you had the money and save me and the taxpayers an extra trip."

"What if I did? I wouldn't give it to you. You don't work for the Columbia Printing Company."

"If I did I wouldn't let you run up no three thousand bucks outstanding in circulars and posters. But they did, and you didn't pay, and come the first of next month, everything in this barn and your office in Los Angeles goes on the block."

"Until then you're trespassing."

The deputy spoke for the first time. "Who's gonna run us off, Chunky? That big ape in the beard?"

Every head turned toward Yuri, who stood six inches taller than anyone present except the sheriff, whom he outweighed by a hundred pounds.

Bensinger addressed Peavey. "I don't know your little friend. When did you start recruiting from Pancho Villa?"

The deputy took a step forward but was stopped by the sheriff's bony elbow, pivoting out from where his hand rested on his revolver. Shorter than Peavey by nearly a foot, he was thick-built through the upper body, with hot eyes behind long beautiful lashes like a woman's. He looked to Tom like a matador on a poster he had seen on a wall in San Francisco.

"Angel's more American than most of us," the sheriff said. "His people came here with Cortes."

"Pizarro." The deputy spat the name.

Bensinger still didn't look at him. "Tell him to come by at the end of March. I'm shooting the Alamo and I need Mexicans."

"Son of a bitch!" The man called Angel displayed an accent for the first time.

Sheriff Peavey raised a hand, also for the first time, pointing a finger as long as a cant dog at Bensinger. "Come March you won't have any equipment to shoot it with. And don't try hiding it. That's contempt of court. Angel will be happy to show you to your cell."

"Tell him there's a buck in it for him if he puts me in with his sister."

The deputy lunged before Peavey could stop him. Tom nudged Yuri, who moved in just as Angel snatched the front of the moving picture maker's shirt and drew back a fist. The big Ukrainian caught his wrist in motion. The fist stopped as if it had struck a wall.

There was nothing swift about Peavey's movement, just a kind of looping grace in the way he scooped the revolver out of its holster and extended his long arm straight out from his shoulder so that the end of the nine-inch barrel touched Yuri's temple. His thumb rolled back the hammer in the same motion.

"I'd let go." His drawl was as slow as ever.

Tom said, "Yuri."

Yuri opened his hand. Angel withdrew his arm and rubbed the wrist, dead white where the Ukrainian had gripped it. Peavey lowered the revolver, but kept it cocked. "I ought to pull you in for officer assault and obstruction of justice."

"Your boy made the first move," Bensinger said. "When I finish suing the county I'll *buy* the fucking printing company."

The sheriff said, "There's a lady present."

Nobody had seen Adele Varga come out of the barn. She said, "Mutt's right, Buck. I never say the word. I just do it. Hello, Angel. I heard you joined the county."

Angel said nothing. But Tom had seen a flash of recognition behind his long lashes when the woman spoke.

Bensinger asked, "You know this peppergut?"

"Angel was a police officer in Tijuana. He took care of collections." She was smiling at the deputy, but the smile fell short of her eyes.

He showed his teeth at her. "You ain't the only one hears things. I heard you was working this side of the border. You take on all these guys at once, or one at a time?"

Her expression didn't change. She had both hands on her hips. "If you heard anything, you heard I left that work. I'm an actress now."

"You always was." He rolled his eyes skyward. " 'Oh, baby, oh, God, baby.' "

She slapped him. As movements go, it was ten times faster than the sheriff's. Tom hadn't seen her hand leave her hip when the noise rang out like a pistol shot and Angel staggered backward a step, touching his left cheek. Adele lifted her chin in front of the sheriff.

"Arrest me," she said. "Officer assault."

Peavey's sluggish tongue bulged first one cheek, then the other. "I'm sorry for my deputy's bad manners, ma'am," he said finally. "He doesn't get in with ladies much."

"Lady." When Angel took his hand away from his cheek, a red imprint remained.

"Shut up." Peavey looked at Bensinger. "I ain't got time for this. I'll stop in on my way back down. The voters in Los Angeles County won't get the water they need if they spend all their money on gas for the Packard."

"Peavey, if I gave a shit I'd cry."

The sheriff touched his hat to Adele, then turned around and slouched toward a dusty blue touring car shaped like a bathtub parked behind the Model T. Angel followed him, but not before raking his hot eyes across the semicircle of faces turned his way, as if scorching them into his memory. Looking into those eyes briefly, Tom remembered the time he'd been sitting next to the driver of the ice wagon when they rattled around a rocky bend and saw a mountain lion watching them from atop a low ridge. For an instant before the big cat withdrew, both he and the driver thought they were going to be attacked.

As the long car backed around and started back down the private road, Bensinger turned and saw Tom. His expression changed as swiftly as the twisting of a kaleidoscope. "Printing company fucked up and struck off five hundred posters with a misprint in the title. Would you pay to see a picture called *Nuns of Galveston?*"

"That's why you didn't pay them?"

"I could sue, but why foot the bill? I figured if they took me to court the story would come out, but the judge wouldn't let me talk. He's from Maine, for chrissake. Fucking pilgrim."

"Missouri," Adele said.

"Fucking hillbilly. Anyway, I'm still waiting on the appeal. These things work themselves out. Did Adele introduce you to Jarette? He smuggled ten thousand feet across the border after Mexico City fell. Huerta's got a reward out for him. Five thousand pesos."

Adele said, "You told me he covered the revolution in China."

"He's been around. I stole him from Edison. You'll love him, Tom. He's a walking history lesson. He worked with Méliès." He grasped Tom's arm and pulled.

Tom set his feet. "How are you going to pay for ten tons of ice if the sheriff forecloses on you?"

"Mutt Peavey's a joke. They only pinned that star on him because he transposed two numbers on a sheet when he was a county clerk and got the governor reelected. He won't foreclose."

"Is he the reason you bought the cannon?"

"Cannon?" The moving picture maker looked around and appeared to notice for the first time the truck with the artillery piece in its bed. "That's a prop. We're shooting Gettysburg in March."

"You told the deputy you were shooting the Alamo then."

"You've got a good memory, Tom. You must really be a writer. I can use somebody to fix up the Klondike scenario. You're right about Jack London. We've got to sponge all of him out of it. I'm paying forty a week."

"I heard someone say you were expecting detectives."

The kaleidoscope twisted again. Bensinger's face darkened behind the freckles. "Pinks."

"Pinks?"

"Pinkertons. Spooks. Forget about 'em. They've got no authority."

"Then what's the cannon for?"

"It's the kind of thing they understand. They never got over John Wilkes Booth. Let me worry about the Pinks, the sheriff too. You want the job? Forty-five a week. What the hell. That's almost as much as I'm paying Latimer."

"You don't even know if I can write."

"What's the difference? Latimer can't act. Fuck it. Fifty a week."

Adele said, "You're only paying me forty-five."

Tom was amused. "Your father doesn't own an ice company."

The kaleidoscope took another turn. Bensinger drew himself up, becoming almost tall. For once his shock of hair stayed back after he swept his fingers through it. "I'm an entrepreneur in a tough business. I can't afford to make mistakes. That's an authentic Civil War cannon. I don't use fakes. I've got the most popular player in pictures, the latest equipment, the best cameraman—"

"Billy Bitzer won't leave Griffith," Adele said.

"I was going to say the best cameraman available. The point is I don't make choices based on anything but merit or a damn strong hunch. I'll get the fucking ice someplace else. Jesus Christ, it's just water. Investors I can dig up anywhere. This country's crawling with millionaires who can't even write their own names except on a check. Some of them must like moving pictures. You want the job or not? Look, I've even got a spot for your friend Ivan."

"Yuri." Yuri, Tom, and Adele corrected him simultaneously.

"Yuri. You've got good reflexes, Yuri. Can you fall off a horse?"

"Probably. The last time I was on one I was two."

"Wardrobe won't have anything in your size. I'll have them run up a set of buckskins. You just became Fetterman's guide."

"I don't know how to shoot under a horse's belly."

"Hell, if I wanted that I'd go down to the Watering Hole. The only thing those drunks can't do is walk a straight line."

"How much?" Yuri asked.

"Fifteen a week."

Tom said, "He makes more than that cutting ice."

"What are you, his booking agent? Twenty-five."

"Cutting ice is steady work," Tom told the Ukrainian.

"Cold, too. And you can't see whales. I'll take the job."

Bensinger grinned. "What's the answer, Tom? So far you're the only one here who doesn't work for Rocky. It's a closed set."

"I don't know how to write a scenario. I don't even know what one is."

"That's nothing. Adele never saw a camera before I pulled her out from under a streetcar conductor in Tijuana and stood her up in front of one."

"He owned the streetcar company," she said. "And I do a lot more than stand in front of a camera. If it weren't for me running the office, Rocky would have been on the county block long before this."

"That you do for love, Pepita. It isn't in your contract."

"What contract?"

"This one." Bensinger thrust his hand out at Tom. "It's solider than the iron in that cannon."

"It's brass." The man in the truck bed had witnessed the whole episode without abandoning his leaning perch against one of the big wheels.

"Even better." The hand remained steady.

Tom took it. His own father had taught him it was impolite to let a man's friendly hand wave in the breeze.

Chapter 6

FATHER

CANNOT PASS UP OPPORTUNITY WRITE MOV-
ING PICTURE SCENARIOS ROCKY MOUNTAIN
ASSOCIATION STOP SEND FOR THINGS LATER
STOP WILL COMPLETE ARRANGEMENTS FOR
SALE ICE STOP PLEASE UNDERSTAND DECISION

YOUR SON
DMITRI

Tom read what he'd written on the yellow telegraph
flimsy, then crumpled it and dropped it into the
wooden wastebasket under the post office counter. He
took another blank off the stack and started over.

SIR

HAVE ACCEPTED OFFER WRITE FOR ROCKY
MOUNTAIN MOVING PICTURE ASSOC STOP
WHEN ICE SALE COMPLETE WILL SETTLE HERE

DMITRI

This one he balled up and threw away without reading. He selected a third flimsy, touched the tip of the squat yellow pencil to his tongue, and wrote.

ROCKY MOUNTAIN AGREES PAY ADVANCE FOR SHIPMENT

                                                    YOUR SON

He took it over to the polished-oak cage, behind which a clerk with white muttonchops and a green eyeshade counted the words, took his money, gave him his copy, and told him the wire would go out that afternoon. Yuri was standing on top of the marble steps, leaning back against the iron railing, when Tom came out. "What did you tell him?"

"I said Bensinger will pay for the ice up front." He started down. The Ford was parked at the base of the steps.

"That's all?" Yuri followed him.

"I'll write him a letter later. Let's see about finding a room."

"With your father's money?"

"Well, for the first week. Either way we'd need a place to stay." Tom slid under the wheel.

Yuri climbed in beside him. "I'd like to see your father's face when he reads that letter."

"I wouldn't."

Buck Bensinger had told them they might find luck renting a place on Bunker Hill, a ridge of land across the city's west side that from its base looked as if God had set it there to prevent the settlement from spreading in that direction. "Don't tell them you're in the business," Buck had added, without offering an explanation.

The Model T labored up a curving stretch of macadamized street between houses of Victorian vintage that made Tom think of home, bristling with turrets and spires with shingles like fish scales. A little bit of geography and a great deal of stubborn will separated this neighborhood from the sprawling, tile-roofed haciendas to the south and the low frame bungalows close to the center of town; it seemed to represent a kind of firebreak between Spanish colonial California and the new element filtering in from the East, made up of real estate salesmen and elderly retired in search of a warm place to spend their remaining years. The new reservoir, Buck had said, had already begun to draw interest from developers hoping to make the desert bloom with fistfuls of cash.

At length Tom pulled up in front of a carriage house beside a Queen Anne that reminded him comfortingly of familiar things, with a sign in a front ground-floor window reading ROOM FOR RENT. As he and Yuri started up the flagstone path to the front door, the puzzling legend on a smaller sign below the first became legible: NO MOVIES. Tom twisted the bell.

The woman who answered the door was nearly as tall as he, in a charcoal-colored dress covering her from the tops of her shoes to her throat, where a bit of lace showed. Her blue-white hair was swept up in an elaborate, old-fashioned way, and she wore silver-rimmed bifocals. There were bitter lines around her mouth.

"We'd like to ask about the room," he said.

A pair of pale blue eyes swollen behind magnifying lenses moved from him to Yuri and back. "Movies?"

"I don't know what that means."

"Moom pitchers."

He hesitated. "I'm a writer."

"For moom pitchers?"

He hadn't expected her to make that connection. "Yes."

"No movies." She started to close the door.

He inserted his foot into the space, a trick he'd learned from Adele Varga. "What's wrong with moving pictures?" he asked.

"Them that makes 'em. My brother rents to movies. They live like apes and duck out without paying."

"Why does he rent to them if they do that?"

She let out an impatient breath. "Who else'd he get to live in the valley?"

"What valley is that?"

A wrinkled hand laden with rings swept northward. "San Fernando. Movies and Mexican orange pickers. Nobody decent."

"Does everyone here feel the way you do about movies?"

"Nobody on the hill will rent to 'em."

"What's your brother's name?"

"Augustus Wolz." She spelled it.

"Where can we find him?"

She breathed again and gave him rapid directions. While groping for his pencil and something to write on, he withdrew his foot from the door and it banged shut.

He looked at Yuri. "Did you get any of that?"

"We go north," he said.

The San Fernando Valley was as beautiful as Salinas, but in a different way. In place of patches of lettuce and sugar beets, orchards of lemons and oranges and groves of walnut trees grew in endless rows, their black shade actually chilling Tom as he drove between the farms along a gravel road as straight as a cutline on the ice. Then without warning they broke into the blazing sunshine of the vineyards, miles of braided vines as thick as a man's wrist twisted around fence rails snaking up and over swelling hills to the horizon. In a little while they entered the town of San Fernando, whose business section comprised two blocks of false-fronted stores selling farm equipment. In one of them a counterman with old black earth ground deep into his knuckles told them where they could find Augustus Wolz.

The place was two miles outside town. A fierce wind was blowing and they almost missed the sign, which was suspended beneath a horizontal post on the burned-out front yard and blowing almost perpendicular to the ground:

BUNGALOWS FOR RENT
BY WEEK OR MONTH

The office was a low frame building, white with gray trim, identical to the line of buildings behind it, set back a quarter acre from the road. Tom opened a screen door on a rusty spring and he and Yuri stepped into a shallow room with a counter to the right and three calendars hung on the back wall, each turned to a different consecutive month from December 1912 to February 1913, with notations scribbled inside many of the squares.

The counter was unoccupied. Tom was about to pick up a copper bell with a wooden handle standing on the near corner when a door behind the counter opened and a man came through. He was fat and bald, with breasts beneath his white cotton shirt and a cigar in the corner of his mouth. Tom saw no resemblance to the woman on Bunker Hill. When the man looked at him he said, "Augustus Wolz?"

The man took the cigar out of his mouth long enough to say, "I'm Gus Wolz," then put it back.

"Your sister says you have rooms for rent."

Wolz looked him over from head to toe, as if measuring him for a room, then did the same with Yuri. The cigar came out again. "Migrants?"

"I'm sorry?"

"Pickers. You work the farms?"

"No." After a silence Tom said, "Movies."

"Week or month?"

There was another pause before he answered. He'd expected some kind of reaction. "Could we see the room?"

"Rooms," Wolz corrected. "They're all the same: two bedrooms, a sitting room, sink and toilet. Showers at the end." He pointed with the cigar, then returned it to its permanent groove. He seemed to be using it as a plug to keep speech from leaking out. He removed it again and said, "Week's twelve bucks. Month, forty."

Tom, who had distributed the money his father had given him among his various pockets, peeled three bills from his roll of fives and laid them on the counter. "We'll try it for a week."

"First harvest coming in," Wolz said. "Migrants swarm in like fruitflies. This time next week there won't be a vacancy in the valley."

"We'll take that chance."

The bald man took a cigar box with a conquistador on the lid from under the counter and put it on top. He thrust the bills inside and took out three singles for change, but he didn't give them to Tom right away. He unplugged the cigar. "I was kidding about the harvest. That don't come for a couple of months.

Things are slow. Give you the month for thirty-five."

"We might not be here that long. The job might not work out."

That ended Wolz's interest. He surrendered the bills and let the lid drop. Then he took an old-fashioned brass key attached to a wooden tab off a pegboard and slapped it on the counter.

"Four. You lose it, you pay for a new lock. Names?"

"Tom Boston and Yuri Yaroslavl." He started to spell Yuri's surname, but Wolz interrupted him.

"Boston." He came out from behind the counter and used a green pencil dangling at the end of a string tacked next to the wall calendars to write Tom's name and the numeral 4 next to the current date. "Park your heap out back. Oil raises hell with the grass."

The bungalow was small but not unpleasant, and fairly new: the smell of turpentine still clung to the white-painted walls, which were partitions only and made of thin laminate, through which sound filtered freely. Each bedroom contained a single bed on a painted iron frame, a painted bureau, and a ceiling fixture designed to shed unwelcome harsh light into a sleeper's eyes when the wall button was pushed. The tapestry sofa and mismatched horsehair chairs in the little sitting room had probably been bought second-hand, but they were comfortable enough, if a bit musty-smelling. A large print of a painted landscape in a plaster frame on the wall above the sofa added nothing to the atmosphere. Yuri laid claim to the first bedroom they inspected by stretching out on the mattress, his boots protruding beyond the footboard. Tom unpacked his suitcase in the other bedroom, filling the bureau drawers with his clothes and laying out his toilet articles on top. If things worked out and he decided to stay, he'd invest in a shaving mirror; the glass above the sink in the cramped little water closet was wavy and mounted at an inconvenient angle. It would do well enough for Yuri, who trimmed his beard once a month with a pair of barber's shears. The stool was made of discolored white porcelain with a chain-pull and flushed with a roar.

When he finished unpacking, he sat down on the edge of his bed and watched the patch of light on the wall opposite the window fade. He could hear Yuri snoring on the other side of the bungalow, and he knew he should be tired at the end of a long day on top of a lengthy automobile trip, but he was wide awake and bored, and lonelier than he had ever felt shut away in the shack by the lake. The window was open, with a cool early evening breeze coming through it. He could not believe that back home everything was still covered with snow. And that was only one of the many things that were different at this distance of a few hundred miles, where Mexican prostitutes kept company ledgers and fifty-year-old cannons were still employed for their original purpose.

Galvanized suddenly, he borrowed a straightback chair from the sitting room, set the Blickensderfer on it, and removed the cover, but when he drew it up to the edge of the bed and sat on the mattress he found he had to bend almost double to reach the keys. He corrected that by propping up the machine with the empty suitcase. He rolled a blank sheet into the platen, but by then the light was almost gone. The merciless overhead fixture threw his shadow across the page no matter what angle he turned. He tried sitting up in bed with his back against the headboard and the Blick in his lap. It felt natural enough, but the mood had fled. No words came.

He set the machine aside, laid back against his one skimpy pillow, and tried to read *Burning Daylight*, but Jack London's frozen tundra just reminded him of the remoteness of his situation. The descriptions and characters of a writer who wrote no matter what were no comfort to a writer who could think of nothing to write about. He leaned out of bed and switched off the light. Lying on his back he watched the freshly painted ceiling receding into shadow, feeling guilty for letting Buck Bensinger believe he sold what he wrote, for not mentioning Bensinger's offer and his acceptance in the telegram to his father, and for lying in the telegram he sent. No reference had been made to an advance payment for the ice. The scene with the sheriff cast into doubt the ability of the Rocky Mountain Moving Picture Association to pay for it at all. He had only sent the wire to buy time.

For what? A writing job he knew nothing about, for which he probably had no talent, and which he'd been offered only because his father owned a company and might one day be persuaded (or so thought a man who had never laid eyes on Andrei Ivanovitch Pulski) to invest in moving pictures? A job that would vanish as thoroughly as the setting sun on February 1, when Mutt Peavey and his disagreeable deputy returned to padlock the front door and attach all the equipment?

Dark thoughts to doze off with his first night in southern California; and they were still there when Yuri came in and shook him awake to remind him that they hadn't eaten since breakfast.

Chapter 7

————

Just wander around your first couple of days," Bensinger said. "Ask questions."

"You're going to pay me to wander around and get in the way?" Tom craned his neck and shielded his eyes to look up at the moving picture maker, whose preferred designation, he had begun to learn, was "producer." Bensinger was standing atop a six-foot platform erected that morning of pine timbers that resembled nothing so much as the scaffold of a gallows. He in turn was peering up at a small man with a pointed moustache who looked as if he cut his own hair, straddling a section of four-by-four barn timber braced by two-by-fours nailed to the platform, atop which a hand-crank camera was mounted. The overhead canister lights—*kliegs*, so many strange new words to learn—were burning, shedding glowing particles everywhere; it appeared to be the sole responsibility of one laborer, a towheaded youth scarcely out of knickerbockers, to keep track of the larger particles and stamp them out before they could ignite the bits of old straw and grain that drifted down from the rafters and clung to the barn floor. At any given moment the atmosphere was a fine golden cloud of grain dust, interspersed with incendiaries from the lights. Tom wondered if Los Angeles County had a fire marshal and if he was aware of the situation on the ranch.

"If you get in the way, someone'll be sure to let you know," Bensinger said.

The camera rig, which overlooked the same simple log-cabin set of the day before, had an unsteady, slapped-together look that Tom found unsettling. It required two men to hold it, like a ladder. One of the two was yesterday's Indian, although he had shed his headband and leggings in favor of a homespun pioneer shirt, canvas trousers, and lace-up brogans, suggesting that some of the players doubled in other roles as well as helped behind the scenes. Moving picture making was a smaller and less-populated world than it appeared on screen. The little fellow atop the contraption, who was in danger at any moment of falling off and injuring himself, appeared to be less concerned with his own condition than he was with his equipment; whenever the timber wobbled, he grabbed first at the camera, cursing his clumsy supporters in a combination of heavily accented English and what Tom thought was French. This would be Buck Bensinger's cameraman, the legendary Jerry Jarette, who if the hyperbole could be believed had filmed revolutions in Mexico and China and worked with Méliès, whoever he may be. From Tom's perspective on the ground, he looked like a fussy shoe clerk perched on a rickety ladder.

Everything the young man observed, from the amateurish landscape painting mounted behind the "log cabin's" window—there was a flock of birds frozen in midflight between clouds, stationary airborne fowl in a moving picture—to the huge, medieval-looking generator housed in a lean-to shed behind the barn, chattering and belching blue smoke and visibly shaking loose the bolts that secured it to its wooden platform as it supplied power to the lights and electric fans inside, impressed him with the makeshift, naively improvised quality of the entire Rocky Mountain operation. By contrast, the ice business was conducted along lines tested and proved generations before he was born, with the identical equipment with which it was inaugurated, efficiently and with a minimum of risk to those involved. The making of moving pictures smacked of something the country's established industries had devised to keep misfits and incompetents occupied at a safe distance from their own work sites.

Quitting the barn for fresh air and an escape from the heat and relentless hissing of the kliegs, he found that a crowd as large as the group inside had gathered out front. A dozen or more men in worn work clothes and broad-brimmed hats stained through with sweat stood and sat about the bare patch beyond the doors. As they turned their heads briefly to see who had come out, he recognized a number of faces from the Watering Hole: burnt umber and brown faces weathered beyond their years, with cigarettes burning in the corners of their cracked lips. Some had brought their own saddles and were using them as seats. Others sat on the ground with their backs against the wall of the barn, while still others stood either in groups or apart, practicing rope tricks or twirling long-barreled revolvers by their trigger guards around their index fingers. Flat pints of whiskey made the rounds.

While Tom took inventory, a shadow passed between him and the sun. He hadn't seen Yuri approaching, and a second passed before he recognized the big Ukrainian. That part of his face not covered by whiskers was as white as hoar ice, with black holes through which his eyes pleaded. He had on a yellow buckskin jacket with fringes on the sleeves and the old corduroy trousers he had worn on his way in that morning; the gnarled, chain-smoking wardrobe ward-robe mistress had evidently not had time to sew up a pair that would fit him.

"It's as bad as I thought, right?" Yuri said. "Don't lie, Dmitri. Everything you think shows on your face."

"Tom," he corrected. "It's not so bad. You just surprised me. I thought you were out learning to ride."

"Buck says they don't need me on a horse for the first shot. A little birdy-looking fellow plastered me with powder and some black gunk from a jar. He wouldn't give me a mirror. I look like a clown, don't I? I saw one once when the circus came to Ingot." He swept one of his buckskin sleeves across his cheek. It just made smears in the white.

"It won't look so bad under the lights. Have you seen Miss Varga? She's supposed to be working to-day." He had fixed on her as his interpreter in foreign country.

"I didn't see her. Buck said to go in when I finished painting up. They won't see this back home, will they? I'd rather drive the ice wagon than this." Ice delivery was reserved for those laborers who had grown too old and crippled to cut ice. Carrying the heavy blocks up several flights of stairs for customers was no less difficult and carried the additional stigma of servitude.

"Ingot doesn't have a theater. You'd better go in."

"Did you write that letter?"

"Not yet. It's only been one day."

"You might want to hold off. I don't think we'll be

doing this long." Yuri took a deep breath and went inside.

Tom noticed for the first time that the big truck was no longer parked outside the barn. Shielding his eyes against the sun, he could just make out the profile of the big cannon perched on a hill half a mile to the west. From that angle, with the telephone poles out of sight behind him and only the sky and mountains showing on the other side, the venerable gun looked like a thing that belonged, with Buck Bensinger and the barn full of equipment and the handful of parked cars, the interlopers. It struck him that here, without planning, was all the historical atmosphere that a crew of hired workers was laboring so hard to achieve inside. But the cannon was not a stage prop. It had something to do with the Pinkerton National Detective Agency and a thing called the Trust.

He wished Adele Varga would show up. He had so many questions to ask.

"You got makin's?"

He blinked. A face had come between him and the gun on the hill: long and sandpapery, with red-rimmed eyes under the shadow of the brim of his shapeless hat. Both the face and the hat looked familiar. "I'm sorry?"

"Baccy." The man held up a wilted leather pouch on a calloused palm. "I was a dern fool to stick it in my hip pocket. It's sweat clean through."

"I don't smoke."

"My sore luck. You're the only one here I don't owe money to." He plucked up the pouch with his other hand and let it dangle between thumb and forefinger, as if to dry.

"Your name's Chickamaw, isn't it?"

The face brightened. The man had a black tooth

in front, probably iron. "You heard about me, huh? I'm the genuine article, not like the rest of these dandles. I rode with Miller Brothers, and before that I busted broncs at the King Ranch. I can ride upside-down and shoot under a horse's belly."

"I know. You told me yesterday. We met at the Watering Hole."

The man looked disappointed. His eyes puckered, as if trying to place Tom against the landscape. Then he grinned again. Tom wondered if everyone in southern California displayed his emotions as visibly as wash on a line. "Fella in the flivver! I told you how to get to Rocky. You put in a word, huh? Reckon I owe you after all." Absentmindedly he returned the sodden tobacco pouch to his hip pocket.

"They hired you?"

"Rounded up a bunch of us. Sent a car. But I can ride better than any of these dandles. I can even make Wild Bill Latimer look good. He can't ride a lick. Buck got him off the stage in Philadelphia, playing Hamlet or somesuch. And that ain't all." He winked. Tom actually thought he heard the lid grating in its socket. He drew back a little. The man had on the same clothes he'd been wearing the day before and he smelled like the room where the ice cutters hung their coats and heavy, sweat-soaked shirts.

A powder blue touring car with brass headlamps and a white top folded down sped up the hill from the private road and ground to a halt. Its plume of dust caught up with it then and settled into a sugary brown coating on the fenders and white leather seats. Tom was astonished when he recognized Adele Varga behind the steering wheel. He had never seen a woman operate an automobile. She wore an ankle-length linen duster and a straw hat with a two-foot brim secured under her chin with a gauzy scarf. She smiled at Tom with her white teeth and motioned him over.

"Do you like it? It's a Rambler. Buck bought it for me out of the profits from *Geronimo's Revenge*." She squeezed the bulb of a brass horn mounted on the side panel. It made a noise like a flatulent gander.

"I'm gonna get me one of these when I'm a featured player." Chickamaw ran a hand over the finish. All the men near the barn had gathered around the car.

Tom said, "Did Buck teach you how to drive it?"

"I taught myself. I took it out to the desert where I couldn't hit anything and made circles for hours. I'm still no good at left turns. I make three rights instead. Would you like to take it for a spin? I'll come along and show you where everything is."

"Don't they need you inside?"

"They can shoot around me for a while. If I know Jerry, he's still monkeying around with his precious black box. As long as Billy Bitzer's around he'll never be the best cameraman in the business, but he's sure the slowest. Hop in." She slid over to the passenger's side.

He hesitated with one foot on the running board. "Buck might ask for me."

"What's he doing?"

"He was helping set up the camera when I left him."

"By now he's forgotten he even hired you. I'm restless. If you don't come with me there's no telling where I'll wind up. The last time I felt like this, Buck had to wire me train fare back from Nevada. I didn't have the car then."

"What's in Nevada?"

"Two Navajos and a hundred tons of sand." She patted the seat on the driver's side. He climbed in.

The seat was soft and pliant, not like the taut fabric in the Ford. He twisted the wheel right and left, testing it, worked the pedals, gripped the gearshift's black bulbous handle. "Where do you want to go?"

"South."

"What's south?"

"Mexico."

He let out the clutch, found first after an ominous groaning and shuddering from underneath the floorboards, and started a long looping turn back down the hill. The Rambler had a longer wheelbase than the Model T and he almost grazed a cowboy.

Adele said, "Don't run over the talent. There's not more than a couple hundred thousand of them between here and Montana."

He stayed in low gear downhill. The path was poorly graded and he wasn't sure how flexible the undercarriage was. His passenger slapped the panel on her side.

"*Drive* the damn thing, Tom! It's not made of glass."

"I don't know how much it will take."

"I ran it over a cactus and through a prairie dog town the size of Mexico City. I think you can put it in second on a pimple like this."

He eased it into the higher gear. They were almost down to the level anyway.

Adele raised her face to feel the slipstream, like a dog. "I was born in a village you could hide behind that barn. I saw my first automobile when I was six. It was an Oldsmobile, spindly little thing, no bigger than a doctor's buggy. I thought it was the grandest thing that ever was. I no more expected to own one than live in the presidential palace."

"It's a nice car. Buck paid for it with moving picture money?"

"Are you surprised?"

"No. Well, yes. It only cost me a nickel to see *The Musketeers of Pig Alley.*"

"Six hundred thousand people plunked down their nickels to see *The Great Train Robbery.* That was ten years ago."

He drove for a while in silence. She was watching him now. Sunlight coming through the open weave of her hat brim spattered her face with diamond-shaped spots.

"Tijuana taught me a thing or two about reading men's faces," she said finally. "You look like the groom at a twelve-gauge wedding. What happened this morning?"

"No one thing. Moving picture making is kind of casual."

"It depends on the company. Jesse Lasky runs Famous Players like the army. Meanwhile, compared to Essanay, Rocky's U.S. Steel. Billy Anderson keeps chickens in his office."

"That's what I mean. There's no consistency. Everything's just nailed together. If my father operated the Sierra Nevada Ice Company that way he'd be bankrupt in a year."

"Let me ask you something. How old is the ice business? I don't mean Sierra Nevada. I'm asking about the business in general."

"I don't know. At least a hundred years. As long as people have needed ice."

"What do you think it was like in the beginning? Don't you think they made up the rules as they went along? Someone had to fall through the ice before someone else came up with something to keep it from happening again. You never know what you need until you need it."

He turned onto the main road. He couldn't think of an argument.

"Moving picture making is new," she said. "Twenty years ago the business didn't exist. Five years ago everything had to be shot outdoors because the right lights hadn't been invented. The interior scenes were staged without a roof and when the wind came up you had to wet down the costumes to keep skirts and coattails from flapping. Kliegs have done away with that, but when you stand under them too long your eyes swell up and turn pink and hurt like hell and you have to stay away for two or three days. Give us another year or two and we'll come up with something better. Give us ten and we'll make the ice business look like a place that makes goose-quill pens."

"Maybe."

She returned her gaze to the road ahead. "Poor Tom. Stranded among the niggers."

"It isn't that. I'm just wondering when I'll get to write. That's what I was hired to do."

"You'll get the chance to do everything. I type letters, answer the phone, and try to make the accounts come out even at the end of the month. When there's time I act. The actors move props. The grips fill out crowd scenes and sometimes get a close-up. Buck does all of that and everything else. All Bill Latimer does is make faces in front of the camera, but that's as much as he can manage without tripping over his feet. Rocky isn't the Ford Motor Company. I like it that way. I could never hang doors all day and then come back the next day and do it all over again."

Tom stopped at an intersection to let a truckload of oranges cross. The driver was a Mexican with a bullfighter tattooed on the forearm resting on the window ledge. "Are we really going to Mexico?"

"We wouldn't make it before dark. I know a place on the pier in Long Beach where we can have lunch. Then we'll head back. Do you like clams?"

"I've never eaten one."

She looked at him again. Her smile lit up the car. "Tom, you have so much ahead of you. Today we'll just start with clams."

Chapter 8

Tom spent the afternoon watching Adele Varga walk across a room.

Jerry Jarette, ensconced at last to his satisfaction astride something that looked like a bicycle seat at the top of the pyramid of four-by-fours, spent some time gesturing to a pair of grips in the rafters until he was contented with the angle of the kliegs, then nodded at Buck Bensinger, his hand on the camera crank. Buck in turn signaled to Adele Varga, who laid aside the Spanish-language newspaper she was reading and climbed down from a wooden stool set up outside camera range. She wore a gingham dress with a voluminous skirt, which she spent some time arranging, and her blue-black hair was done up in sausage curls. But for a metallic makeup that made her look as if she were wearing a silver mask, she might have stepped out of a fifty-year-old tintype. Tom admired the way she seemed to glide across the barn floor, lifting her skirts only to step over the tangles of cable, until she reached the edge of the log cabin set, where she waited for her cue. Extras in costume and grips not engaged in work stood around watching.

The man whom Tom had first seen dressed as an Indian, then a frontiersman, and who now wore overalls with cigars in the bib pocket, sat on a folding chair directly opposite the stool and beyond reach of the camera. In front of him on a low table stood a Victrola in a varnished case with a hand crank and a morning-glory horn. A wooden crate on the floor at his feet contained a number of phonograph records in brown paper sleeves and he selected one, unsheathed it, and placed it on the turntable. He lifted the tone arm and looked at Buck, who nodded. He threw the brake, starting the turntable revolving, and gently lowered the tone arm. A scratching noise came out of the horn, then chamber music.

Now began the slow ratchet of the camera crank. Buck made an abrupt pumping motion with his right fist and Adele walked across the set and looked out the window.

"Cut!"

The instant Buck barked the single syllable, Jarette stopped cranking. The phonograph needle whooped as the man in overalls plucked up the tone arm. Adele turned from the window, eyebrows lifted.

"Slower next time, Pepita," Buck said. "You're not jumping out."

She nodded and returned to the edge of the set.

"And roll," Buck said.

The cranking resumed, then the record. "Action," said Buck, and Adele crossed to the window again, a little slower this time.

"Cut."

This time the needle came up without noise, simultaneous with the stopping of the crank.

"Muchacha, you're developing a hitch in your gitalong. Are your bloomers creeping up?"

"Maybe if you told me what you want." Adele's tone was patient.

"I want you to walk to the window."

"I walked to the window twice. Just what am I supposed to be looking at?"

Buck held up a sheath of papers rolled in his left fist. "Did you get one of these?"

"I *typed* the scenario. It says, 'Virginia walks to the window.' If I *didn't* walk to the window I could see why you'd want to complain, but I walked to the fucking window. I'll *skip* to the window if it's Pickford you want, or flutter if it's one of the Gishes. If it's Normand I'll cartwheel right through it and land on my prat. You're the director, darling. Direct."

"I want you to walk to the window."

The next time Adele took only one step before Buck said, "Cut."

"You do it," she said. "Show me what's missing."

"*I'm* not the bride of the young lieutenant who went out last week with Captain Fetterman and hasn't been seen since."

"That's what I'm looking for?"

"What else, Chiquita? Not the painted birds."

Once again the camera ratcheted. "The Pathetique," a favorite of Andrei Pulski's, simpered from the phonograph. Adele, hands clutched to her breast, walked slowly, hesitantly to the window and peered through the glass. Even the grips who had been sawing two-by-fours at the opposite end of the barn stopped to watch. Tom thought he had never seen anything so delicate.

"Cut. Damn it, Adele!"

She whirled about, fists down at her sides. "Now what?"

"You looked like a mouse with a snootful of cheese. I'm shooting a feature, not an animated short."

"*Hijo de la puta!*" She looked around, eyes hot, then went over to the barrel stove in the corner and pushed it over. The sections of stovepipe separated with a shower of soot and bounced all about the set. She ran around the end of the log wall at the back and disappeared behind it.

"Shit. You might as well come down and stretch your legs, Jerry. She'll sulk for an hour." Buck strode over to where the grip was sitting by the Victrola and helped himself to one of the cigars in the man's pocket. He patted his own pockets, then fished inside the grip's bib and came up with a match. He struck it on the seat of his whipcord trousers and set fire to the cigar with none of the ceremony Tom's father employed when he indulged himself in a rare smoke. As the Frenchman climbed down from his perch, a pair of laborers entered the set, righted the stove, and began gathering pieces of pipe.

"May I see that?" Tom asked Buck.

Puffing industriously, the producer squinted at him through thick smoke as if trying to remember who he was. "What, this?" He took the roll of crumpled sheets from under his left arm. "It's just today's pages. Tomorrow's too, probably. I lose more time dealing with Adele's tantrums than I do scouting out parts for that broken-down generator. I bought it from Buffalo Bill."

"She said it was the scenario. If I'm to write one, I'd like to see what one looks like."

"Be my guest. I hardly ever look at it myself."

Tom took it. "What good is it if you don't read it?"

"I wrote it. I only carry it around in case I get lost. I never get lost."

"Then why carry it around?"

"I'm superstitious." He blew a ring and looked through it at Tom. "You won't find any Booth Tarkington in it. I quit school in the eighth grade to work in my uncle's hardware store. I'd still be selling hammers in New Jersey if I hadn't tripped over a bucket of washers four years ago. The old boy's probably still sweeping them up."

The pages were disappointing. They consisted of simple stage directions; no descriptions or dialogue. Tom looked up. "How'd you come to work in moving pictures?"

"Uncle Stu rented the store out Saturday nights to a nickelodeon exhibitor. He tacked a bedsheet to the back wall, set up folding chairs and a projector, and charged the rubes a nickel a head to watch a pair of fat women strip down to their undies. I went to work for him. Later I bought an old projector and a print of *The Great Train Robbery* and went out on my own. But the real money's in making them, not showing them, so I came out here."

"Why here?"

"More sunny days. We didn't have kliegs then. Also it's three thousand miles away from the Trust."

"What *is* the Trust?"

Buck grinned around the cigar. "If my luck holds, you'll never find out. Jerry!"

The cameraman paused on his way past. At ground level he was almost freakishly small, with a stooping gait that shrunk him further still. "Yes?" He drew out the sibilant.

"This is Tom Boston. He's learning the business. Would you mind spending some time with him while we're waiting for Adele?"

"I have last week still to edit."

"Let him watch. He'll keep his mouth shut."

"Shut, open, it is no different." Jarette resumed walking. Tom interpreted this as an invitation to follow. He held out the scenario to Buck, who kept one hand on his cigar and the other in a pocket.

"Keep it. Just don't hang on to my genius all day. Latimer's due in an hour, if he doesn't take the wrong streetcar again and wind up in Pasadena."

Still Tom hesitated. "What was wrong with that last take?" He was beginning to pick up the terminology.

"Not a damn thing. I'll probably use it. With Adele you've got to choke up on the leash from time to time, that's all."

The Frenchman went out a narrow side door with Tom trotting to catch up, jamming the pages into a back pocket. They took a path between tall alfalfa grass to a clapboard toolshed with a corrugated iron roof that reminded Tom of the shack by the lake where he wrote and supervised the ice harvest. Jarette produced a key ring from the deep pocket of his shapeless slacks, opened a heavy brass padlock that secured an iron hasp, and led the way inside. He pulled a chain attached to an electric bulb suspended from the roof by a frayed cord and sat down on a stool before a plank bench littered with bits of film, a large pair of shears, and a pot of glue. Stacks of flat metal cans, some tall enough for a man to sit on, stood about the hard earthen floor like gigantic coins. The camerman lifted one of them off a nearby stack and prised it apart with his fingers, grunting when the lid came loose.

"A year I spent telling Mr. Bensinger I needed an electrical cord out here." He removed a metal reel from the can. "It took a fire to convince him. We lost a day's shooting to the oil lantern. Celluloid is like nitroglycerin. *Choom!*" He threw up his hands, losing his grip on the reel. Tom caught it on the fly and gave it to him. Several hundred feet of glistening black photographic film were wound around the hub.

"*Merci.* I am a nervous man. My mother was a singer in the chorus of the Paris opera house. She committed suicide when I was six."

The young man made a noise of sympathy and understanding, although he didn't know what the tragedy had to do with Jarette's clumsiness. He watched as the Frenchman spiked the reel onto a nail sticking out of the wall above the bench and slid dozens of feet of film off it, allowing coils to accumulate on the bench. From time to time he paused to hold a strip up against the light and peer at the frames. At length he grunted, picked up the shears, and sliced through the film. He counted off eight frames with a dirty-nailed finger, cut again, and tossed the bit among the scraps on the bench. Then he removed the brush from the pot of glue, scraped off the excess against the side of the pot, and applied some of the viscous amber liquid to the film in his hands. After returning the brush to the pot he lined up the end of the film coiled on the bench with the end of the footage still on the reel and held them together between thumb and forefinger while he rummaged among the litter on the bench, coming up at last with a metal clamp with tufts of cotton fixed to the ends.

When the two sections of film were clamped securely, Tom said, "For a nervous man you have steady hands."

Jarette held up his palms and looked at them as if they didn't belong on the ends of his arms. "I don't trust them. I trust my eyes, I trust the glue. I do not trust the scissors. I would rather use my teeth, but I lost them in China. The ones I have now cost a lot of money, but I do not trust things which are false."

"Were you attacked by bandits?" Tom had read Sax Rohmer.

"No. Scurvy. In Mexico I ate beans. I made a lot of *merde*, but I did not get sick."

This time Tom didn't even make a noise. There was an abiding unhealthiness about the man, from his sallow complexion to his ill-kept nails and, in that enclosed space, a clinging musty odor of old magazines stacked in a dugout basement. He could not picture Jarette clambering up Chinese mountains and descending into Mexican canyons carrying a moving picture camera on its tripod over his shoulder.

"Buck told me you worked with Méliès."

"Méliès," corrected the other; but Tom noted no difference in the pronunciation. "He was a magician, you know, first and last. Moving pictures were to him just another parlor trick. I saw it as something more, and that is why we parted. But he was clever. Griffith does nothing that Méliès did not already do in 1896."

"Everybody here talks about Griffith. Who is he?"

"Another genius. The business is full of them." He removed the clamp from the film, used the open blade of the shears to scrape an unsightly blob of glue from the corner of a frame, and resumed unreeling and peering.

"Why does Buck play music during a take? The audience won't hear it."

"*Humeur.* How you say, mewd. Mewd?" Muddy brown eyes slid over the top of the strip he was examining to look at Tom. There was a shrewd glint in them that suggested his English was not as poor as he made out.

"Mood."

"*Oui*, mewd. It is for the actors, to put them into

the moment. Though for this scene I would not have chosen Tchaikovsky. Mr. Bensinger's library of recordings is small. At Biograph they use live musicians. You know Stravinsky?"

"I've heard my father mention him."

" 'The Firebird' I should think would be appropriate for the character of Virginia, but it is, how you say, controversial. People threw rotten fruit the first time it was performed in Moscow. Stravinsky is the composer to use for moving pictures. Tchaikovsky belongs to the old century."

"How do you know so much about Russian music?"

"I filmed the first peace conference at The Hague. I befriended a percussionist with the Russian imperial band in order to get close. He spoke French, and he was an enthusiast, a *moderne*. I was arrested by the Dutch police, who seized my equipment and burned the film. But I expanded my knowledge of music." He snipped a section containing thirty-two frames.

"What brought you here?"

"Europe is *fini*. Finished. I came here to work for Mr. Thomas Edison. The electrical light, eh?" He reached up and flicked a finger at the bulb, starting it swinging and hurling shadows from wall to wall like ocean waves. "The phonograph, eh? The moving picture. All his, all American. Europe has invented nothing since iron. What is impossible there is here just something that no one has tried yet, just wait. Here they do not throw rotten fruit at something they do not understand." He put a hand up again to steady the bulb, then reached for the glue pot.

"If you think so much of Edison, why did you leave?"

"I did not get along with his man Edwin Porter.

Titles for every scene, as if the audience were Simple Simons and could not figure out what was happening from the evidence of their eyes. Pah! No imagination. I quit."

"And Buck?"

"Another philistine. But he lets me alone to work. At my age it is my only remaining wish." He used the clamp. "You wish to learn to work the camera, eh?"

"No, *monsieur*." Tom's reading of Henry James had not been for nothing. "I'm not a genius, like you and Griffith. I only want to write."

The Frenchman scratched his shaggy head and shook it. "A waste. A mistake. Writing is *fini*. The future it is here." He touched the film. When it came apart at the splice he said something harsh-sounding in French and reached again for the glue.

1927

The Enchanted Hill

I understand the Warner brothers are fooling around with a talking picture," William Randolph Hearst announced. "As a writer, you must have an opinion on the subject, Mr. Pulaski. Do you think it will catch on?"

All eyes upon him now—not the least of them the host's obsidian orbs in their mournful settings, slanting away from the straight nose—he laid down his heavy silver fork and touched his lips with his napkin, made incongruously of fine paper. Conversation about the fifty-foot table, which had been lively and cacophonous, echoing in the vaulted ceiling of the medieval refectory, trickled into silence; when the Chief spoke in his clear tenor, no one interrupted.

"Pulski," he corrected gently. "I haven't written in years. My interests in Hollywood are purely financial and have to do with real estate. I doubt talking pictures will have much effect on me."

That opened the subject to general discussion, and the chattering resumed, more energetically than before. Dinner at the Hearst Castle—referred to variously as San Simeon, The Ranch, El Casa Grande, and La Cuestra Encantada (The Enchanted Hill)—was determinedly casual, despite the presence of ornately carved choir stalls, priceless tapestries, Greek statuary, piles of costly china, and waiters in livery; the newspaper tycoon himself wore tweeds of a genteel, Old World shabbiness, and his mistress, actress Marion Davies, sat across from him in the middle of the table in gold lamé lounging pajamas. The guests had filed in from their rooms and bungalows in a dazzling variety of leisure wear tailored by those same specialists who cut and sewed the evening clothes they wore to premieres and moguls' birthday parties in Beverly Hills, that pink-new colony of Spanish Modern villas and rococo mansions currently spreading like a glittering rash across the once-barren slopes ten miles west of Los Angeles in the shadow of the planing mill. At Hearst's right elbow sat Louis B. Mayer, jowly head of MGM, with former Congressman Will Hays on his sinister side, peering through pince-nez glasses at the truffles on his plate as if they might contain something antithetical to the moral principles established by his Motion Picture Producers and Distributors of America. Farther down were Norma Talmadge, Vilma Banky, Myrna Loy (free for once of the Chinese silks the Montana-born actress was forced by her studio to effect in public to maintain her screen image as an Oriental temptress), Gary Cooper, Gloria Swanson, Wallace Beery, and Irving Thalberg, Mayer's brilliant young production chief, who seemed to take in everything behind his windowpane spectacles as if evaluating its cost. Across from them sat Arthur Brisbane, second-in-command of the Hearst communications empire; Buster Keaton, classically handsome when not wearing his comic porkpie hat;

Hearst columnist Louella Parsons, dumpy in an ordinary floral print frock; King Vidor; Dorothy and Lillian Gish, joined at the hip as always; Ethel Barrymore and her brother Lionel; and John Gilbert, deep in his cups, a fact his tablemates sought to conceal from their host, a teetotaler who had been known to invite guests to leave when they were caught imbibing. Rumor had it Greta Garbo, Gilbert's on-again, off-again fiancée, had agreed to attend the weekend festivities with him, then backed out at the last minute, as she had been said to do when the pair were to be wed. He swayed in his seat and tried to light a cigarette while the Barrymores signaled for a waiter to refill his cup from an elaborate silver coffee-pot.

Summoned by the prospector's son, the inventor of the war with Spain, the two-time candidate for the U.S. presidency, what have you, these stars, moral pundits, and studio bosses had made the long crawl up the coast, and then up the winding road to the castle on the hill, its twin Spanish Renaissance towers and cathedral facade bathed in colored floodlights and visible for miles, like Fuād's palace or a motion picture premiere. Few ignored the mandate, which offered free use of the pools and tennis courts and dancing to the live music of Paul Whiteman, Duke Ellington, or other name bands in Marion Davies's forty-room beach house adjoining the main structure. A visit to the "Versailles of Hollywood" was worth any number of minor annoyances, including strictly enforced prohibition and the prospect of having to shut off one's motor and wait for a soporific moose or water buffalo to rise from its afternoon siesta across the road and lumber on: Prominent signs posted at intervals along the macadam reminded motorists that The Ranch's numerous exotic animals enjoyed the right of way.

He himself had come out of curiosity. The invitation had come through William Murray, manager of the property and an old acquaintance from his earliest forays into real estate investment, and by reason of his tenuous relationship with a number of the other guests, for whom he had written plum scenes before he had latched the case of the Blick for the last time. Before dinner, not wishing to dance and having no skill in swimming or batting balls over nets, he had strolled the exquisitely barbered grounds. He had been struck by the unrealness of the Roman fountains and medieval clerestories, the incredibly ancient Egyptian cat goddesses and Grecian temples that dotted the landscape as if it were a dumping ground for the detritus of lost civilizations. The unlikely hodgepodge reminded him of nothing so much as a studio backlot. He thought of Griffith's *Intolerance*, and those towering plaster-of-Paris idols and massive papier-mâché gates still decaying in the hills behind the painted wooden letters of the HOLLYWOODLAND sign, inserted like a title card above the sprawling city years after the development project of that name had closed its doors. It was that sign that had given the motion picture community the name by which it was now known around the world, or as much of it as constituted the domestic and foreign markets. In his time, Hollywood had been only a street, on one corner of which out-of-work cowboys gathered at the Watering Hole to tell lies and wait for a cattle call to wrangle horses for a western and maybe pick up work as an extra. He wondered where they had all gone. Even the background faces in Tom Mix's last picture looked as if they had come straight from a Broadway chorus.

He no longer recognized in that urban spread the sun-beaten provincial village he had first encountered only fourteen years before. The new reservoir had drawn developers and residents, and the residents had drawn merchants as surely as it had attracted seagulls in flocks from the ocean to the desert. The wooden false fronts had come down and concrete department stores and office buildings had sprung up from their foundations, asphalt had been poured over the dusty streets, bungalows reluctantly rented to "movies" had been swept away and replaced by ten-thousand-square-foot haciendas where five-thousand-dollar-a-week stars sunned themselves and walked their greyhounds among palms and forests of hydrangea planted to screen them from the hungry eyes of their admirers. Gone were the wooden oil derricks and acres of orange groves, vanished the green countryside that separated Los Angeles from San Fernando, Culver City from Burbank; it was all one city, complete with the squalor of Mexican neighborhoods where dwelt the workers who clambered over the raw girders going up downtown. Vacationers tramped the sidewalks carrying cameras and autograph albums, and scrawny, undernourished youths with patched knees and ancient eyes stood on corners hawking maps to the stars' homes. Between 1913 and the end of the Great War, the place had done to itself what its chief industry had done to Tombstone and Dodge City. taken a virile boomtown and turned it into a fat, complacent tourist trap.

Give us ten years, Adele Varga had said. It had taken five.

And it wasn't finished. Everything was so different; yet as he strolled along the circular driveway, passing the line of white Cadillacs, black Deusenbergs, hornet-green Marmons, and wicker-bodied Isotta-Fraschinis, he'd had the premonition that the entire community, the factory town grown like a coral reef around the studios that elected its mayors and appointed its police chiefs and judges, was quivering on the lip of something that would change its face and soul as drastically as a rupture in the reservoir. The feeling had remained with him through the reception and the single cocktail each of the guests was allowed, and had not abated as course after steaming course arrived at the table on baronial platters in the white-gloved hands of Hearst's army of waiters. With the sorbet came yet another opinion on the latest obsession, this from Buster Keaton:

"I'll talk on film when Felix the Cat talks."

Everyone laughed, John Gilbert's cultured baritone rising conspicuously above the group. Ethel Barrymore shushed him.

Mayer said, "Oh, I suppose talking pictures will find an audience, but they won't take the place of the real article. Ninety percent of the market is in foreign-speaking countries. All we have to do is change the cards. What are we going to do if they start talking, shoot the picture in English and then turn around and do it all over again in Spanish and German?"

Norma Talmadge touched her golden helmet of marcelled curls. "Certainly not me. My French is *un petit bon*, but I doubt I can handle Japanese."

"There isn't a market in Japan, dear." Gilbert's cigarette, still unlit, clung to his bottom lip as desperately as Renée Adorée clutched at his boot as the truck carried him away in *The Big Parade*. Hearst eyed him with the suspicion of an old-time muckraker. "Their idea of entertainment is to commit suicide."

King Vidor, Gilbert's director, fingered his crystal

water glass. "You have to hand it to the Warners for grit. They lost everything but their spats when they added music to *Don Juan*."

"The trouble with Fairbanks is he won't admit he's getting old," said Lionel Barrymore. "The first time I met Junior he introduced him as his younger brother."

There was a moment of silence for the graying of Douglas Fairbanks. One of Hearst's dachshunds gnawed disrespectfully at a bone in front of the fireplace.

"I'll answer the question." He looked up apologetically from his sorbet.

The host returned his gaze, and the millionaire's expression was mild once again. Little about his demeanor suggested the magnate who had demanded military intervention in Mexico when the revolution threatened his interests south of the border, or the New York gubernatorial candidate who had orated in Madison Square Garden in favor of the imprisonment of Boss Murphy.

"Don't stand on ceremony, Mr. Pulaski. We're informal here. When I was young I used to camp out on this very hill with my father."

"Thank you, sir. It's my observation that some novelties have a way of hanging around after their vogue is past. I sold the ice business I inherited from my father the day a refrigerator was installed at the White House."

The silence this time was merely polite. Even the dog had abandoned the bone to lick its genitals. It was Hearst who broke it, offering his shy smile across the table to his mistress. "We haven't heard from you yet, Marion. What do you think of pictures that talk?"

The blond hostess swallowed a spoonful of orange sherbet and chased it with iced tea from a heavy silver goblet.

"I think they're a p-passing f-f-fad," she said.

1913

———

Chapter 9

DMITRI

WHEN ARE YOU COMING HOME

YOUR FATHER

The telegram had been addressed to him at the office of the Rocky Mountain Moving Picture Association, where Tom stopped on his way to the studio in response to a telephone message relayed to him by Gus Wolz. He read it twice, then refolded it and stuck it and the envelope in his jacket pocket. He'd bought the jacket, a two-tone design in brown and cream, in a shop in Santa Monica. The outerwear he'd brought was far too heavy for the local climate.

"Bad news?" Adele was watching him from behind the desk.

"Nothing I didn't expect. My father's wondering what became of me."

"You haven't told him?"

"I've started the same letter a dozen times."

"Finish it and send it. Anything's better than nothing, I'm told. I never knew my father. My mother gave me up when I was three."

"There's a matter of three hundred dollars he sent me down with."

"Wire it back to him. I'll get Buck to give you an advance to see you through your first month."

"I can't wire back the car."

"One of your father's men can drive it back after they deliver the ice. I know where you can pick up a used Ford for a buck, if you don't mind bumping out some dents and maybe replacing the radiator."

"They cost eight hundred new."

"Mack Sennett buys them used at fifty bucks a pop and wrecks them on camera. He'd rather replace them than spend time fixing them. His property manager sells them by the dozen."

Tom smiled. "Know somebody who can write a letter?"

"I write all of Buck's, including requests for money from his uncle in New Jersey."

"I was joking," he said. "This is one thing I have to do myself."

"This might take out some of the sting." From the top drawer of the desk she drew a cloth-bound book the size of a ledger, which she spread open on the blotter. It contained blank checks, ten to a page joined by perforations. She dipped a pen in the inkwell, scribbled on one, tore it loose, pressed it face down on the blotter, and held it out.

He took it. It was drawn on the Rocky Mountain account in the Bank of Los Angeles in the amount of five hundred dollars, paid to the order of the Sierra Nevada Ice Company.

"That should cover the ten tons plus trucking fees and expenses," she said. "When you leave a place of employment it's always nice to bring something in."

"Does Buck know you're doing this?"

She shook her head. "It's from the fund he was planning to give the printing company to stall the foreclosure."

"I can't accept it." He thrust the check back at her. Instead of taking it she busied her hands closing the book and returning it to its drawer.

"The day Buck can't handle a mutt like Clarence Peavey is the day he pulls out and goes back East. Peavey's been trying to shut us down for a year. His wife ran off with a gaffer at Famous Players–Lasky and he's had it in for moving pictures ever since. Mutt thinks we're an easy mark."

"But this will give him an excuse."

"To do what? The barn belongs to Thomas Ince. Buck leases all his equipment from Essanay. Even Wild Bill Latimer's on the books as an employee of the Bensinger and Rausch Hardware and Electrical Supply of Union City."

"He can garnishee this account." He waved the check.

"No, he can't. I just closed it out."

"How are you going to operate without money?"

"We're experts at that. If worse comes to worse I'll write another letter to dear old Uncle Stu. He's stinking, and he'll do anything to keep Buck out of the store. So you see, you have to take the money."

"Why are you doing this? You don't need a writer, and my father's never going to invest a cent in moving pictures."

She opened her mouth to reply. Then Buck Bensinger's voice called from the other side of the door behind the desk. "Adele! I need your eyes!"

Tom said, "He's here?"

"A print came in this morning from Chicago of the stuff we shot Saturday. He always stops by to screen it. You've never seen a daily, have you?"

"I don't know what a daily is."

" 'Weekly' would be more accurate. We're thinking of using a developer closer to home, but they charge too much in San Francisco. Come take a look." She rose and opened the door. She had on the working uniform she wore when she wasn't performing: white blouse, dark skirt, and boots. He walked around the desk, putting the check in the same pocket with the telegram.

The inner room, what he could see of it in the stuttering light, resembled the storefront, with a desk and stacks of props and pieces of scenery piled against the walls. Dark shades were drawn over the windows and a big projector like the one Tom had seen in Stockton stood on the desk. Buck stood behind it, turning the crank. On a folding screen ten feet away, men on horseback were galloping jerkily through hilly countryside recognizable as the ranch north of Santa Monica, but the images had an unreal quality: The sky was black, the ground white. The faces and hands of the riders were as dark as the sky.

"Pepita, I can't work this damn crank and pay attention to what's on-screen. Where's Merle?"

"You sent him back to the barn. You said he cranked too fast."

"You work it, then."

"No, sir. I might crank too slow and burn the place down. You said you needed my eyes."

"I wasn't thinking. I trust mine better than yours. Your hands I trust."

In a different tone she said, "Buck, we're not alone."

"I'll crank it," Tom said.

"That you, Tom?" Buck's eyes remained on the screen. "You'd better practice awhile without any film on the reel. This is our only print."

"I don't know why you don't lease a motor-driven one," Adele said.

"I'd rather be the one who decides how fast or slow to turn it, not Bell and Howell. Anyway, Essanay won't lease me one. Anderson's too busy using them for his own pictures." He reached down and flipped a switch. The screen went dark and he stopped cranking. "Let's have some light."

Tom found the wall button and pushed it. A bowl fixture suspended by chains from the ceiling came on. Buck began turning the crank the other way, several times faster. The film whirred through the gate. When at length the end flapped free, he removed the full reel from its peg and laid it gently on its side on the desk. He looked around, found an empty reel lying on the seat of the captain's swivel behind the desk, and put it on the peg. "Yours, Tom." He stepped away.

The wooden handle was warm and slightly moist from Buck's grip. Tom, who was accustomed to the resistance of the Model T's crank, was surprised by how easily it turned. After one revolution it seemed to be operating itself.

"Too fast," Buck said. "Anything faster than eighteen frames per second looks like a Keystone comedy."

He slowed down.

Adele said, "Too slow. You'll burn the film."

Buck said, "Try singing to yourself. 'Way down

upon the Swanee River.' Downstroke on *swan*."

"You told me 'Old Folks at Home,' " Adele said.

"It's the same song."

" 'Old times there are not forgotten,' " she sang. "Downstroke on *not*."

"That's 'Dixie,' but it makes no difference."

"Except when I tried it you said I was cranking too fast."

"That's because you sang it with a flamenco beat. Tom's people came from Russia. They do everything to 'The Song of the Volga Boatmen.' "

" 'That's where my heart is turning ever,' " Tom sang. He swung the crank down on *turn*.

"That's good," Buck said. "You're a natural at this."

"It's easy."

"It helps not to be Mexican."

"Son of a bitch." Adele's tone was sweeter than when she had said the same thing in Spanish the day before.

Buck ignored her. "It's got ball bearings. If you have to stop and blow your nose, the crank will turn a full revolution by itself. Just don't lose your place in the song."

Adele said, "I think he's ready for the real thing."

"Thirty-two more bars," Buck said. "Might as well finish your solo."

Tom felt ridiculous and eager at the same time. At the lake he had prided himself on his ability to keep up with the regular ice cutters as much as he had on his writing. The task at hand seemed absurdly simple, but he had been made to understand that a great deal depended upon how well he performed it. He was learning that this business of making moving pictures consisted of hundreds of small details, each as important as all the rest. He stood by while Buck replaced the empty reel with the one containing the film and threaded the end through the rubber pulleys and between the two plates of glass in front of the lens. "You'll notice the drag when you turn the crank," Buck said. "That's the weight and friction. You'll adjust."

Adele stepped over to the door and placed her thumb on the wall button. Buck leaned across the desk and curled a finger around the metal switch in the projector's base. "Ready, Tom?"

"Yes."

"And roll." He flipped the switch. Adele extinguished the overhead light. Tom began turning. Jerky numerals like those he'd seen in the Stockton theater leapt into sight. This time they were white on black.

"Too slow," Buck said. He sang, " 'Way down upon the *Swan*ee River,' " a notch faster than he had the first time. Tom picked up the song and the pace. The only sounds in the room were his singing and the *clickety-click* of the sprockets. After a while he fell silent, singing to himself in his head. On-screen the riders galloped once again across the uneven landscape, up steep slopes and down gulleys, quirting their reins across the horses' necks for more speed. Tom found himself growing excited, forgetting that it was he who was driving the action. If he stopped cranking, the whole illusion would come to a halt.

Adele said, "Bill's riding is improving. I'm not seeing as much daylight between him and the saddle."

Buck said, "That's because it isn't him riding. He missed the stirrup completely and fell and split his lip. I stuck his hat on one of those bums from the Watering Hole. Luckily they were all in cavalry uniform. I postponed the close-ups until he heals."

"Was he on the needle?"

"No, just clumsy. He can't walk and smoke a cigarette at the same time."

"How'd he ever get to be so big on Broadway?"

"There aren't as many things to trip over on the stage. They never let him handle props in New York. When he did *Hamlet* the actor who played Horatio had to hold the skull."

"I don't know why you use him. Even when he manages to show up before you lose the light, he ruins nearly every take."

"Every take. If Jerry weren't as good an editor as he is behind the camera, we'd still be trying to get through *Bandit Canyon*."

"That's my point. Can him."

"His name on a poster is worth ten thousand on the coast alone. In Iowa and Maryland they think he built the Transcontinental Railroad with his bare hands and captured Geronimo on his break."

"That's because you told them he did. That studio biography makes him sound like the bastard son of Kit Carson and Annie Oakley."

"What else could I say? Folks in Des Moines don't know Shakespeare from the milkman, but they've all read Street and Smith. The guy looks like he stepped right out of a Remington painting. He's gotten us where we are."

"Three thousand in debt, with the Trust breathing down our necks."

"Thanks for the advice, Pepita. I'll put your name on the sign out front, just as soon as you finish typing up those invoices."

"Go to hell, darling," she purred.

"Good job, Tom. I think we can use all of this. Jerry won't agree, but he's a genius."

The film had run out. Tom flipped off the switch just as Adele turned the lights back on. "Why does it look so funny?" he asked. "The moving pictures I've seen in the theaters didn't look like this."

Buck threw up one of the blinds, flooding the room with sunlight. Dust motes swarmed in the yellow beam. "That's because theaters show positive prints. At Rocky we screen and cut the negative. There's no sense printing stuff we might not use. We're not Edison."

A bell jangled. Adele scooped the upright telephone off the desk. "Rocky Moun—oh, hello, Dusty. How's Wild Bill?" A voice buzzed tinnily in the earpiece while her face paled beneath its natural coloring. She held the telephone out to Buck, who took it without questions.

"Me, Dusty. What's going on?" His expression didn't change as he listened. "Who else did you call? Good. Lock the door. Don't open it for anyone but us." He pegged the receiver. "Did you drive in today?" he asked Adele.

"I took the streetcar."

"Shit. Tom?"

"I drove the Ford. It's out front."

"Terrific. You're driving us to Long Beach."

"What's in Long Beach?"

"All that's left of our star."

Chapter 10

Long Beach stank of fish.

The masts and derricks of fishing boats and tugs leaned at odd angles to a row of piers plastered over with slime and glittering scales. Seagulls prowled the streets plucking at cigarette butts and bits of entrails and perched atop awnings streaked white with their droppings. The beach was a maze of nets strung out on stakes to dry. Galvanized tubs of ice stood on the sidewalks in front of fish markets with sea bass gaping atop the crystals, their tails flapping occasionally. Over everything hung the miasma of the mariners' trade. Even the pounding of the surf had to compete with the buzzing of clouds of flies.

At the end of a street of bait-and-tackle shops stood a plain saltbox house built of weathered clapboard, beyond which sprawled the Pacific. Tom set the brake in front of it and they got out and walked around to the ocean side and mounted a wooden porch with sandbags heaped up against its base. Despite that precaution, the bottoms of the whitewashed posts were

warped and discolored where the tide had crept un-
interrupted.

Buck rapped on the screen door. Metal scraped on
the other side and the inner door swung open.
Through the rusted screen, Tom could just make out
a blur of face above an open collar high up. There
was a pause, then a hand moved up to disengage the
hook and Buck pulled open the screen against the
tension of the spring. The man standing in the doorway was very tall and built narrow, with high shoulders in a faded flannel shirt. His legs were long in blue
jeans bleached almost white by washing and sun. A
pair of narrow bony feet in dirty gray stockings stuck
out beneath the rolled cuffs. His right hand was
wrapped around the butt of a long-barreled revolver.

"Who's that with you?" The man's faded blue eyes
were on Tom. He was bald, with a dust-colored fringe
and a clear line above his brows where his tan
stopped. He looked as if he were wearing a white cap.

Buck said, "You know Adele. This is Tom Boston.
He's with us. Tom, Dusty Phillips. Dusty makes Wild
Bill look good in the long shots. He can ride anything
and shoot the fuzz off a peach at forty yards."

"Fifty. I rid up San Juan Hill with Colonel Roosevelt." He lowered the revolver and stepped aside.

The house needed light and air. The windows fac-
ing the ocean were shaded, plunging the room into
deep gloom. As his eyes grew accustomed to the
change, Tom saw overstuffed furniture, a straw mat
on a plank floor strewn with sand, liquor bottles, and
smeared glasses on every horizontal surface. There
was a stench of cigars and mildew and old cooking.

"Where is he?" Buck asked.

"Bedroom," said Dusty.

"You put him there?"

"No. He always done it on the bed."

Adele asked, "Which one of you owns this place?"

"Bill rented it furnished. He never expected to be out here permanent. He was always going back to New York and play some king."

"*King Lear*," Buck said. "But he never mentioned it when he was sober. Let's take a look."

They followed the tall man through a door into another room, just as dark as the first. This room had a pungent medicinal smell on top of all the rest.

Buck said, "Well, let's have some light. You and Bill must be part bat."

Dusty stepped over to the window and gave the shade a jerk. It shot up, flapping like a sea bass, and light rammed into the room. The space was narrow, with faded paper on the walls and ceiling. Most of the area was taken up by a tall bed on a painted iron frame. The man stretched out on the mattress was thicker through the waist than he looked on the *Bandit Canyon* poster—his shirtless belly overlapped the cinch of his wide leather belt—and his inert face was a grayish shade of violet. His feet were bare.

Adele said, "*Dio mio*," and crossed herself.

Buck lifted one of the man's large hands and looked at the purple nails. Then he lowered it and used his thumb to pry open an eyelid. Tom saw only white.

"You found him like this?" Buck asked.

Dusty nodded. "He told me to shake him out at eight and we'd get breakfast. That was around midnight."

"He's stiff already. You didn't hear anything?"

"No. I sleep upstairs. Except when—"

"Except when you don't. Everyone knows about you and Bill except Peavey and a million suckers." He lifted a tent of newspaper from the nightstand. Tom saw a tangle of rubber hose, a forest of small brown bottles, a litter of spent matches, a charred spoon, and a syringe with a glass barrel. "Who gets the stuff, you?"

"Yeah, but I don't use it. I drink likker."

"Tijuana?"

"San Diego. Mexican quarter. Name's—"

"I didn't ask for a recommendation, I just asked where. He know who his customer was?"

"He don't even speak American. We use sign language."

"That's the first good news I've had all day. Throw all this shit in a sack and bury it where the tide won't dig it up. Got anything to write with?" He slid open the nightstand drawer, glanced inside, and pushed it shut. It contained more brown bottles.

Dusty went out.

"This could be worse," Buck said. "We haven't shot any close-ups yet. All we need is somebody with Latimer's build."

Adele said, "He's really dead?"

"If he isn't, he's a lot better actor than I thought."

"We ought to do something."

"We are." When Dusty returned, Buck took the pencil and lined tablet he was carrying, looked up at the ceiling, then back at the top page and wrote something on it. Then he handed them back. "That's the number of a doctor in Pasadena. Don't shake hands with him; he came out here for his TB and it didn't take. He'll sign the certificate and see to the details. Have him bill me. As far as everyone else is concerned, I wasn't here. It was just you and Bill and him. If he died under a doctor's care there won't be an autopsy."

"What about me?" Dusty wiped his nose on his

right sleeve. The revolver still dangled at the end of his hand as if he'd forgotten to put it away.

"How long's it been since you rode?"

"I rented a nag in San Berdoo just before Christmas."

"I just promoted you to cavalry sergeant. Come to the barn tomorrow and we'll find you a uniform. Here's an advance." He took a bulky wallet from his hip pocket and gave him two tens. "Don't buy any liquor till after the doc's come and gone."

"Thanks, Mr. Bensinger. I don't know why Wild Bill said you was a son of a bitch."

"He might've known my mother back East."

On the way back they stopped for lunch in a restaurant that advertised home cooking. They sat at a table with a red-and-white-checked oilcloth by a window overlooking the beach. Watching the waves frothing against the sand, Tom wondered if Yuri was having any luck spotting whales. He wasn't on call that day and had announced he wasn't coming back until he saw one or the last streetcar ran, whichever came first. Thinking about Yuri looking for whales kept him from thinking about a half-naked moving picture actor lying stiff and cold in a bed in Long Beach. He shook his head at the menu that was offered him and asked for coffee.

"Stupid," Buck was saying. "I always knew it was coming. Not this, exactly; I thought it would be a morals charge. Point is I knew he was going to blow up in our face someday. I should've had a backup plan."

"How could you plan to replace Wild Bill? He was a fluke to begin with." Adele crunched on a cracker from the bowl in the center of the table.

"I built the cocksucker from the ground up. I don't mean I made him a nancy and a needle hound; he was that when he came out here. I showed him how to put on his first pair of chaps. He came out of Wardrobe with them on backwards. I did it once; I could've done it again. Fuck it. I still can. I just need time."

"You promised the distributors you'd deliver *Sioux Massacre* first week of February."

"I'll do that if I have to take Lester off the gate and put him in Wild Bill's uniform. They'll be so pissed off he isn't Latimer they won't even notice he's colored. I'm talking about *The Trail of '98*. If I cast anything less than the Second Coming of Jesus in the lead, I might as well open a hardware store in Bakersfield."

"I hear Bill Clifford's unhappy at Universal."

"That's because *Sheridan's Ride* didn't make back expenses. We'd be better off with Lester." He twirled his fork. "When I took out Bessie Love last month I got the impression she could be lured away from Griffith. With Tom's help I could make it the woman's story."

"You've cast that part." Adele's tone would grow icicles.

He patted her hand. "Just brainstorming, Chiquita. You have to throw all the cards to see which ones stick."

"That's one you can put back in the deck."

The proprietress, a thickset woman with severe features and her hair in a net, brought their orders, then went over to refill another customer's coffee cup from the blue enamel pot in her hand. He was an old man with a brown wrinkled face under a long-billed fisherman's cap, reading a copy of the *Los Angeles Star*. There were no other diners.

"What do you think, Tom?"

He looked at Buck, who was attacking his ham and eggs with energy. He hesitated.

"Don't be shy." The producer spoke with his mouth full. "You've got a stake in this too."

"I was wondering if Latimer had a family."

"Not that I know of. He had three wives in New York, but they're all married to someone else by now."

"No children?"

He laughed, but when Tom didn't join in he stopped and took a gulp of coffee. "They weren't that kind of marriage."

"I'm sorry."

"Me too. If he had a son I'd name him Wild Bill Junior and sign him up."

"That isn't what he means, dear. Sometimes I wonder why I'm in love with you." Adele blew on a spoonful of chowder.

"Don't get me wrong, Tom. I'm sorry as hell about Bill. Pain in the ass that he was, I liked him. I'll miss him. But not until I find a way out of this hole the pansy fuck screwed me into."

"*There's* the man who makes my heart pound," Adele said.

Buck wasn't listening. "I'm too far out on a limb to start from the bottom. I need a hook."

"I need salt." Adele had the top off the shaker. It was empty.

The producer looked around and caught the eye of the proprietress, who was talking with the old fisherman. As she started over, the customer picked up his newspaper.

"Holy Christ," Buck said.

The severe-looking woman was at their table. "I beg your pardon?"

"Would you ask that fellow if we could take a look at his paper?" he asked.

"His *news*paper?"

"Just the first section."

She went back that direction, adjusting her hairnet. Adele said, "I still need salt."

"Sorry, Del. I forgot."

The woman returned carrying the newspaper. Buck thanked her, flipped a salute at the fisherman, and asked for salt. As she left carrying the empty shaker, he turned to the back page of the front section and laid it on top of his plate. After ten seconds he sat back. "There it is."

"There *what* is?" Adele asked.

"My hook." He smacked a corner article with his palm.

Tom picked up the section and turned it so he and Adele could read.

DESPERADO FREED.

SAN QUENTIN, JANUARY 11—J. W. Starling, one-time member of Butch Cassidy's infamous Wild Bunch of bank and train robbers and later chief of his own gang, will be released next Monday from the California State Penitentiary after serving fifteen years for the 1897 robbery of the Sacramento Northern Railroad near McAlvoy, in which two bandits were slain in a shoot-out with railroad detectives.

Starling, 45, is believed to have taken part in as many as twenty robberies throughout northern

California, Nevada, Oregon, and Idaho between 1880 and his arrest in December 1897, but no other charges against him were ever proved. In 1879 he was convicted in Eugene, Oregon, for cattle rustling, but by reason of his youth was released for time served in jail awaiting his trial.

Under the terms of his parole, Starling must seek honest employment in the State of California. If he is not employed within six months, he will be returned to prison.

The woman came back with the freshly filled salt shaker. When she left, Tom said, "You're serious?"

Buck gestured toward the newspaper. "I'd be an idiot not to be. The press will sell out his first feature and it won't cost us a penny."

"You don't even know if he can act."

"That never slowed down Wild Bill."

Adele shook salt into her chowder. "At least you shouldn't have to teach him how to put on a pair of chaps."

Chapter 11

Los Angeles, old Spanish Mission that it was, came out in numbers for funerals and weddings. The farewell ceremony for William David Garrick "Wild Bill" Latimer, star of *Bandit Canyon, Cry Apache!, Slaughter in Tombstone*, and 124 performances of *Othello* at the Winter Garden Theater in New York, packed the interior of the Rodriguez Brothers Funerary Emporium and lined the streets to witness the procession to Hollywood Cemetery. It helped that it was a fine day and that the curious among the large Mexican population had had a week to rest up from the festival of the Epiphany.

Buck Bensinger met with the Rodriguezes and agreed to include the parlor's old-time false front prominently in a future production in return for a reduced rate on its best package. This included a simple but elegant rosewood coffin, the use of an organist who knew the chords to "Tenting Tonight on the Old Campground," a horse-drawn hearse on rubber tires, and a thousand-year concrete vault with perpetual care. Buck borrowed the cash from Famous Players–

Lasky in exchange for Jerry Jarette's services on a project to be decided later. When Adele heard about that, she asked if the Fourteenth Amendment held no jurisdiction in California.

"Slavery's about selling and owning," Buck said. "This is just a rental."

"What does Jerry say?"

"You know Jerry. He asked if they'd let him cut the positive for a change."

There was a hitch when, Dusty Phillips having found a letter in Latimer's effects mentioning that he was raised Presbyterian, the pastor of the local Dutch Calvinist Church refused to preside at the funeral. Although Buck's tubercular doctor had issued a certificate assigning Wild Bill's death to a long-standing cardiac condition, the rumors of the actor's leisure activities were a well-chewed subject in the close atmosphere of the old pueblo. Buck then interviewed a Lutheran minister who had no great love for his Presbyterian colleague and agreed to officiate. Adele had an admirer on the *Star* city desk who ran a piece suggesting that Latimer was baptized Lutheran, and the event was allowed to proceed.

In death, Rocky's late prized possession proved to be even more popular than he had been in life. The national wire services picked up the obituary that appeared in the *Star*, and within twenty-four hours the Yucca Avenue storefront was flooded with telegrams expressing sympathy, including one from Sarah Bernhardt, who had toured with Latimer in *Joan of Arc*. Reporters spilled off westbound trains, wearing winter hats and carrying overcoats far too heavy for the southern California climate and mobbed the entrance to Rodriguez Brothers. Buck took Lester off the gate at the ranch and stationed him on the sidewalk with his shotgun to prevent anyone from getting in and taking a photograph of Wild Bill in his coffin.

"That's very sensitive," Adele said. "It's not like you. What about the publicity?"

"It's bigger publicity when you say no," said Buck. "It used to be my job to tape butcher wrap over the windows at Bensinger and Rausch the day before we ran a sale. They were the same old nails and pliers inside, but not being able to see them made the customers crazy."

"The *Plain Dealer* ran a shot this morning of Wild Bill's head superimposed on someone else's body on a bier."

"I bet it looked better than he does. The Rodriguezes didn't do that good a job."

Mourners were expected from across the continent. When a friend back East wired Buck that a contingent of chorus boys whom Latimer had known on Broadway had booked a sleeper for Los Angeles, the producer rang up Chicago on the trunk line and had them arrested there on a charge of lewd and lascivious conduct. They were put on the next train back to New York, thus averting a potentially embarrassing scene at graveside.

Two of the deceased's former wives wired regrets that they were unable to attend. The *Herald* of Omaha, where Rocky's releases were banned because a love affair between a white trapper and a Cheyenne princess had gone unpunished in *Romance on the Warbonnet*, reported that the third, who was chronologically Latimer's first, had declined to send anything when Western Union refused to transmit her message as written.

The services were brief and dignified, thanks to Lester, who barred the door once all the seats were taken.

Two rows were reserved for reporters, who made notes from the minister's text, a conventional passage from Ecclesiastes, and muttered among themselves about the closed coffin. Buck, visibly uncomfortable in a dark blue suit and necktie, delivered the eulogy haltingly from notes drawn from the studio biography he himself had composed.

Before the ceremony, Buck introduced Tom to a number of colleagues who had arrived to pay their respects. He shook hands with little Carl Laemmle from Universal, a German Jew with a comical command of English, who the year before had dispatched a band of armed cowboys recruited from the Watering Hole to seize control of a rival studio; Famous Players–Lasky's famous Jesse L. Lasky, a generally quiet man in his thirties, with the straight back of a U.S. Marine and somewhat extravagant lapels, whose speech sometimes slid out the side of his mouth, a habit not quite broken from his Vaudeville past; and Cecil B. De Mille, a mild-faced, balding young producer at Famous Players, apparently the only person of Buck's acquaintance who addressed him as Arthur. Finally, Buck put a hand on Tom's shoulder and called his attention to a tall, angular fellow of indeterminate age in a charcoal tweed suit that needed pressing and old-fashioned high-topped shoes with brass hooks. "Tom Boston, David Wark Griffith."

Tom took the man's bony hand, examining him more closely. His nose was a hawk's beak, peeling at the bridge from an old sunburn. He had a bulldog mouth, small eyes with a hard shine like beetle's wings, and black hair matted to the skull, as if it was accustomed to the pressure of a hat. His grip was firm but brief, the grasp of a man who knew the social obligations but had better things to do with his hands.

Nothing about his appearance suggested he knew his name was on the lips of practically everyone Tom had met since he came to Los Angeles.

"Buck tells me you're a good writer." His speech had a touch of the Old South, with a slight theatrical vibrato in the vowels.

"I haven't written anything for him yet."

"He has an instinct for genius. I've been trying to get Jerry Jarette away from him for years."

"It won't happen," Buck said. "If you even talked to him, Billy Bitzer would walk out on you. Then I'd hire Billy, and you'd be back juggling bowling pins on the Chautauqua Circuit."

Griffith changed the subject without even a nod to subtlety. "Who are you going to get to replace Wild Bill?"

"I'm working on it. Tom and I are heading north next week to talk to someone."

This was the first Tom had heard of any such plan.

Griffith peeled skin from his nose. "San Francisco? Who's playing there?"

Buck smiled. "You shouldn't ask questions you won't get any answers to, D.W. I'm not the same rube you unloaded five hundred bucks' worth of Cooper-Hewitts on in 1910."

"Those were perfectly good lights. They got you indoors out of the weather."

"I lost my first week's shooting dyeing all the costumes black. Even the browns photographed white. You took me."

"You should be grateful for the lesson. When I came into this business there wasn't anyone who could tell me anything. I had to fall on my face every time. It cost me a lot more than five hundred Yankee dollars."

This time it was Buck who changed the subject. "How's *Judith* coming along? I hear La Gish and Blanche Sweet got into a scratching match the first day of principal photography."

"I don't know where you heard it. Lillian wouldn't fight with a stuck drawer."

"Okay, D.W. Thanks for coming out for Bill."

"They aren't making any new Latimers." Griffith shook his hand. "Come see me when we wrap *Judith of Bethulia*. I'll screen it for you."

"I'd like that."

"Good luck, young man. Drop by Biograph when you get bored with Rocky. All our equipment works." He favored Tom with his quick, powerful grasp, then left to find a seat near the back.

Buck watched him. "You don't wear rings, do you, Tom?"

"No." He was becoming accustomed to answering bizarre questions.

"You're smart. I always have to check to see if I still have mine after I shake hands with that old Reb."

"I thought he was a genius."

"So was Jesse James."

The procession to Hollywood Cemetery impressed Tom with its dignity. Buck had intended to hire a marching band, but the only one willing to work for what he was offering wore big sombreros and played maracas, so he abandoned the idea. The only unconventional feature was the presence of a number of cowboys from the Watering Hole, who had brushed their suits, dug their brightest vests out of their bedrolls, and applied lampblack and white shoe polish to their Stetsons in order to follow the hearse on foot.

Brass buckles and silver watch chains glinted in the late-afternoon sunlight. A few of them had even strapped on their six-guns. Tom was pretty sure most of these diehard westerners had had little good to say about Wild Bill Latimer in life; they were merely hoping to attract the attention of the producers present.

Tom drove Adele's Rambler, with Adele on the passenger's side in front in a fetching black taffeta dress purchased from the funeral fund, complete with hat and veil. The tailoring complimented her tiny waist and she carried a black lace handkerchief for effect. He couldn't read her expression through the veil, but he doubted she was crying. Buck sat in back with Yuri. The big Ukrainian wore his best corduroys and a new white shirt buttoned to the throat. He had brushed his beard until it threw off blue haloes. His right cheek was patched with sticking plaster where he had scraped it when he fell off the horse assigned to him his first day of shooting.

"There's the law in Los Angeles County," said Buck.

They were rolling past Mutt Peavey's big touring car, parked alongside the curb. The sheriff's long frame was leaning back against the front door on the driver's side, one booted foot resting on the running board with his thumbs hooked inside his gun belt. His Stetson was tipped as far back as it would go without falling off. His eyes, tinier even than D. W. Griffith's, followed the hearse in front of the Rambler at the precise crawling pace of the horse-drawn vehicle.

"Skinny-ass bastard won't even take off his hat." Buck cranked down his window and raised his voice. "Take your hat off, you goddamn pencil-pusher!"

The eyes shifted their way, but the rest of him didn't move.

The producer sat back. "Wild Bill was always after me to cast him as a lawman. I bet I threw away a dozen scenarios. Three pages was as far as I ever got before the sheriff started to look and talk like Mutt Peavey."

Tom said, "I wonder where his deputy is?"

"Angel never goes to funerals." Adele was looking straight ahead. "He's superstitious."

Buck leaned forward and folded his arms on the back of the front seat. "You know plenty about him for a border-town working girl."

"Tijuana's not that big."

"It's not that small."

She shifted on the seat and lifted her veil, meeting his gaze. "He had a favorite. She liked to talk. I didn't mind listening. There's not much else to do in a place like that while you're waiting for the sun to go down. If you don't believe that, why don't you go ahead and challenge him to a duel?"

"I'm a lover, Chiquita, not a fighter." There was a grin in his voice.

"Stay away from Angel, then. He's both."

"More talk?"

"He lost his job with the city after he shot down three kids running away from a broken store window. One of them was only twelve."

"What'd they steal, guns?"

"Sausages."

At the cemetery, Buck took his place among the other pallbearers, most of whom he had chosen from among the employees at Rocky, his telegrams to Wyatt Earp and Buffalo Bill Cody having gone unanswered. They included the blue-eyed "Indian" Tom had encountered on his first visit to the barn; Dusty Phillips, all but unrecognizable in a western-cut blue suit with a new white Stetson covering his bald head; Jerry Jarette; Thomas Ince, yet another industry *Wunderkind* and Buck's landlord at the ranch; and Yuri, who manned the right rear corner of the coffin, relieving most of the burden from the shabby little Frenchman in the middle.

Yuri had been silent throughout the day. Tom assumed he didn't care for funerals any more than Peavey's deputy, but the Ukrainian had been untalkative ever since his last journey in search of whales. He hadn't seen any and was beginning to believe they didn't exist. Tom suspected he was homesick.

The graveside services took place under an opensided tent. A tarpaulin had been draped discreetly over the mound of earth next to the open cavity, and the mourners stood without coughing or shuffling their feet while the minister expressed his faith in the Resurrection. Buck and the others lowered the worldly remains of Wild Bill Latimer into the ground with ropes and the assembly broke up.

"Bensinger!"

Buck, Adele, Tom, and Yuri were passing a long gunmetal-colored car with an enclosed rear seat and a colored driver in cap and duster seated up front, exposed to the elements, when the harsh baritone voice rang out. Buck stopped and turned, nearly causing a collision among those walking behind. A white head leaned out the open window in back. The others made way while the producer retraced his footsteps and placed a foot on the car's running board.

"Senator Alvin Wheelock, as I live and breathe," Buck said. "I heard they booted you out of the New Jersey state house, but I didn't think you'd bounce this far."

The man in the rear seat sat back. He wore his fine

white hair long after the fashion of William Jennings
Bryan, swept back behind his ears to his collar. Black-
rimmed spectacles with glittering panes straddled the
thick bridge of his nose, with a silk ribbon trailing to
a gold clip in the notch of a black broadcloth lapel.
His face was pale and ageless, the skin stretched tight
at the temples but beginning to sag under the chin.
He had an underslung jaw and when he bared his
teeth in a smile it jutted out like the base of a cliff.

"I thought you'd heard," he said. "I'm working for
Mr. Edison now."

"You were then. The voters just didn't know it."

"I'm chief security officer for the M.P.P.C. in the
State of California."

"A snake with a title. I'm impressed."

Wheelock's jaw slid forward. "I'm sorry about your
actor."

"The hell you are."

"You didn't let me finish. I'm sorry because he's
still wanted on an outstanding charge of sodomy in
Trenton. I guess he thought the hotel detectives in
New Jersey were less vigilant than the ones he was
used to in New York."

"Why don't you arrest him? I think even you can
handle a stiff."

The jaw retreated. He'd stopped smiling. His eyes
matched the automobile's gunmetal body.

"Since you're recently bereaved, we'll consider today a truce. Tomorrow I intend to deliver a summons
demanding you appear before Judge Mortenson in
Los Angeles and show cause why you shouldn't be
arrested for patent infringement and piracy. If you
take my advice, you'll be in your office to accept it. I
wouldn't want to have to go out looking for you."

"Better make it Friday. I'll be out of town a couple of days on business."

"Friday it is. I'm nothing if not accommodating."

"You should have made that your campaign slogan."

When Wheelock's chin jutted out once again, Tom couldn't decide which expression was more menacing. The senator raised the heavy gold knob of a hardwood walking stick and rapped it twice against the glass separating him from the driver. The motor ground into life. Buck took his foot off the running board, gears meshed, and the car pulled out of line. As it rolled away, picking up speed, Buck told Adele: "I'm starting to agree with your friend Angel. Funerals are just plain bad luck."

She wound her arm around his. "You said the Trust would never reach this far. It's the whole reason Rocky moved out here."

"I never said I was right all the time. I let one of my biggest backers set sail on the *Titanic* before signing the check."

"What *is* the Trust?" Tom asked.

Chapter 12

T*he* Thomas Edison?" Tom was aghast.

Buck nodded. "The Lizard of Menlo Park. The man who stole the light bulb from Nikola Tesla. You know that old story about the conductor who boxed his ears when he was a kid and threw him off the train for stowing away? He didn't throw him hard enough."

"I still don't understand what he's got to do with Senator Wheelock."

They were in a day coach of the Southern Pacific, paralleling the Coast Road between Los Angeles and San Francisco. Buck had decided a first-class sleeper would make a better impression than a long automobile trip, saving money by booking the compartment for the journey south; they could sleep sitting up on the way to the Bay Area. He had placed Jerry Jarette in charge of *Sioux Massacre* in his absence. Adele and Yuri had stayed behind for shooting.

"Edison claims exclusive ownership of the moving picture process. He came up with it as a kid's toy in the 1880s, then forgot all about it for twenty years.

Then his company shot *The Great Train Robbery* in Jersey and found out there was money to be made from the toy. There was plenty to go around, but Old Tom didn't see it that way. Four years ago he had lunch back East with the presidents of Vitagraph and Selig, his biggest competitors in America, and a couple of big cheeses from France, Méliès included. By the time dessert came, they'd put together the Motion Picture Patents Company."

"That's the M.P.P.C. Wheelock mentioned."

Buck bit the end off a cigar and spat it out the train window. They were crossing the Santa Maria River. "The company doesn't make anything, doesn't employ anyone except strong-arm thugs. It doesn't even have an office. It's a monopoly, a trust. Its only function is to keep anyone else from making moving pictures. You remember little Carl Laemmle from the funeral?" Tom nodded. "He was the first to set himself against the Trust. He was just a distributor then, and he refused to pay the two-dollar-per-week licensing fee the Trust demanded through its own General Film Company in return for permission to show pictures. When they cut off his supply, he produced his own series of animated shorts about a villain named General Filmco. That was his Boston tea party.

"The M.P.P.C. declared war. They buried his Independent Motion Picture Company of America in lawsuits, and when that didn't scare him off they pressured developing labs into refusing IMP's business. No store in New York or New Jersey would sell equipment to Laemmle or any of his people. When he got around that by ordering from Chicago, hired toughs beat up the deliverymen on their way into the building and ran off with the shipments. They bribed IMP employees to commit sabotage. The editing room in the New York office caught fire. Master prints were lost or destroyed. Loyal employees got pushed down stairwells."

"I can't believe Thomas Edison approved that," Tom said.

"What's the difference? It was done in his name. You met Laemmle; he's a kindly Jewish shopkeeper. His employees call him Uncle Carl. Rather than expose them to any more danger he shut down, came out here where the Trust didn't have any contacts, and reorganized as Universal Pictures. That was good for him but bad for the rest of us back East, because then the M.P.P.C. went after all the other independents. In New Jersey they hired Pinkertons to break into our homes and plant dope and stolen property, then tip off the cops and get us arrested. I caught one of the slippery sons of bitches in my living room and threw him down the front steps. The next day somebody tossed a firebomb into my studio."

"Pinkertons?"

"We'll never know. The local police were just starting to investigate when jurisdiction was taken from them and transferred to the state attorney general's office. The order was signed by State Senator Alvin Wheelock."

"He was in the Trust's pocket."

"Two bucks a week, fifty-two weeks a year from each of ten thousand theaters and distributors buys a lot of politicians. Anyway, the attorney general's men blamed anarchists for the fire and threw a couple of hunkies who couldn't speak English into the Jersey City pen for fifteen to twenty. Lucky nobody got killed. They'd have hung the poor bastards."

The conductor, long-faced and sallow with a tobacco bulge the size of a crabapple in one cheek, punched their tickets and moved on down the aisle, wobbling on sore feet. Tom waited until he was out of earshot before he spoke.

"Is that when you came west?"

"I held out longer than most." Buck struck a match and puffed his cigar into life. "Ince was out here already, Lasky and Biograph were shooting in the Valley. I sold what I couldn't bring, including those useless Cooper-Hewitts Griffith stuck me with, scouted out the ranch and leased the barn and a thousand acres, and bought a dry goods store to establish an office downtown. The owners wouldn't sell unless I bought out the stock. My first six months in business I made more money selling bedsheets and flannel shirts than I did making pictures."

"Then why not stick with dry goods?"

He looked at Tom through wreaths of smoke. "Why not stick with ice?"

"It's honest." Tom felt the need to defend his father's profession.

"So's dry goods. So's hardware. So's moving pictures, if you look past the hustle. Don't you think the first guy who cut and sold ice didn't have to pitch a razzle-dazzle to convince his customers they needed what he had? He wasn't offering anything they couldn't get for free."

"Adele said something like that last week."

"I hope you listened to her. She started out in a harder line of work than any of us. You think it's all lying on your back, but if that was true you'd see a lot more whores running around in their sixties and seventies. Most of them don't make forty."

"How did you wind up together?"

"I'm not really sure. Jerry and I went down to shoot locations. We stopped in this little shit bar on the waterfront and I bought a bottle of tequila. The next thing I knew all three of us were riding on top of a truckload of artichokes headed back to L.A."

"I can't believe that's the whole story."

"Me neither, but you'll have to get the rest from Del. When you do, tell me. She won't." He tipped a column of ash outside the window. "You're not your father, Tom, and I'm not my uncle. I couldn't stand behind a counter for the rest of my life any more than you could spend it freezing your nuts off on some frozen lake. Jerry worked in a bakery in Paris. Can you imagine him sweating away all that genius in front of a big oven? Or Adele oohing and ahhing under some damn streetcar conductor? Well, maybe you can, but it'd be a waste of the gifts God gave her. We didn't leave all that behind to feel safe. We're fucking well not going to tuck in our tails and go running back to it just because a snake like Alvin Wheelock says boo."

"You can't ignore a court summons."

"I don't intend to, but that's the least of it. Long before I stand up in front of a judge he'll be turning up the heat under Rocky. I'd bet the barn he's already been to see the Pinkertons. They've got an office in San Francisco. When we get back I'm calling a council of war. We're in for something that will make what happened back in New Jersey look like dinner with Woodrow and Edith Wilson."

"Are we stopping at the Pinkerton agency while we're in town?"

"And do what? Even if they admit they're working for Wheelock, the law's on their side until they break it. And you've seen what passes for law in our little corner of the world. No, we're in Frisco for one thing and one thing only. We're going up and bust J. W. Starling out of San Quentin."

As he said it, he tongued the cigar over to one corner of his mouth, just like one of the gangsters in *The Musketeers of Pig Alley*.

Chapter 13

Rising like a granite cliff out of a horn-shaped point of blue clay and gray rock twelve miles north of the City of San Francisco, the south wall of San Quentin put Tom in mind of Mount Shasta.

With the bright metal blue of San Francisco Bay glittering behind it, the prison shared the mountain's stony isolation from the stomach-tightening blue of the sky near the Oregon border. The Romanesque gun towers, the towering chimney, the glimpses Tom received through the gridded iron gate of the Gothic windows of the visitor's wing, created an illusion of impossible distance from the ramshackle village of shops and rooming houses that stood less than a mile away. That distance multiplied over the spare dozen yards between him and the gate.

"What time is it?" Buck blew a mouthful of smoke into the wind.

The driver of the Ford depot hack that had brought them from San Francisco searched his pockets and came up with a turnip watch. "Quarter of one." He snapped shut the lid and returned it to his mackinaw.

The cold air blasting off the bay made Tom grateful he'd brought his own warm coat.

"Well, are you sure we're in the right place?" Buck, who had come away from the station with only a twill jacket, had the collar up around his neck and his fists jammed into the pockets of his whipcord trousers. The cigar between his teeth kept them from chattering.

"I'm up here a couple of times a month, bringing visitors or picking up convicts when they're sprung. They always come through that gate."

"They wouldn't let him go early, would they?"

The driver snorted. He was a basset-faced forty in a tweed cap with a wilted VOTE FOR TAFT ribbon pinned to the side and a ready-made cigarette smoldering patiently between his lips.

"If they said one o'clock, they won't spring him at twelve fifty-nine. When he came through the first time, you can bet the captain of the guard stood there with his watch in his hand and wrote down the time to the second. They'll knock off five years if you save the warden's daughter from falling off the wall, but they won't cut you half a minute no matter what you do."

Directly on the stroke of one, two figures, one in a guard's uniform, the other wearing a blue suit and carrying a suitcase, emerged from the building and walked toward the gate. There they were joined by another guard, who unlocked the mechanism and together with his colleague seized the gate and heaved it open. Outside, the first man turned to the man in the suit and stuck out his right hand. The man in the suit stared at him until he lowered it. Then the guard stepped back inside, grasped the gate in both hands before the other guard could help him, and hurled it shut, leaving the man in the suit standing alone before the wall.

"That can't be him," Buck said. "He's too short."

The driver said, "They don't let them out more than one to the hour. That business about not associating with other ex-convicts starts at the gate. If they said one o'clock, that's your man."

"How come you know so much about it?"

"I worked in the machine shop for thirty-six months."

Buck approached the man holding the suitcase. "J. W. Starling?"

The man was silent so long it seemed he would never reply.

"I'm Starling."

His speech grated, as if he were employing machinery that hadn't worked in years.

"Buck Bensinger, the Rocky Mountain Moving Picture Association. I sent a wire."

"I didn't get no wire. You have to slip the guards a dollar to get a message from outside. I never gave no law a bent penny off a train track."

"Mine was worth it. I offered you a job."

This silence was twice as long as the first. The man was small-boned, no taller than a normal boy of twelve, with an unhealthy bluish pallor. His hair was cropped very close to his skull and he had large eyes with bloated lids that never moved. He had a thin nose, a deeply cleft chin with a tiny white scar, and a mouth that was nothing more than a line drawn straight across. His suit bagged on him, with puckered stitches where the sleeves joined the shoulders, and his necktie was a strip of black cloth knotted tightly at the collar of his coarse white shirt. The suitcase in his hand was painted cardboard.

"What do you make?" he asked finally.

"Moving pictures."

"I heard of them."

Buck uncorked his infectious grin. "Splendid! I was afraid I'd have to explain—"

"I don't believe in them. I heard of machines that fly and ships that sail underwater too and I don't believe in them either. The new fish will tell you anything to make you think they amount to something better than horseshit. Who are these others?"

"This young man is Tom Boston, a writer in my employ."

Now the eyes moved Tom's way. They were gray, the pupils almost nonexistent in the bright sunshine, and might have been punched out of lead for all they gave back. Then they slid toward the third man. "Who's he?"

Buck said, "He's just our driver. He says he served three years inside."

"I never seen him."

"I wasn't in maximum security," the driver said.

"Who's Papa Roy?"

"Lifer, runs the mail room. He came in with the first batch in '54."

There was another uncomfortable silence. Then: "What's the job?"

Buck hesitated. "Actor."

The man's puffy lids moved for the first time, a full blink. With glacier slowness, the message traveled down to the cruel slash of a mouth, which spread and opened to reveal a full set of surprisingly good teeth. The effect, in the wintery face, was not so much sunny as that of the moon glimmering through a rift in the clouds. "You mean like Ed Booth? I seen him yelling up at a window in the Sacramento Theater in '85."

"Not exactly. You won't have to say anything. The pictures move, but they don't talk."

"I just jump around in ladies' pantaloons?"

"You wouldn't be wearing anything you're not already accustomed to. I make westerns."

The smile died, uncomprehending.

"Moving pictures are like camels," Buck said. "You have to see one to know what I'm talking about. Come with us down to Los Angeles and I'll show you."

"I was in Los Angeles once. It had a couple of thousand prairie dogs and one saloon."

"We got rid of the prairie dogs."

"What's the job pay?"

The producer's kaleidoscopic face assumed an expression Tom had not seen before. "Mr. Starling, does it really matter? If you're not working by this date in July, you'll be back behind bars. No one around here is going to employ a convicted thief."

The first trace of color came to the ex-convict's cheeks, like blood on a trout's belly. When he set down his suitcase, Tom thought he was going to hit someone, and could not fathom Buck's immobility. Then Starling turned and walked over to the granite wall behind which he'd spent the last fifteen years. He unbuttoned his fly, took a deep breath, and let it out in a long, rattling sigh. Water splattered the rough gray stones and eddied into a steaming puddle on the clay at its base. He shook himself, buttoned up, and came back to claim the suitcase. "I reckon we'll head on down and see what they done to that saloon."

They started toward the depot hack. "Is there anything you want right away?" Buck asked. "I mean, now that you've peed on San Quentin."

"Flapjacks."

"Pancakes?" He laughed.

"Not pancakes. Flapjacks. Big as a wagon wheel and hot as a squaw's belly. Flapjacks!" Starling threw his suitcase into the back of the hack.

"Are you sure? I've a fair acquaintance with some of the better houses of joy in San Francisco."

"Whores can wait. I ain't sailed into a big stack of jacks smothered in butter and honey since before the Farmer's Bank of Boise."

"But you were arrested for robbing the Sacramento Northern Railroad."

The leaden eyes settled on Tom, who was sorry he'd spoken. "I reckon I got mixed up," Starling said. "Fifteen years is a long time." He started to climb into the rear seat, paused, and bounced up and down on the support springs, which creaked like a ship in a high sea. He laughed. "I'll be a son of a bitch. Maybe I'll catch me a ride on one of them flying machines yet."

They found a restaurant on Telegraph Hill that served breakfast all day, run by an old Chinese dressed incongruously in silk pajamas and a fisherman's cable-knit sweater. Buck and Tom dismissed the hack and driver and drank coffee while Starling disposed of an enormous heap of pancakes dripping with honey and melted butter, using only a spoon. It occurred to Tom that he might not have held a knife or fork since before his incarceration. Conversation was minimal and drowned out for the most part by animal feeding noises and the clicking of metal against china. At length the retired bandit pushed away his empty plate, wiped his lips with a surprisingly decorous movement of his napkin, and drank off his third cup of piping-hot coffee in two gulps. Tom suspected his throat and tongue were lined with asbestos.

"Better than prison food?" Buck asked.

"The grub wasn't so bad. They didn't give you much time to eat it. Thirty minutes, cell door to cell door, including time spent in line, and I was on the top tier. It don't do much for a man's table manners. They used to call me Gentleman Jack in the better places up in Portland, but that's all gone now."

Buck asked if Jack was what the *J* stood for.

"It don't stand for nothing, the *W* neither. Ma thought if I had a banker's name I might amount to something. Well, I done my share of business with banks."

"Did you really ride with Butch Cassidy?" Tom had read a great many of Emerson Hough's tales of the West.

"For a time. The outfit observed too many rules to suit me. Wild Bunch, my ass. I had a better time in the army."

Buck said, "You served in the army?"

"Dishonorably discharged in '96. I got bored and taken off to Texas for a month. If they told me we was going to Cuba, I might of stood around." He watched Buck looking at the clock on the wall next to the kitchen. "How much time before we catch that train?"

"About an hour."

"We can stop off on the way, then. I got something to pick up, if it's still there."

They took a cable car toward the train station. Starling hung off the front, gripping the pole in one hand and his suitcase in the other, squinting at street signs as they passed. At length he made a noise between a hoot and a bark and leapt to the street, stumbling to catch his balance on the steep hill. Cursing, Buck made his way to the rear of the car, colliding with several standing passengers, and propelled himself off the platform. Tom stepped off behind him, turned his ankle, and skinned his nose on the cobblestones when he fell. By the time he rose, Buck was hurrying down a crooked side street and Starling was out of sight.

He caught up with the producer at an intersection. Buck turned his head this way and that. There were houses on every corner.

"For someone who's been shut up all these years, he sure can run," Buck said. "Did you see which way he went?"

"No, I fell." Tom looked around, then pointed at a large Victorian with gingerbread trim. "That one."

"I thought you didn't see him."

"I didn't. But if he was heading someplace he remembered from fifteen years ago, it would have to be that house. It's the only one close by that's been here since before the quake."

"How can you tell?"

"They don't build them with that much trim anymore. It falls off and hurts people."

Buck lifted his brows, impressed.

Tom said, "Also, that's his suitcase there on the porch."

Just then Starling came out of the house, accompanied by a small woman with a broom, who pointed over the edge of the wooden railing. The former bandit spotted Buck and called out, "Got five dollars?"

Buck hesitated, then nodded.

"Give it to this lady." Starling picked up his case, trotted down the steps, found a latch securing a gate in the crosshatching of lath that surrounded the base of the porch, and set down the case to duck through the opening. Buck and Tom entered the yard and the producer passed a crumpled bill up over the railing to the woman with the broom. Starling came back out cradling what looked like a roll of torn and filthy carpet across his forearms. In the open he balanced it in the crook of one arm and slapped at it with his free hand. Billows of brown dust and bits of rotted canvas set him coughing. When the clouds cleared, Tom identified the remnants of an ancient blanket roll wrapped in tattered oilcloth and bound with a single strap; its mate, decayed through, dangled impotently from the other end of the roll.

Buck stared. "*That's* worth five dollars?"

Starling showed his fine teeth. Despite smudges on his face and cobwebs in his hair he looked years younger than he had only minutes earlier. "Maybe just. But when all you got is a paper suitcase to your name, five's as good as a fortune." He slung the roll over one shoulder and scooped up his only other possession. "We'd best get to gettin'. I ain't missed a train since before the Sacramento Northern."

Chapter 14

Yukon Jack!" Buck shouted.

The company was on an enforced break. The generator had stopped, extinguishing the kliegs and throwing the interior of the barn into gray gloom in the middle of Adele's big scene, when a messenger arrives to inform her that her brave lieutenant is dead along with the rest of Captain Fetterman's command. While two grips went out to investigate, leaving open the double doors at the end for sunlight to come in, the cast and crew found seats; all except for Jerry Jarette, who unscrewed the lens of his camera to blow dust out of it and polish it with a soft cloth. Adele borrowed cigarette makings from the bit player whom Buck had cast as the messenger from among the extras and rolled herself a smoke. She nearly dropped the flaming match when the producer leapt to his feet with the strange cry.

She finished lighting the cigarette and flipped the match into a fire bucket. "Who the devil is Yukon Jack?"

But Buck was looking at Tom. "Jack Westondale,

that's the drifter in 'To the Man on the Trail'?" It was a question.

"As I recall. But I thought you wanted me to sponge Jack London out of the scenario."

"Just the plagiarized stuff. There's no sense gutting it. We'll drop the Westondale, call it *Yukon Jack*, make it the drifter's picture. Start it with the friendship, partners to the death, that kind of horseshit; audiences love loyalty. Friend loses everything in a crooked poker game, their grubstake. We'll make Walter Long the professional gambler, if we can get him away from Griffith; he's got a face that makes you want to cross the street when you see him coming. Partner gets drunk, loses his way back to camp in a blizzard, Jack finds his frozen corpse the next day and vows revenge. Sticks up the crooked game for the exact amount his partner lost, shoots it out with the gambler, and wins. The rest is a breakneck chase across the Yukon behind dogsleds, Mounties breathing down his neck all the way. Is that a big debut for J. W. Starling or what?" His eyes were bright.

"Is there a part for me?" Adele asked.

"Isn't there always? This one's a honey: Skagway Sal, Queen of the Klondike. She runs the biggest, wildest saloon north of San Francisco; deals cards, smokes cigars, and waters the liquor personally."

Her face lost color. "That's a character part!"

"Hear me out. She's got a soft spot for stickup men who hit crooked games. Her father was a miner who lost his claim to a sharp—hell, make it Walter Long, drive it home—drew a gun when he realized he'd been snookered, and got shot in the back by one of Long's henchmen. She hides Jack in the basement while the Mounties search her place, but even after they leave she knows they're watching, so she can't let him go. They fall in love, Long shows up looking for his money, he and Jack fight to the death."

"Long's, naturally." Adele was attentive.

"Naturally. Now Sal takes charge. She orders Jack to switch clothes with Long, then sends him back to the basement, calls in the Mounties, and turns the body and the money over to them with a cock-and-bull story about being forced to shoot Jack to defend her virtue. The Mounties, stupid cops, fall for it, pack up the corpse and the booty, and leave Sal and Jack to face the future together. Iris out."

Adele broke the silence that followed. "One change."

Buck looked at her. "The cigars, right?"

"To start. Marie Dressler smokes cigars. I don't smoke at all." She took a drag on her cigarette. "I don't deal cards, don't touch the liquor, don't run the place. I'm more or less a slave, stranded and forced to sing for my bed and board."

"Fortunately, moving pictures are silent." Buck grinned.

"A title card informs the audience I have the pipes of a goddess. Jack stumbles in from the back, out of breath, eyes shifting left and right. Then he hears me singing. He forgets he's a fugitive. He looks around, sees me in close-up. Close-up." She repeated it for Jarette.

"Filter shot," he said, looking up from his lens. "I make you look like Evelyn Nesbitt."

"Make me look like Adele Vargas. I've got a bigger following." She threw her cigarette into the fire bucket to free her hands for gesturing. "He's transfixed. He draws his fur hat off very slowly, as if he's in church and I'm the Blessed Virgin."

Buck said, "You're not that good an actress."

"Go to hell. And my name's not Skagway Sal. It's Sally. Also I don't give orders. I suggest."

"Pepita, don't you think Tom might object to your taking over his scenario?"

Tom laughed involuntarily. "What part of it is mine? You just wrote the whole thing."

"I just sketched out a rough plot. The fine touches are your department. His department, Del."

"You know I'm right," she said.

"Let's not forget whose debut this is. Tom, you can use Starling as technical advisor for the robbery and the getaway. It'll make a hell of a human-interest story for *The Saturday Evening Post* under your byline."

Tom hoped the editors wouldn't reject it out of habit.

"How *is* your pet desperado?" Adele asked. "I haven't even met the gentleman."

"I got him a room in town. Next week we'll find something more permanent. Right now he's just happy to be able to go in and out the door without yelling for a guard. He's already easier to please than Wild Bill."

"One wonders why San Quentin let him go."

"I've got the campaign all mapped out. We'll put him in stripes and take his picture while he still has the convict haircut, run it full page in the *Star* with a big black WANTED over it. Nothing else to start, not even his name. Start 'em guessing. Then we'll dress him up in a Stetson, pearl gray—no, *black*, a black hat, just like Ince uses for his heavies in the long shots—leather vest, striped pants, boots, cartridge belt, the works, with a bandanna covering his face. Shoot him full figure, pistol in each hand."

"That's Wild Bill's trademark," Adele said.

"As if he's going to hoist himself up out of the sod in Hollywood Cemetery and sue us. I respect the dead as much as the next man, but this is the *moving* picture business. Corpses are strictly for stills." He brushed back his feral shock of hair. " 'Bad Man Makes Good in *Yukon Jack.*' That's the pitch, don't you see? It's not only the plot of the picture. It's his life."

"Very impressive, darling, but have you forgotten you're still shooting *Sioux Massacre?*"

"We'll finish it, but not with Starling. He's too big a story to throw away on a programmer."

Her strong black brows lifted. "You told me this was a feature."

"It was, as long as it starred Latimer. You're a jewel in Rocky's crown, Chiquita, but you're not Mary Pickford. Outdoor yarns need a big male name to pack them in when the back forty isn't plowed and the cow's in the bog."

"I never had any trouble packing them in down in Tijuana." Her color was back now, with flush to spare. Two of the grips looked at each other and slipped down off their packing cases in search of work at the opposite end of the barn.

But Buck was not without tact. "You still could, down there. Up here the wives control the household accounts. Do you think they'd let their men spend the egg money to see you?"

She crossed her legs, bouncing a distinctly non-Victorian length of ankle beneath the hem of her gingham dress, and said nothing. Not quite checkmate, Tom thought, but the board had been spared an upset.

"Putting Starling in a cavalry uniform and casting him as Fetterman would only weaken the buildup later," Buck said. "I'll promote one of the boys from the Watering Hole. Who knows? Maybe he'll catch on. I'm fresh out of good second leads since Hoot Gibson went to Biograph."

"How are you going to finance this publicity campaign?" Adele asked. "You're still on the hook for the last printing bill, and newspaper advertising managers aren't as forgiving as your loyal employees."

"I've got a little left over from the cash I got from Lasky for Wild Bill's funeral. I'll get the rest by offering him Jerry for a second project after he finishes the first. He's still our best asset."

"Hadn't you better ask Jerry how he feels?"

Jarette, who had replaced the camera lens and was using his soft cloth to wipe down the rest of the instrument, shrugged. "I am a photographer. I am in this business to make pictures."

"Just don't get to liking it too much at Famous Players," Buck said. "Lasky straps his cameramen to airplane wings and the roofs of moving trains. He'll never give you the respect you get here."

"He's right, Jerry. Remember, you've got a light bulb in your little outhouse." Clearly, Adele was still miffed about Buck's Mary Pickford comment.

The grips who had gone out to look at the generator returned. One of them was carrying a flat leather strap doubled over in one hand.

"Out of gas, boys? Go down to Santa Monica and fill up the can. Here's a couple of bucks." The producer dug some bills out of his wallet.

"It ain't gas." The grip with the strap held it up. Tom knew his name was Morrie; Adele had addressed him by that name Tom's first day, in the course of deflating his crude sexual allusions to the antique cannon in his charge.

"We just replaced a belt last month," Buck said. "How many does it take to run that machine?"

"Just one. Only it didn't break."

"It's a cut," said Morrie's companion. "Somebody cut it. Look at the edges."

Buck took the belt and examined it. It had parted in a neat line without any fraying.

"Kids, maybe," Morrie said.

Buck thrust the belt back at him. "Can you fix it?"

"It won't hold."

"Damn it, I pay Lester to guard the gate."

"It's a thousand acres," Adele said. "He can't watch the whole ranch."

Buck said to the grip, "We bought this one from a farm equipment store in San Fernando. See if they've got another one in stock. Meanwhile we'll shoot the outdoor stuff." He turned to Tom. "Where's Yuri?"

"Practicing his riding."

"Track him down. Tell him if he sees anyone he doesn't recognize skulking around, he's to hang on to him. Tell him to tell the others, all the extras. There's a close-up and a title card for the man who catches someone who doesn't belong on the ranch."

"He doesn't care about those things. He'll do it for me."

"I'm counting on that."

Tom hesitated. "Is it Senator Wheelock?"

"Not him personally, you can bet on that. He might get a smudge on his collar."

"Pinkertons." Adele whispered the dreaded name.

"They've been busting strikes and dynamiting buildings since Jesse James," Buck said. "Vandalizing equipment is just a warm-up."

Tom said, "But Wheelock hasn't served that summons yet. That's due tomorrow."

"I didn't think he'd do anything till afterwards either, but he's a sneaky old bastard. He served five terms in the New Jersey state senate, and he was a railroad lawyer before that. That's when he got in tight with the Pinks. They've got a long history together."

Adele said, "It might not be the Pinks."

"Of course it's them. Wheelock's a newcomer to California. Who else would he use?"

"One of us."

Tom didn't care for the look that passed among the members of the cast and crew.

Chapter 15

A quarter of a mile north of the barn, the ground stopped rolling for a brief eighty-acre rest before climbing into the foothills. There under the serene vigilance of Buck Bensinger's Civil War eight-pounder, the earth was packed hard as pavement and beaten bare of grass by the ironshod hooves of the Rocky Mountain remuda. There, old-time cowboys in need of a refresher course in the saddle and "tender-heels" who had never ridden anything more challenging than a Ford with a shattered spring prepared for the long-shot equestrian-chase footage endemic to the form. The men from the Watering Hole referred to that stretch of real estate as the "Bozeman Ball-Buster," and upon occasion were known to fling fire-crackers into the horses' paths to make things more lively. White Company ambulance drivers in the employ of St. Mary's Hospital in Santa Monica knew the way there without being directed. Enthusiasts of western moving pictures visited the trash cans behind the hospital often to claim discarded plaster casts autographed by their favorite performers.

Tom found a half-dozen cowboys seated on the edge of a buckboard that had appeared in more features than Wild Bill Latimer, passing a bottle back and forth and shouting words of dubious encouragment to a rider bent over the neck of a lean sorrel. The animal was galloping full tilt on a course parallel with the wagon. Tom could hear its lungs heaving at a distance of two hundred yards.

The man he knew as Chickamaw sat near the tailgate, his lanky legs dangling almost to the ground. Tom climbed up beside him.

"Shoot under any horses' bellies today?"

Chickamaw turned his head. Recognition brightened his sandpapery features. "Hey, there, hoss. I ain't had the chance to do nothing but pound leather with my ass all day long; I might as well of stood it out at Miller Brothers. You hear yet who they're getting to take Wild Bill's place?"

"Buck's thinking of promoting one of the cowboys."

He hooted and nudged the man seated to his right. "Will, you hear that? They're cutting out somebody from the string."

His companion's humorous face broke into a baggy grin. "I liked that eastern feller the second I laid eyes on him. His ma must hail from Oklahoma."

"Texas," Chickamaw said. "Hoss, that's the best news I heard since they sent the car. The boys have been saying that rooster Tom Mix was coming over from Selig." He squinted, suddenly sly. "Anybody specific?"

"He didn't say."

"You be sure and put a word in for old Chickamaw. If it wasn't for me, you'd still be driving all over Lost Angeles, looking for Yucca Avenue."

Tom inclined his head toward the horseman, who

was kicking up dust now in the opposite direction. "Is that Yuri?"

"That's the Rooshian. He come around here making out like he don't know a hackamore from a choppin' block. Turns out he rides like a San Antonio boy."

"Tulsa," said Will.

Tom said, "I'm not surprised. He comes from Tartar stock."

"Well, they ought to buy a case of it and send it to these Oklahoma boys. There isn't a one of 'em that couldn't get hisself throwed from a Morris chair."

A looping right fist caught Chickamaw on the temple, knocking him off the buckboard and his Stetson off his head. Will slid off behind him, pressing his advantage. Chickamaw, still unsteady on his feet, threw a left that missed. The two went into a clinch, and in a little while both were on the ground, kicking and biting. The other cowboys lost interest in Yuri's riding and gathered around the combatants, cheering and digging in the pockets of their Levi's for money. The odds favored the Texan. Tom, less interested, struck off across the trampled ground.

The big Ukrainian, spotting him, turned the sorrel in his direction and drew rein a few yards away. He leapt down, his dark eyes bright. Rivulets of sweat had made tracks in the dust on his cheeks and streaked his beard with mud. "What you think?" he said. "I been going around on foot my whole life and it turns out I didn't have to."

"You even impressed the cowboys."

"Them. They all want to be somebody else."

"Doesn't everyone?"

"Hard enough staying Yuri." He drew the sleeve of his heavy ticking shirt across his brow. In his denims and high-heeled boots, worn almost through at the toes by someone else's feet, he looked more American than he had at any time in their acquaintance. "You write your father yet?"

Tom tapped his temple. "In here. I haven't set down the words."

"He's going to think you stole that money."

"All I've spent of it was on the trip down and our first week in the bungalow. We get paid tomorrow. I sent him the check Adele made out for the ice," he added.

"It isn't the ice he cares about."

Tom brought the subject around to his mission. He told Yuri about the broken generator belt and that he was to spread the word among the cowboys to keep an eye out for strangers.

"This has to do with that Wheeler fellow?" Yuri asked.

"Wheelock. Buck thinks so, but it could be coincidence."

"It almost never is." He stroked the sorrel's moist neck. The animal nuzzled his ear, tickling him. White teeth flashed in the black beard.

Tom said, "It looks like you made a friend."

"He smells my ancestors. Are you writing scenarios now?"

"I just got my first assignment: *Yukon Jack*. J. W. Starling's first starring feature."

"I hear he's a rough old cob."

Tom grinned. "You've been spending too much time with those fellows from the Watering Hole. You're starting to talk like them."

"They're not too bad, except for wanting to be somebody else. Not all that different from ice cutters." His face brightened. "I might have seen a whale."

"Where? Here?"

"Don't be difficult. I took a red car out to the pier in Santa Monica yesterday. I heard a splash. I was looking the wrong way at the time, but when I turned my head the water was still falling. It was too big for a sea lion."

"What happens when you see one for sure?"

"I go home."

Tom felt a pull at his heart, as if he were already alone. He changed the subject again. "How long are you going to be riding? You've almost worn out your horse."

"I'll just take him the rest of the way in. He likes to walk after a hard run." Yuri toed the stirrup and swung over and into the saddle. The movement was balletic.

The fight had ended. The gladiators, their flannel shirts hanging in flaps and their denims smeared with horse manure and dust, were seated in their original position near the end of the buckboard, sharing a plug of chewing tobacco. As Tom approached alongside Yuri, coaxing the sorrel forward at an easy walk, Buck Bensinger's stocky figure strode out from among the chattering cowboys. The extravagantly brimmed sombrero the producer had donned against the hot sun had obviously come from Wardrobe.

"That's the prettiest sight I've seen all week," he said by way of greeting. "Better than Louise Lovely naked."

"The fight?" Tom asked. "Who won?"

"Who cares? I mean that goddamn beautiful fucking Cossack. Sarah Bernhardt never climbed a flight of stairs the way you stepped into leather just now." He was looking up at the rider. "Could you do that on camera?"

"I don't see why not. I was just mounting." Yuri relaxed the reins in his lap.

Buck took off his sombrero and held it up to block the sun. "You aren't married to that beard, are you? It isn't a religious thing?"

"It just grew."

"Would you consider shaving it off?"

"I've had it since I was fourteen. I don't know what I'd look like without it."

"We'll take that chance. America likes its heroes clean-shaven. Your name's Yarbro, right?"

"Yaroslavl."

"Wrong. I don't know what it is yet, but it isn't that. It has to fit on a poster, and people have to be able to pronounce it."

"Why? I'm just an extra."

"Wrong again. You're William J. Fetterman, Captain, United States Cavalry. You're finishing out the picture in Wild Bill's place."

"Holy shit!" Chickamaw spat out a tooth.

His opponent, Will, shook his head and grinned his baggy grin. The expression pushed his swollen left eye the rest of the way shut.

"It's all square with me," he said. "At least he ain't from Texas."

"What do you think of moving picture making now?" Tom asked his friend.

"The same thing I'd think of the ice business if your father took a deliveryman and made him president," he said. "But I'll stay until my first whale."

"What whale?" Buck put his sombrero back on. "I shoot westerns. Let Biograph do *Moby Dick*."

Chapter 16

Tom steeped himself in research, which considering the facilities available to him was no small feat.

San Fernando had no library. What passed for one in Los Angeles filled the ground floor of a frame house with floorboards that creaked and a deaf old woman behind the desk who interpreted shouted requests with the aid of an ear horn mounted atop a bamboo cane and a nearly nonexistent skill for reading lips. The reference section, a single case standing in the short hallway leading to the bathroom, consisted of *Webster's New International Dictionary* and a complete set of the *Annual Cyclopedia* through 1890. Tom gleaned some basic geographical information about Alaska and the Canadian Yukon Territory from the latter, but for details on the gold rush of 1898 he was forced to crib from the stories of Jack London and the poems of Robert Service, found among dog-eared magazines in the periodicals section. That evening in the sitting room of the bungalow, with Yuri snoring in his bedroom, Tom arranged his scribbled notes next to the

Blick on a folding card table he'd bought in a sec-
ondhand shop in Santa Monica and typed:

```
                    YUKON JACK
             A Moving Picture Scenario
                        by
                    Tom Boston
```

He didn't pause to admire the title page, as had
been his habit whenever he'd started a short story,
but laid it in the box his blank paper came in, cranked
a fresh sheet into the platen, and hurled himself into
his opening scene, much of which he'd written in his
head while driving home from the library: a furious
blizzard, with the shadowy figures of a team of powerful dogs plunging through mounting drifts, pulling
a sled, the man behind uncurling a whip furiously
above their heads. In his mind he could hear the
cracking, like crisp pistol shots, and he hoped the illusion would carry to the audience, who would have
only the sight and the strokes of a theater pianist to
go by. Then the pursuers, close behind, identified by
more dogs and men, and two sleds, their greater numbers creating automatic sympathy for their outnum-
bered prey. Cut to—

He paused, fingers curled above the keys. He
needed a name for the saloon where Skagway Sal—
sweet Sally, now—would win Yukon Jack's hardened
heart with her beauty and voice. He thought back
over the day's events, from the sabotaged generator
belt to Yuri's sudden promotion from ice cutter to star
(provided he agreed to shave), a prospect that meant
less to him than the magnificent aquatic creature he
had come all this way to see. At that point Tom

stopped remembering and pounced on the keys. "The Whale's Whiskers," he typed.

This scene fairly wrote itself, a thing he credited to Adele's sure instinct for romance and drama. He saw the untidy sprawl of shaggy miners and prospectors, slopping their drinks out of their glasses as they raised them to hail the delicate songbird, modestly but provocatively attired in a Victorian starched blouse closed at the throat with a cameo brooch, a feather in her hair; saw the hurricane lamps swooping from chains stapled to the ceiling, slinging lariats of shadow and greasy tallow light; saw the moment when the fugitive's hunted eyes rested at last upon the angel who had entered his hell. He removed his hat, just as Adele had said, and with it his hard, persecuted look. A young face now behind the smudges and stubble, hardly more than a boy's, and handsome. How Jerry Jarette's camera would manage that transformation with only J. W. Starling's convict face to work with was something Tom left to the Frenchman's much-touted genius.

He wrote, heedless of time, until past two o'clock, when the occupant of the bungalow next door, an editor at Universal, opened his window and shouted at his neighbor to cut out the racket, people were trying to sleep. Within moments, other windows were flung up and residents down the line called to one another in relays for silence. The scene could just as well have taken place at two in the afternoon; moving picture people kept bizarre hours, and at any time of the day or night were as likely to be at work as asleep. After covering the typewriter, Tom shuffled together the pages he'd written, marveling at the weight and thickness of the sheaf. The best he'd been able to manage in the little tin shack near Shasta was five pages. He credited this new prolificacy to the company he'd been keeping. Never in his life had he spent time with so many creative people; he drew energy from them, as a coward drew courage from a mob. Tired as he was when at last he slid between the sheets of his narrow bed, he lay awake a long time, congratulating himself upon the wisdom of his decision to join Rocky. The euphoria sponged away much of the stain of guilt that had darkened his thoughts for deserting his father's company without having given notice. He resolved to write him a letter in the morning, apologizing for his long silence and explaining his chosen course, and thus eradicated the last tiny speck in the instant before he went to sleep.

He was awakened after five hours by Yuri bumping around in the little water closet. The sun was full in his face. While awaiting his turn at the toilet and sink, Tom dressed and read over what he'd written. He was a little surprised, after penciling in two small changes, to find himself satisfied. In the past he'd been known to throw most of it away and start over with the fraction that was left. It helped that he hadn't needed to worry about style, since his words would be read by only a handful of people before translation to the screen, but the pictures he'd drawn with his minimal descriptions seemed original and vivid, the spare dialogue that would appear on title cards brimming with character. He would not have been ashamed to submit these pages to a magazine. Even so he debated with himself before deciding to show them to Buck. The story was less than half-finished, and he worried that the producer would attempt to influence the remainder. He had an idea for the conclusion that if it worked would break new ground in moving pictures, or what he knew of them based on the ones he'd seen.

Just then Yuri came out into the sitting room, and the sight of the big Ukrainian without his beard made him forget all about his scenario.

While he'd had them, the glossy black whiskers had given him a ferocious air that only Tom, who had known him since he himself was small, knew for a sham, concealing the laconic gentleness of a large and powerful dog. Without them, his eyes seemed smaller and less intimidating, although they retained their luminescence. He had sharp cheekbones, tilted in the Tartar manner, the right one bright pink where new skin had formed after he'd scraped it in a fall his first day on horseback, an aquiline nose, and a round chin with a shallow cleft, marred slightly by a piece of sticking plaster where he'd cut himself with his razor. The greatest surprise was his mouth: It was beautifully curved, like a woman's, with a full lower lip and the upper defined by a deep dimple.

Tom felt a stab of jealousy. He was somewhat vain of his dark curly hair and even features and was accustomed to thinking of himself as the better-looking of the pair. But with his face scraped, in his heavy denims and faded underwear with the sleeves rolled up to reveal his muscular forearms, Yuri Yaroslavl, the ignorant ice cutter on the run from a doubtful Russian past, was a sight to turn the head of every romantically inclined female in southern California.

"It's as bad as I thought," Yuri said. "I can see by the way you're looking at me."

"You look good," Tom said.

"I look like a woman. No one's going to want to take my picture looking like this. I can't even be an extra, and I can't go back up north. The other cutters will beat me to death with their cant dogs."

"You look like Richard Harding Davis."

"How many people is that?"

"Just one. He's a newspaper correspondent." He looked around, spotted yesterday's issue of the *Los Angeles Star* sprawled in scattered sections on the tapestry sofa, and paged through it until he came to the illustrated advertisements. Finally he pointed at a pen-and-ink drawing of a young man with wavy hair and a clean profile wearing an Arrow Collar. "He posed for this years ago."

Yuri snatched the section out of his hand, held it close to his face, then at arm's length. Tom suspected he was farsighted, but refused to wear reading glasses out of an ancestral prejudice against displaying one's weaknesses. "I look like that? You're serious?"

"I've never lied to you."

The Ukrainian smiled.

Buck had told them to stop by Rocky's office in town and collect their pay on the way to the studio, where the rest of the payroll would be divided among the other employees. Where the money had come from, loans from other studios against the services of Jerry Jarette or a gift from Buck's Uncle Stuart to keep him away from New Jersey and the hardware business, or one of the variety of mysterious sources the producer tapped like a sweet-toothed vagabond in a grove of maple syrup trees, wasn't Tom's business. He started to pull into the curb before the storefront, but found all the space was taken by a long Packard touring car and Alvin Wheelock's gunmetal-colored limousine with his colored driver seated behind the wheel, yawning and polishing the lenses of his driving goggles with a white lawn handkerchief.

"Isn't that—?" Yuri began.

"It is. And that's Sheriff Peavey's Packard."

Tom executed a U-turn and parked against the curb on the opposite side of the street. The man leaning in the doorway of the real estate office there came upright, straightened his necktie, and squared the straw boater on his head. When after a full minute the two men had not gotten out of the car, he went inside and slammed shut his door, jangling the bell attached to it.

In a little while Senator Wheelock came striding out of Rocky Mountain in a black morning coat and striped trousers, a gray homburg perched on his head at an insolent angle, and a cigarette burning in a black holder clenched between his teeth, the tip pointed skyward. He was shorter than he had appeared sitting in the backseat of his car; his big head and barrel-shaped torso were balanced on a pair of bowed and stunted legs, giving him a bantam strut. Close behind him walked Angel, Peavey's deputy. The Mexican was the same size as Wheelock, but built in proportion, powerful-looking in the neck and shoulders, the muscles of his thighs standing out beneath the tight material of his uniform trousers. Tom guessed he was a bodybuilder.

No conversation passed between the two men. Once on the sidewalk, they went in separate directions, Angel to the Packard to retrieve the crank from the floor on the passenger's side, the senator to his cubicle behind the Negro driver, who got out to hold the door for him, then bent to the crank. The limousine pulled out behind the touring car and turned right at the next corner. Angel went straight. The pair might have been strangers whose schedules happened to coincide in the office of the Rocky Mountain Moving Picture Association.

Tom and Yuri crossed the street and let themselves in the door. The front room was unoccupied and the door stood open to Buck Bensinger's private office, where they found the producer seated in his swivel with his feet crossed on the desk in their lace-up boots. The desktop was invisible as usual beneath its burden of papers and film cans. The projector stood in a corner on the floor. Buck didn't look up from the two-foot sheaf of papers he was reading when they entered.

"Wheelock's yellow," he said without preamble. "I never noticed it back home, where he had the state legislature behind him. Out here he won't even walk into a man's office to serve legal papers without a greaser in a uniform to back him up."

"I'm surprised he didn't bring the sheriff," Tom said.

"I guess Mutt figures even Angel can do the work of an office errand boy without help. He's saving himself for when he can throw us off the ranch."

Yuri, who had never before been inside the private office, wandered around, looking and touching. He put Tom in mind of a child exploring a cluttered attic on a rainy day.

"What's the paper say?" Tom bent his head to read the typewriting on the back of the page Buck had just turned over.

"Gibberish. It's no wonder the damn lawyers are taking over California. They made up their own language and only teach it to each other. Underneath all the horseshit it says I have to stand in front of the Honorable Henry Horatio Mortenson on March tenth, if he happens to be sober that day, and talk him out of throwing me behind bars for making moving pictures without kissing Thomas Alva Edison's musty ass and asking please, sir, may I?"

"That's six weeks away."

"Wheelock's doing. The sneaky old bastard wants plenty of lead time to break my spirit. That slashed belt yesterday was just the salad before the main course."

"Did he tell you that?"

"Of course not, and I didn't give him the satisfaction of accusing him. He'd just be back later to serve me for slander. Angel would make a dandy witness. Who the hell are *you*?"

The question was startled from him. Yuri, lifting the folding projector screen to test its heft, had accidentally released the catch that held the screen taut. The canvas had shot back up on its roller with a noise like a chandelier falling.

The Ukrainian, red-faced, folded his hands behind him. "I'm Yuri."

"Horseshit. Yuri? Horseshit." Buck looked at Tom with an expression encouraging him to say horseshit.

"You asked him to shave off his beard." For once he couldn't tell by the producer's face if he liked what he was looking at.

Buck threw the summons onto the desk, where it camouflaged itself immediately among the other papers, withdrew his feet from the top, and stood. He grasped Yuri's shoulders and went up on tiptoe to look at him close up. He looked as if he were climbing the Ukrainian. Yuri stiffened during the scrutiny. Tom was pretty sure he didn't like to be touched.

Finally Buck let go. His gaze drifted around the office, lighting at last upon a pearl gray Stetson that looked as if it had been hanging on the hall tree beside the door for years; there was a small but distinct bulge on the side of the crown where the bulbous end of the brass hook had begun to gnaw through the fur felt. He charged that way, scooped the hat off the hook, charged back, and thrust it at Yuri, telling him to put it on. Tom thought he would have plopped it onto the big man's head himself if he could reach that high. People had a way of turning into inanimate objects once they'd attracted Buck's interest.

Yuri scowled at the item. "I don't think it's big enough."

"Who cares? If it doesn't look like shit we'll have one made that is. Put it on."

"Dmitri?"

His eyes implored Tom, who knew what he was thinking. It was one thing to appear ridiculous in front of his friend, quite another to do so before a near stranger.

"Who the hell's Dmitri?" Buck said. "Put the damn thing on."

Tom nodded, smiling encouragement.

The big man sighed, turned the hat upside down to find which way it went, revolved it 360 degrees, and put it on. He had to tug it down to get it as far as his temples, after which it tried to ride up. But the effect was dramatic. Without his beard, and with the swooping brim throwing shadows under the bony ridge of his brow and into the hollows below his cheekbones, Yuri looked like a bronze statue celebrating the glory of the American cowboy. He appeared more authentic than any of the extras from the Watering Hole, the weathered and trailworn products of cattle ranches and stock drives from Montana to the Rio Grande.

He glanced from Buck to Tom, and misinterpreted their silence. "I knew it." Coloring deeper, he reached up to snatch off the Stetson.

"*Madre mia.*"

None of the three had heard the bell tinkling when Adele opened and closed the front door. Now Tom and Buck turned to see her framed in the doorway to the office, already wearing her gingham dress for the day's shooting. She was staring at Yuri. Absentmindedly she crossed herself; then, gathering her wits, she strode into the room, offering her right hand.

"I'm honored to meet you, Mr. Starling," she said. "May I say you're everything I'd pictured."

1930

———

Flight of Fancy

He had managed to miss the war the first time, hung up in training when the Kaiser decided to wrap. The second time, the front came to him.

Columns of colored light rammed pastel holes through the night, climbing hundreds of feet with clouds boiling at the tops. Other shafts were mobile, jousting and crossing and circling among the firmament, visible from as far away as Catalina: five times as many, it was said, as had ever been used for such an event, and each of them many times more powerful than all the kliegs that had threatened to burn down Rocky's barn and sent actors and crew into the shadows for days at a time with damp cloths over their eyes, waiting for the pain and redness to subside. Biplanes buzzed among them, fragile box kites with zipping propellers, swooping low enough for the crowds on the street to see the pilots' faces below their leather helmets and bugeye goggles, rictus expressions intent upon avoiding a hundred different opportunities for collision that close to the pavement. The craft seemed little more than huge harmless moths, less substantial than the dummies made of balsa and papier-mâché hanging motionless and stately from the conventional streetlamps. (J. W. Starling: *I heard of machines that fly and ships that sail underwater too and I don't believe in them either.*)

Crowds were good, crowds were dangerous. Two hundred fifty "special police"—Los Angeles regulars and reserves, studio security, and fifty extras on Howard Hughes's payroll wearing uniforms leased from MGM's vast wardrobe department—kept them behind the barricades with threats and batons. Three companies of marines on loan from the San Diego base patroled the side streets looking for local protection racketeers intending to make good on promises to throw acid in the faces of Jean Harlow and Bebe Daniels if Hughes didn't come across with thousands. Five hundred thousand spectators were good for the industry, bad for beleaguered authorities still struggling to cope with a population that had trebled itself three times in ten years. There was, too, a hunger in the eyes of the men and women ranked ten deep at the barricades that had not been there seven months before, when the New York stock market disintegrated. A depression was on, members of the Young Communist League worked their way along the lines handing out literature from the Popular Front, the young men in white shirts and neckties, the young women fashionable in cloche hats and white cotton gloves, smiling and wishing everyone an entertaining evening. Revolutions were always orderly at the start.

Whoever kept the population count had taken a busman's holiday tonight to inventory the cars parked in the Grauman's lot and lined up along the boulevard: 45,000 hardtops and convertibles, coupes and sedans, Italian limousines and German speedsters, Au-

burns with their muscles showing, and plain old pro-
letarian Model Ts, hanging on like weeds three years
after the last of them left Detroit.

He was a guest of Howard Hughes, but he had no
idea if the spoiled young millionaire would be attend-
ing the premiere of *Hell's Angels*, at four million and
change the most expensive moving picture ever made;
the cost of the retakes alone, when the popularity of
talkies forced the production to shut down while concrete soundstages were built and recording technicians
pirated away from MGM and Paramount, would
have financed Rocky throughout its existence.
Hughes, who had personally suited up to man the
controls of a Spad during the zeppelin-busting scene
(a color insert in which the heat of the flames had
reportedly been *felt* by audiences during the sneak
previews), but it was said his courage had failed him
at the thought of appearing in public. His guest found
the young man with the pencil moustache difficult to
do business with and had been on the verge of back-
ing out of negotiations to sell him sixteen hundred
acres of citrus groves in the Valley when Hughes suddenly and unaccountably doubled his offer. Two tickets to the premiere had arrived by special messenger
the next day to celebrate the end of the transaction.
With no one to accompany him, and not having attended a Hollywood function in nearly three years,
during which both the community and the industry
that fed it had become unrecognizable, he had given
the tickets to his attorney, who had planned to attend
with his star-struck teenaged daughter. Then the attorney had been called to Florida to iron out a development deal and asked him to escort the girl, who
had bought her first evening gown and a new pair of
pumps with a handbag to match and was not to be

disappointed. Now they were seated in a limousine
fragrant with leather and rosewood, hired by a friend
from his screenwriting days, *Life* motion picture editor–turned–playwright Robert E. Sherwood, there to
review the movie for *The New York Herald*.

"I have to say I'm impressed." The playwright, at
thirty-four a decorated veteran and contender for the
Pulitzer Prize, offered him an Abdullah from a clam-
shell case, lighting one for himself when it was declined. "It shows what God could do if He had
money."

"Yours?" He smiled. The remark had the ring of
something composed and polished.

Sherwood nodded, blowing smoke. "I'm thinking
of giving it to George Kaufman. I ghostwrite half
those gems he drops at the Algonquin."

He made no response. He'd sat in on one of the
notorious marathon sessions at the round table and
wondered how many reams of deathless prose had
been forgone by Kaufman, Moss Hart, Sherwood,
Robert Benchley, and Dottie Parker while they re-
hearsed their spontaneous wit. Likely none. A writer
wrote as much as he wanted to write.

"Sid Grauman's socking them eleven bucks a seat,"
he said, looking out the window at the throngs making
way for the motorcycle escort. "I wonder if they know
this is the best part of the show."

Sherwood consulted a pocket notebook bound in
red leather. "The scalpers were hawking tickets for
fifty apiece as of an hour ago. They're part of the
entertainment. These days the real theatrics begin after the production wraps. You know Hughes shot this
picture silent the first time. It was already in the can
when he decided to add a soundtrack. That meant
dubbing all the aerial sequences and scrapping every

foot shot on the ground. He's quite insane."

"Fortunately he's in the only business where reason is a liability."

"Yours?" Sherwood's smile made his long grave face humorous.

"It belongs to a man I worked for. It wasn't as true then as it is now. But it was true enough then."

The playwright uncapped a gold fountain pen and scribbled in his notebook. "I believe I'll steal it. Anyway, Hughes's change of heart was a windfall for that Harlow girl. The rumor is he fell for her and switched it from a war picture to a love triangle just to show her off. She's only nineteen and already world famous."

"Eighteen." The attorney's daughter, plump, plucked, and reeking of Evening in Paris to cover the chemical stench of her permanent wave, leaned forward to stare out the windows, clutching a rolled copy of *Photoplay* in her lap with Jean Harlow's picture on the cover. She was determined not to go home without an autograph. As raw material, the writer in him found nothing in her worth salvaging.

Entering the last mile before the theater, the motorcade slowed down, possibly to avoid hitting pedestrians, although the line of idling automobiles waiting for valets was already visible. The interviews had started, and star fever had proven too much for the barricades; gawkers stepped into harm's way to catch a glimpse of the famous faces riding in the limousines.

"This was a desert town a dozen years ago," Sherwood said. "The studios cranked out one-and two-reelers and sold the prints outright. When I saw *The Battle at Elderbrush Gulch* in a tent in France, it had been stepped on so many times I thought Mae Marsh was a boy. I suppose you can lay everything that's happened since to *The Birth of a Nation*."

"Not everything," he said; but he didn't feel like pursuing the point.

Grauman's Chinese Theater, more jaw-droppingly hideous than usual in the colored beams of Hughes Tool Company searchlights, thrust its dragons and pagodas into the night sky. Their driver, as remote behind his pane of tinted glass as Senator Wheelock's Negro in his exposed front seat, eased up on the hand throttle and boated into the curb, stopping inches behind the Rolls-Royce waiting at the end of the line. From there they could see the hard white light of the newsreel setups in the forecourt, an occasional flutter of sequins and white ermine. The stars of *Hell's Angels*, Ben Lyons, James Hall, Bebe Daniels, and Harlow, the platinum-haired Gloria Swanson (Adele Varga?) of the season, would be reciting their statements, memorized from scripts written by studio flacks, for radio broadcasters. He had to grasp the door handle to keep the attorney's daughter from vaulting over him and quitting the car to get a better look. She flung herself back against the seat, folding her arms and throwing out her lower lip.

When their turn came and the doorman, an authentic Oriental got up in colored silks and a mandarin's cap, stepped forward to let them out, the radio reporter and a newsreel cameraman, both wearing evening dress complete with white ties, crowded in, then retreated upon failing to recognize any of the new arrivals.

Sherwood's companion laughed at the irritation on the playwright's horsey features. He clapped a hand on his arm; at his preposterous height of six-foot-seven, Sherwood's shoulder was beyond reach. "It's a different kind of fame," he said. "You'll have your taste of it for a week or so after they give you the Nobel, because of the newsreels. Then you'll have to step aside to make room for some starlet at Paramount."

"Is that why you quit pictures?"

They were crossing the flagstones now, dotted with coconut palms and marred indelibly with the hand- and footprints of the adored and the extinct, Harold Lloyd and Dustin Farnum and Rin Tin Tin. The attorney's daughter's feet were twice the size of Mary Pickford's.

"No." He took his hand off Sherwood's arm. "That's not why."

More dragons inside, with electrified eyes; Ming vases and mock; antiques in red and black lacquer and contemporary imitations done in Bakelite; a vaulted plaster ceiling cast into pagan images; Chinese red curtains with runners to match on the staircases that swept to the balconies. A room to look at and walk through on the way to the room they wanted. Through tall tapestry-covered doors (doves and lotus blossoms, peacocks and bridges) into the auditorium, bigger and more steeply vaulted, with a chandelier and 2,200 seats covered in red velour, nearly all of them occupied. A diminutive female usher, cross-culturally painted like a Geisha—what did Sid Grauman know of Asia, he had an Egyptian Theater farther down Hollywood Boulevard and a Spanish baroque picture palace on Broadway—blonde hair limning the edge of her headdress, looked at their tickets, directed Sherwood to the press gallery, and led the others to seats in the center of the orchestra, right behind Charlie Chaplin and Dolores Del Rio. The attorney's daughter was vibrating.

There were more stars in the auditorium than in

the film, not unusual at a major premiere; the tickets and the exposure were free, their working fees high. John Gilbert, drunk as usual, appeared to be fading in his seat as he was from the screen, the microphone having sentenced the matinee idol to the community of the walking dead, dancing their morbid tangoes on the edge of the glitter. Elsewhere, scattered strategically among figures less photographed, was Louise Fazenda, in feathers and diamonds, one of the Barrymores—Lionel or John, it was difficult to tell beyond a few yards, intermarriage being as common within acting families as in the courts of Europe—the Frenchman Maurice Chevalier, Billie Burke. Others he recognized from posters and their pictures in the Sunday magazines but whose names he hadn't learned; it was like trying to catch up with a favorite ball team after a couple of years abroad, strange faces in familiar uniforms. He saw Florenz Ziegfeld seated next to Jerome Kern, their heads together as if scoring a new musical, programs covering their mouths in case Jed Harris was listening, and two old acquaintances, Jesse Lasky and Cecil B. De Mille.

De Mille, looking too, met his gaze, wrinkled his bald, tanned forehead briefly, then measured out one of those smiles reserved for someone you may or may not have met, but in case you have and he's important . . . He wondered, idly, why De Mille had been the only one out here privileged to call Buck Bensinger by his Christian name. Lasky, whose Famous Players was now Paramount and run by others, never turned his head. He looked ill. That signified nothing. The business had a history of sustaining the aged rich while killing the young and talented: Valentino, Thomas Ince, William Desmond Taylor. He predicted the executive class would corner the market on centenarians.

He looked at the orchestra pit, the paradisiacal Wurlitzer built into the wall next to the proscenium, the deep stage behind the footlights and behind that the virginal screen cloistered behind a scrim, searching for something to compare with the flyblown little theater in Stockton where he and Yuri had sat on folding chairs and watched *The Musketeers of Pig Alley*. There was nothing. The worlds would not line up. He had seen the evolution—no, *revolution*—witnessed every step, yet he felt as Starling must have upon exiting prison into a new century.

The stage show was strictly vaudeville and surprisingly seedy, emcee Frank Fay trying in his white tie and swallowtail coat to impart dignity to a bill whose highlight was an appearance by transcontinental aviator Roscoe Turner and Gilmore, his lion-cub mascot. A thousand years ago—was it really less than twenty?—he had sat through a similar succession of acrobats, crooners, soft-shoe dancers, baggy-pants comics, and ephemeral celebrities in San Francisco, with a one-reel moving picture tacked on at the end while the audience was shrugging into coats and heading for the exits; now the live acts (some of them might have been the same ones, telling jokes and executing steps worn smooth by thousands of repetitions) were merely warm-ups to the main event on celluloid.

Hell's Angels ran one hundred twenty-seven minutes, an hour and a half longer than Buck had believed any audience could be made to sit still. It would have gratified him to see how many members of this one coughed and squirmed through the interminable melodrama on the ground. The aerial footage, however, was spectacular, as advertised, and the two-strip color inserts dazzling, particularly during the zeppelin explosion. The thumping machine guns and wowing aircraft engines were sufficiently loud to awaken moviegoers no longer diverted by the novelty of sound. Back on earth, the stodgy technology of the stationary microphone and the immobility of the camera, sentenced to the isolation cell of the soundproof booth, undermined the balletics that took place in the air: The leading man was wooden, the second lead less so but still underdone. The vamp—*femme fatale* was the current term, coined by flacks eager to shed the terminology of the silent screen like a dead pupa— was another story, an alien from Hollywood's future dropped into the ruins of its past to accelerate the destruction. She glowed and shimmered, all white gold and gossamer among the patent-leather sheiks of the already-moldering twenties. Adele, who had seethed at the very thought that any other actress might tread her sacred ground, would have viewed Jean Harlow's brand of teenaged seduction in black silence.

At long last the titles came on, the spectators applauded, some with relief, and the exodus commenced. All the way up the steep aisle the attorney's daughter chattered about this scene and that actor and asked no one in particular if she would look as glamorous as Harlow if she plucked her eyebrows. Most of the other conversations he overheard had to do with traffic and where was that valet ticket.

They found Sherwood in the lobby, smoking an Abdullah by a pillar encrusted with carved Chinese gods, most of which looked like Warner Oland.

"What did you think?" the playwright asked. "Bear in mind that the budget on this one would bail out every farmer in Oklahoma."

He said, "You're the critic. I'm a guest of Mr. Hughes's."

"A nickel's worth of plot, thirty-eight cents' worth of acting, and a hell of a lot of dialogue. The rest went up with the damn zeppelin."

"I liked the costumes," said the attorney's daughter.

Sherwood ignored her. "We're on the cusp of a new theocracy: the worship of those who spend for the sake of spending. It can only escalate. Movies will have to bring in tens of millions to justify the millions it costs to make them. The profits of a *Ben-Hur* will represent start-up money for the next big feature. We've seen the end of hard little gems like *The Squaw Man*."

They were moving swiftly with the pedestrian flow toward the curb. The attorney's daughter protested to her escort that she wanted Harlow's autograph.

"I'm afraid she's left," he said. "The stars always sneak out before the lights go up to avoid meeting the people who pay to see them."

"What a gyp. I'd have seen more if I took a cab and *bought* a ticket."

Sherwood handed the valet his ticket with a dollar bill folded around it. "It's always that way, dear, when you're *in* the parade."

1913

Chapter 17

Tom accepted without question the fact that Jerry Jarette was a genius. Although he had seen no other cameramen at work and thus had nothing with which to compare his performance, the sheer tide of opinion at Rocky, from Adele Varga to the local boy in knickerbockers who rode his bike to the studio after school to mop the floor and keep the fire buckets filled, was too formidable for him to oppose. What he confirmed for himself was that the little fellow was a very brave man.

All day the previous day, graders and scrapers had been at work, leveling a portion of the canyon land west of the Bozeman Ball-Buster for the Indian chase leading to the climax of *Sioux Massacre*. Buck had used some of the cash he had borrowed from his competitors to bribe an official with the county (an enemy of Sheriff Peavey's), who had diverted men and equipment to the ranch from the ongoing reservoir project. The result was a strip of sand and gravel twenty feet wide and three-quarters of a mile long: a road starting from nothing and leading nowhere, along which a vehicle would convey Jarette's camera for the tracking shot.

Grips had been prepared by bolting the legs of the tripod to the bed of the same truck that had brought Buck's cannon, the Frenchman supervising even that minute part of the operation. Next they had fashioned a harness of rope and leather straps and secured it to the sides of the box in order to prevent Jarette from flying out the back when the truck hit a bump. After a brief test run, however, he had found the apparatus restricted his movements and ordered it removed. In its place he directed that four short two-by-four planks be nailed to the floorboards, each pair separated just enough for him to wedge a foot in between, to avoid sliding. Tom suspected the Frenchman was more concerned with not spoiling a take than he was with the possibility of breaking an ankle.

Another team of workers, including the boy in knickerbockers, splashed buckets of water over the area to cut down on dust, one of various improvements to be made upon authentic conditions if audiences were to see anything more than gray clouds onscreen. Finally the camera truck was placed in position. Indians and cavalry crushed out cigarettes, adjusted their leggings and tunics, and mounted their horses. Buck, wearing his standard riding outfit and ridiculous sombrero, walked out into plain view carrying a long-barreled antique pistol borrowed from the property department. Tom thought he looked like a Mexican revolutionist, except for the freckles. The producer reached inside his breast pocket as if going for a cigar but brought out a stopwatch instead.

For the next thirty seconds, the stocky little man was the only point of interest on the ranch. Several dozen pairs of eyes followed his movements as he twisted his trunk 180 degrees, squinting against the glare. Having evidently made certain that no aircraft was in sight to spoil the scene, he rested his thumb on the plunger of the stopwatch, pointed the pistol at the sky, waited a long, silent moment, then simultaneously activated both watch and weapon.

At the sound of the report, the extras dressed as cavalry shouted and dug in their spurs. Their horses bolted. Two seconds later, the "Indians" took off in pursuit. The two groups were roughly the same size, and to the unschooled eye the maneuver resembled an act of cowardice on the part of the army. But Tom had learned a bit about moving picture making, and knew that when Jarette had finished shooting and edited the footage, audiences would view the scene as a tactical retreat on the part of eighty-one men from an attack by two thousand Sioux warriors. There would be plenty enough time for bravery during the climactic scene, when Colonel Fetterman and the remnants of his command made their heroic last stand, selling their lives dearly by killing as many braves as possible until the last soldier—Fetterman, of course—fell. The scene, according to Adele Varga, was apocryphal, and blatantly filched from Ince's *Custer's Last Fight*.

"I was Buck's researcher on this one," she had said. "The real Fetterman, horse's ass, led his patrol square into an ambush. It was all over in five minutes."

Tom had asked, "Then why film it at all?"

"Because all the good massacres were taken. Bill Cody did Wounded Knee. When Ince took the Little Bighorn, Fetterman was what was left. So Buck decided to do Custer anyway and call it something else." She'd smiled and rolled a cigarette. "Welcome to Hollywood."

"Hollywood?"

"Development project up in the hills. Griffith and Uncle Carl have started putting it on their letterheads. I suppose it sounds better than Culver City."

The truck bearing Jerry Jarette and his camera charged forward with the Indians, at a distance that allowed him to keep both parties in the shot. Later he would repeat the procedure at closer range with each party separately, then shoot close-ups to insert during editing, at which point Yuri would report for star duty; notwithstanding his newfound skill on horseback, Buck had decided the Ukrainian's clean-shaven good looks were too valuable to risk in a facefirst fall should his mount step in a chuckhole. He'd already made arrangements to pay a first-year art student at USC to paint a portrait of his Fetterman for the poster, provided he could talk the Ukrainian into sitting for it; Yuri had already balked at the heavy silver-based makeup Buck wanted him to wear and which was reserved for featured players only.

The truck was no ordinary truck. Tom, who had spent his share of time poking along behind them during the drive down from Ingot, had never known one to go faster than twenty-five miles per hour, and that on a steep downgrade. He was pretty sure this one reached forty before the driver downshifted to brake for the end of the abbreviated road. The slipstream snatched the little Frenchman's ragged shirttail out of his trousers and straightened his rumpled hair. The sharp wind must have made his·eyes water, but he kept one hand on the camera's guide handle and the other on the crank and continued turning it according to Buck Bensinger's musical formula: "Way Down Upon the Swanee River . . ." Downstroke on *Swan*. It took more than two pairs of fixed two-by-fours to keep Jarette motionless in the bouncing bed of that truck.

A second shot rang out, warped by wind and distance. At the same time, the hand holding Buck's stopwatch jerked and he looked down at the face. Cavalry and Indians drew rein. The truck's transmission groaned its way down through its succession of gears and rattled at last to a stop. The cloud of dust the vehicle had churned up, undeterred by the gallons of water, caught up with it and settled into a brown powder on truck, camera, and man. By the time Jarette climbed down, cradling the container of film he had removed, he resembled a statue of some unprepossessing French explorer hewn from native sandstone. Even the points of his moustache were crusted.

"What do you think?" Buck had to trot to keep up with him. The cameraman was headed toward his little toolshed behind the barn. He never surrendered what he shot until he'd packed it up and sent it off to the developing laboratory.

"I tell you when it comes back. What I see through the glass I like."

"What's that mean?"

"It means what it means. It looked good."

"Just good? It's got to be great."

"When I say it is good it is great."

"How soon can you get set up for the last stand?"

"Tomorrow."

"We've still got two hours of light!"

"The last truck leaves the post office at five. If this is not on it we will not see it for two weeks."

"I can see to that."

"You can, but you will finish the picture with another cameraman."

"You goddamn temperamental frog!"

Tom, walking behind them, had never heard the producer address the Frenchman with anything less than respect approaching reverence; not that Jarette seemed to mind. He kept walking, shielding the film from the sun with his body as if he didn't trust the painted steel can. Buck was agitated and not in his usual way. Worry looked inappropriate on him.

"When you send it," he said, "tell them to strike off two masters besides the negative."

The cameraman stopped.

"You never say that. You say, cut the negative, why should I pay to develop all of it when I will only use some of it?"

"That was before. From now on you cut one master. The other one and the negative go straight to the bank in separate deposit boxes. That way when Wheelock sends his thugs to burn one print, we'll still have the other plus the negative."

"This is a good idea," Jarette said. "This is not your idea."

"What's it matter whether it was mine or Adele's? We're at war."

Jarette resumed walking. "I will be glad when it is over, whoever wins. Even if it means I must go back to cutting negatives."

"If we win, you'll never have to cut another one. Edison's the only one standing between us and payday."

Tom had been aware of the changed atmosphere at Rocky from the moment he had arrived at the gate that morning. Lester was gone, replaced by a white man in pleated khaki trousers and a dark blue flannel shirt with epaulets and a military holster, its flap buttoned over the checked grip of a .45 automatic pistol. The young man had looked at him carefully with flat blue eyes, then found Tom's name on a list attached to a clipboard before opening the gate. Buck had explained that he had engaged the fellow, a former marine, through a security service based in San Bernardino.

The man at the gate had been only part of the package. On his way up to the barn, and during the walk from there to the shooting location, he had spotted a number of strange men on horseback whose general air placed them apart from the cowboys who hung around the Watering Hole, all armed with .45s in flap holsters. Walking back toward the barn behind Buck and Jarette, he noticed that the producer had holstered his big antique revolver in a chamois leather scabbard with extra cartridges hooked into loops on the belt. Seen from behind in his sombrero, tall boots, and ordnance, he looked as if he belonged in front of the camera.

"Things won't be like they were in Jersey," Buck told Jerry. "Wheelock surprised us there because none of us thought he'd go as far as he did. We were naïve. But we're all veterans out here, and we've run out of room to run. Well, I shouldn't have to tell you what to expect. You've covered two revolutions."

"I photographed them. I did not fight them."

"You won't have to fight this one. You're too valuable to put in the front lines. All you have to worry about is protecting what you shoot. That's why we're going to make two of everything until this is over."

"It is a pity we cannot do the same with people," Jarette said.

Chapter 18

W ill it hold?" asked Buck.

Morrie the grip stood back from the big generator and mopped his sweating bald head with a blue bandanna handkerchief. Immediately a pattern of glittering droplets reappeared on his scalp in rows like infantry on parade. "Only one way to find out. The belt ain't designed for this machine; I bought it from a place that sells equipment to sawmills. It's the right size, the only difference is it's made of canvas. I don't know if that's better or worse than leather. Only one way to find out." .

"Let her rip."

"That's what I'm scared of." But Morrie grasped the big flywheel and gave it a spin. The motor popped twice, wheezed, and stopped. Two more turns were required before it caught. The belt wobbled around the pulleys, seated itself, and became a whizzing blur. After a while Buck and Tom stopped holding their breath and went inside, where they'd know soon enough if it broke. Morrie already had instructions never to leave the generator unattended. "Not that

Wheelock ever repeats himself," Buck had added. "Snakes like him never slither down the same path twice."

Inside the barn, the pages Tom had written on *Yukon Jack* lay undisturbed atop an upturned hogshead next to the canvas chair where Buck relaxed between takes, a conceit he admitted he had acquired from Griffith, although he was too energetic an individual to direct action on film any way but on his feet. Now he seated himself, patted his breast pockets, found nothing but the stopwatch, and called for Andy, the grip in charge of his cigars. This was the man Tom would always think of as an Indian because he had been dressed like one the first time he'd seen him; at the moment he had on cavalry trousers with a stripe up one side and yellow galluses over red flannel underwear faded an unappetizing shade of pink. He fished a cigar from his tunic hanging on the back of a prop chair, brought it over, and lit it for the producer.

At Rocky, Tom had learned, you never knew what side you were fighting on, or whether you would be holding an antique weapon or a hammer.

When Buck had the cigar going, he picked up Tom's pages and read through them swiftly. Tom, who knew his high school dropout employer for a slow reader under the best of circumstances, was pretty sure this was his second time through. He wondered if there was anyone on earth for whom he didn't feel the need to strike some pose.

When he came to the last page he blew a ring and thrust the sheaf back at Tom. "Too long."

"It isn't finished."

"It's already longer than *Judith of Bethulia*, and that's three reels. I bribed a grip at Biograph for a look at the scenario," he said. "Get it down to forty minutes, and don't waste my time with all that description shit. I'll decide what the saloon looks like. And what's this Whale's Whiskers?"

"I thought it sounded like a saloon you'd find in Alaska."

Another lazy blue ring of smoke drifted toward the rafters. Tom found himself watching it, like a dog.

"I like it," Buck said at last. "I don't know about that dogsled chase at the beginning. How's the audience going to tell which one's Jack with all that snow blowing around? Snowstorms are a bitch to shoot. You have to use soap flakes, a shitload of Lux. The real stuff doesn't photograph."

"I thought I'd leave that to you and Jerry."

"It isn't like writing for the magazines. You've got to be aware of the limitations. The saloon's too big, for one thing. Cost us a fortune to light it."

"Well, do you like the story?"

"It's a corker. Except I want to see the robbery. Your scenario doesn't start till after it's done. I got a big black iron Hall and Whitman safe back at the office I bought used for fifty bucks; it's collecting dust because I never got the combination. We'll blast it open on camera and get me back my investment."

"You want me to add a scene and still make it shorter?"

"Don't forget the reluctant clerk."

"The what?"

"You know, the little twerp who refuses to open the safe even with a gun in his face, like it's his own money he's protecting. That puts the audience on the bandit's side right away, they want to climb up on-screen and strangle the little cocksucker. They'll cheer when the dynamite goes off."

"I guess I could shorten the chase."

"Forget the chase. Broncho Billy Anderson almost choked to death when a mess of Lux flakes went down his throat last year at Essanay. I'd like to get more than one picture out of Starling before I kill him. We'll cut straight from the robbery to the saloon, dust his shoulders and frost his eyebrows so the audience knows what he's been through. It'll play."

"Why don't we forget about Alaska entirely and move the action to Arizona?"

"I thought about that. But I'm committed to your old man for ten tons of ice. That's more than we'll need for the wrap party."

Tom gave up. The producer was impervious to sarcasm. "How much dynamite does it take to blow up a safe without taking half of downtown Los Angeles with it?"

"You can get that from Starling. I almost forgot." Clamping the cigar between his teeth, Buck rolled over on one hip and excavated a ring of keys from a pocket of his whipcords. "This one opens the front door to my place. Heaven's Court Bungalows, sixty-seven twelve Mulholland, Number Five. Pick up Starling and bring him here to the barn. I promised him I'd show him around the ranch."

"Can't you send a grip for that?" He fingered the heavy ring.

"He hasn't met any of them yet. He's skittish around strangers. I'd send Adele with the Rambler, but she's shopping in La Jolla. I told her we wouldn't need her for a couple of days because I didn't think we'd have the generator up and working for the interiors. Also our star's had a long dry spell between women."

"Do you think he's that dangerous?"

"That's the thing, I don't know for sure. But I know about Adele; she carries a knife."

"It's *Starling* you're concerned about?"

Buck unbuttoned his right shirtcuff, turned back the sleeve, and rotated his wrist to display a thick white scar running up the underside of his forearm. "She gave me that the first time we went out. Eighteen stitches, and I was half Starling's age and in better shape. I can't afford another funeral."

"If he's at your place, why do I need a key? He can let me in."

"He's usually passed out by this time. It takes half a case of tequila per week to keep him from wandering around and getting into trouble. If he violates parole I'm down to one star, and I don't know yet how audiences are going to react to Yuri in Louisville."

"So I'll have to wake him up."

"Just give his shoulder a good shake and stand back. He's not what you call a morning person."

"Am I supposed to write the scenario while I'm driving him here?"

Buck rotated his cigar, puffing it into a fierce glow. Finally he removed it from his mouth and let the smoke roll out. "Look around, Tom. I'm leasing a studio with alfalfa hay in the corners. My power plant's on loan from the Smithsonian. Half my grips swam over from Mexico and the other half are on work-release from the California penal system. My stunt coordinator cleans out septic tanks weekends, and makes more money doing that than I make the rest of the week. You know what my leading lady was. Just what are you bringing to the Rocky Mountain Moving Picture Association that gives you the right to pick and choose what you do for it?"

"How do you know I'm not a genius like Jerry Jar-ette?"

"If you were, someone would have published you by now."

Tom watched him tip ash into the fire bucket at his knee, the producer taking his time to allow what he'd said to sink in.

"When she's not acting or typing letters or answer-ing the telephone or juggling the books," Buck said, "Adele reads. She subscribes to all the major maga-zines, looking for stories we can adapt. She's never seen your byline in *Collier's, Century, The Saturday Evening Post*, or *Scribner's*. Those are the magazines you said you write for. She's never seen it anywhere else, either. You're just an iceman with big eyes."

"How long have you known?"

"She told me the night of the day I hired you. We don't keep secrets from each other. She also admitted she whipped up that story about you being a student of Griffith. She wanted you to have the job. She likes you."

"Why didn't you fire me the next day?"

"I just told you. Adele's a pain in the ass, but there's a reason I keep her around besides the obvious one. She knows people. She saw something in Wild Bill Latimer when all anyone else saw was a broken-down Broadway fag with a habit. She's the one who put me on to Jerry when he was getting restless at Edison. If it weren't for her I'd be back in Jersey running up the insurance in my uncle's store. I've gotten this far be-cause I'm smart enough to see that. So my question is, if she's willing to pick up the phone and change the ribbon on the typewriter back at the office, what makes you special?"

Tom was thinking of an answer when the light from

the overhead kliegs went down and up twice, then died. The generator had ceased chugging.

"Shit. I knew that canvas belt wouldn't hold." The tip of Buck's cigar described an orange arc in the pitch blackness.

The bungalow, Tom was surprised to observe, was no larger than the one he shared with Yuri in San Fernando, although it was better kept, possibly by a landlady. Freshly painted mauve shutters stood out against soft gray siding, and pink-budded rosebushes grew in well-pruned order from limestone beds on both sides of a flagstone walkway. Tom used the ornamental knocker twice, then let himself in. A strong masculine smell of stale cigars and unwashed socks greeted him.

Despite that, and the general bachelor untidiness of the small sitting room—a smeared glass and a half-empty tequila bottle left on the coffee table, clothing flung over the arms of chairs and the camelback sofa, dust bunnies twitching about in the current of air from the open door—the place showed signs of Adele's hand in its decoration. A sentimental but tasteful print of the *Wedding at Cana* hung in a pasteboard frame above the false fireplace, and a colorful arrangement of paper peonies bloomed perpetually in a blue china bowl in the hearth; she had even made allowances for the inevitable neglect of the watering can.

Buck had not told him which bedroom was Starling's, but there were only two, and the volume of sound coming from the one on the right narrowed the choice even further. When Tom opened that door, the racking snores rolled out on a volume of air redolent of grain alcohol, greasy armpits, and bad breath. He was instantly catapulted back to Shasta and the long, narrow room behind the ice house, where the cutters slept in hammocks and berths built into the walls like sailors' quarters aboard ship. The room's single narrow window was a vague oblong behind bamboo blinds, leaving the interior as dark as the room where Bill Latimer had died. Shuddering at the memory, he stepped across and tipped up the panels, letting in sunlight in long horizontal stacks.

J. W. Starling lay fully clothed atop the covers of a double bed with a six-foot mahogany headboard, elegant once but now covered with scaly layers of inexpensive varnish and carved initials, a palimpsest record of the many transients who had occupied the sagging mattress. He had not even bothered to remove the hightop shoes he'd worn the day he left San Quentin; their cheap blacking had come off in smudges on the faded floral bedspread. He had on the trousers of his suit, spectacularly wrinkled, and a white BVD undershirt of a kind that had not existed when he was sentenced, although he'd wasted no time in mottling it with stains since his release. The carpet of beard on his cheeks and chin was as dark as his short-cropped hair and nearly as thick, but the inverted U beneath his thin nose was darker still; he was growing out his moustache. His mouth hung open, and when he took in oxygen in a bubbling snort, his upper lip lifted away from those remarkable teeth, which Tom noted were now stained dark in the spaces between, like old grout. The presence of a freshly opened foil packet of Levi Garrett's chewing tobacco on the cracked nightstand cleared up that mystery.

More perplexing was the object slung from one corner of the bedstead by a short length of new rope. Tom thought at first it was a quiver of arrows, and wondered if the old bandit had reverted to Indian weaponry in pursuit of a new life of crime. Then he recognized the faded pattern on the tube of coarse wool and realized it was the blanket roll that Starling had gone through so much trouble to reclaim from beneath the porch of the old house in San Francisco. It was in better condition than it had appeared before its rotted oilcloth covering had been discarded and the dust pounded out of it, although the ends were tattered and black with age. It still didn't look as if it had been worth the stop, much less the five dollars Buck had paid for the privilege of removing it. The would-be adventure writer in Tom wondered, tantalizingly, if it contained some of Starling's stolen booty.

"Who the hell are *you*?"

The voice, bubbly with phlegm, made him jump. He hadn't noticed the snoring had stopped. He looked down into J. W. Starling's fever-bright eyes and, below them, at the octagonal barrel of the pistol pointed at his own groin.

Chapter 19

Last time I was here I could of stuck up every place in town and still owed the bartender at the Bella Union seventeen cents for whiskey." J. W. Starling scowled at the office buildings rolling past the Model T on Cahuenga. "The bank was a tight old grandee name of Don Sebastiano in a big hacienda up in the hills where them letters are. He owned everything from here to the Pacific Ocean."

"I wonder what happened to him," Tom said.

"Buried under a mess of concrete, probably, like everything else." He squirted a stream of tobacco out the window. Tom winced when the slipstream took it and splattered it over the side of the car.

They had quickly cleared up the business of who Tom was and what he was doing standing beside Starling's bed. The fog that blurred the ex-convict's thoughts upon awakening from his alcoholic sleep had burned off ahead of Tom's shock; he'd recognized him as one of the men who had taken him away from prison and returned the big pistol to its place under his pillow. Tom was reluctant to ask him where he'd gotten it. He wondered if Buck was reckless enough to have supplied the former bandit with a weapon from Rocky's property department.

He'd waited in the sitting room while Starling freshened himself up and dressed, not that the door to the bungalow's bathroom was much of a buffer between him and the sound of the man's urine splashing into the toilet. He'd been relieved, when Starling came out stuffing the tail of one of Buck's loose cotton shirts into his trousers, that there were no suspicious bulges in his pockets. The pistol was apparently just for his protection while he slept.

"I like this buggy better than the other," he said, squirming to make himself comfortable on the Ford's seat. "It's got more backbone. How's it for handling?"

"The clutch and brake take some getting used to."

"I don't know what them are, but they can't be any worse than a six-hitch with a Appaloosa on the outside lead. That's when I had a job hauling stoves. Everything's uphill in Boise, even coming back down."

"You had a job?" He asked the question without thinking.

But Starling wasn't offended. "I reckon I had my share and then some. I tended bar in Carson City and again in Eugene, graded track for the Northern Pacific up by Seattle, busted strikes for Consolidated Mines outside Pocatello—let me tell you, that was as hard a job of work as I ever done; them Cornish Jacks got skulls thick as boiler plate. Let's see, I rode fence in Montana, but not for long; ranch work didn't agree with me. I painted barns one whole summer. You know about the stoves. If it needs a strong back I done it. Even the bartending was mostly splitting ax handles over drunks' heads."

"You did all that before you became a bandit?"

"Before and during. The outlaw trail ain't as profitable as you might think. The take's almost never as much as you anticipated. The newspapers always jack up the amount when they write about it. Then there's what you call overhead. Horses and hotels cost twice as much when you're on the scout. When a bank or a train gets robbed it's the legitimate tradesmen that profit. I made more money as a railroad guard than I did robbing the railroad."

Tom waited for a helmeted traffic officer at Santa Monica to wave them through the intersection. "*You* were a railroad guard?"

"There wasn't a lot to it. I rode the cars all day between Frisco and Sacramento, clubbing tramps when I found them and throwing 'em off. I was twenty then, built like a bull. I loved it. The Sacramento Northern paid good, with a pension plan; I seen myself riding cars and clubbing tramps till I was too old to swing a club. Then I bent this kid's skull that turned out to be related to one of the directors and they fired me. Damn kid had a free pass, but he climbed on the gondola for the pure hell of it when the train slowed down for a grade. Well, I didn't blame them for the firing, but they owed me two weeks' pay. Ten years later I was still collecting it when I got arrested. I reckon you could say it was the Sacramento Northern turned me to a life of crime."

The traffic officer's hard eyes followed them as they crossed the boulevard. It was almost as if he'd overheard the conversation.

"When we picked you up at the prison you said something about robbing a bank."

"Did I? You get in the habit of boasting inside, stretching all kinds of blankets about what a hard character you are. If you're good enough at it the perverts leave you alone for fresher fish." The ex-convict was watching the scenery.

"I won't turn you in," Tom said. "I helped get you out, remember?"

"Fifteen years of busting up rocks for gravel got me out. You just rode me away. I could of walked."

"I work for the man who gave you a job. Without it you'd be riding back in six months. I like this job as much as you did riding cars and clubbing tramps. If you can stretch blankets for the other inmates, you can stretch one for me. I need the research."

Starling spat again. They had turned north and this time the wind blowing from the ocean carried the stream away from the car. He sat back, wiping his mouth on Buck's shirtsleeve. "You want to know what it's like robbing a bank? The worst part is trying not to shit your pants. Anytime you see a bank being stuck up, the scaredest person is the one sticking it up. The tellers and guard are easy to keep an eye on, if you know what you're about. It's the heroes you got to grow that third eye for. More often than not it's some stump-buster walking past the window without a penny in the bank, takes it into his head to pull his pocket bulldog and shoot you through the glass." He grinned, an out-of-balance expression with the tobacco bulging one cheek. "That's what I heard, anyway. This greaser in my block got life for trying to push in the Miners Trust in Frisco. Lord, that little peppergut loved to hear hisself talk."

Tom wondered what it would take to win this man's trust. "I'm chiefly interested in how much dynamite it takes to blast open a safe."

"Stick to your last, kid. You ain't got the guns to ride the high country."

"The only safe I'm interested in blasting open is the one in the picture." He was going to leave it at that, but the man's dilapidated grin stung him in a sensitive spot. He'd had more than his share of lectures for one day. "How do you know what kind of guns I have? I'm the same age you were when you turned outlaw."

"I don't recommend it. Quentin done something for me my ma never could, nor any of them mule-ass ugly old ladies that busted sticks over my knuckles every day of them three years I spent in school: made a reader of me. I don't believe I ever got through so much as a train schedule all the time I was out, but if there's a magazine come through the gates the last fifteen years I didn't see, I'd like to know what it was. I read up on all the new inventions, time locks and radio sets and writing machines and machines that send pictures over telegraph wires. I didn't put store in all of them, but I seen some things since I been out that's got me to thinking maybe I wasn't right. Anyway, I ain't so dumb I don't know the way I used to get along wouldn't work now. I'm still a young man, I reckon, but there ain't time enough to learn what I'd have to in order to make it profit. The next batch of bandits is going to have to know how to operate an automobile and handle one of them guns that fires more cartridges than you can wear around your middle in less time than it takes to spit tobacco." As if to demonstrate, he leaned out his window and shot out the rest of his plug. "That takes more energy than I got. I thought for a while I'd join up with a Wild West exhibition like Frank James and Cole Younger, but I hear even that old liar Cody can't raise enough these days to hire a hall. Maybe there's something to these moving pictures."

"Have you seen one yet?"

"Bensinger set up a contraption in that crib of his and showed me one on the wall. Some silly horseshit about a desperado loaning stolen bank money to a widow to pay off her landlord and then turning around and sticking up the landlord to get it back. I'm thinking I could do at least that good with a bullet in my head."

"*Yukon Jack* is about a man who turns highwayman to avenge a friend, then reforms for the love of a good woman."

"Who's the woman?" Starling straightened up and ran a hand over his brushy hair, as if they were about to be introduced.

"Adele Varga. I don't think you've met."

"Varga, that's Mexican, right? I used to be a fair hand with the brown ladies. What's she look like?"

"She's one of the most beautiful women I've ever seen. And she's spoken for." He sounded stiff even to himself. He felt as if he were committing some kind of violation just by discussing her in the ex-convict's presence.

"Yours, huh? Don't worry. I'll give her back good as new."

"She's with Buck Bensinger."

"Yeah? Well, that's different. I got principles against paying attention to the boss man's woman. That's what separates me from a miserable thief like Harry Tracy, and why he shot hisself in Spokane and I didn't in Sacramento. Principles." He rolled over on one buttock and let out a rippling fart.

Tom rolled down his window and changed the subject along with the air. "I need to know about that dynamite."

"Dynamite?"

"For the safe." He made a note to discuss with Buck

the tendency on the part of the former bandit's mind to wander. It would mean shortening the takes to conform to his attention span.

"What kind of safe?"

"Buck said it was a Whitman something."

"Hall and Whitman. That outfit went out of business in '89. Where'd he find it?"

"A museum, maybe. That's where he found his cannon. Can you blow it?"

"Easy as blowing my nose. That soft iron's tricky if you don't know what you're about. Three sticks'd blow out every window in town, but just bend it out of shape and leave the door on. Half a stick'd pop it like a tin of 'baccy."

"Half a stick doesn't sound like much. How will it look on camera?"

"It'll be loud enough to make a bucket ring in a barn a mile away. I'm talking about fresh dynamite. The old stuff sweats pure nitro; drop one and they wipe you off the brick wall next door with a bar rag."

"They won't hear it on film. Does it make a lot of smoke?"

"Plenty, if you use black powder. I don't trust that smokeless shit. In the old days I favored plenty of clouds to hide behind when I rode out."

"You used dynamite when you robbed the Sacramento Northern?" Tom smiled.

Starling surprised him by smiling back. His grin didn't look quite as sinister without the tobacco bulge. "There's a heap of things I favor about the law, bet you didn't suspect that," he said. "Top of the list is they lose interest after seven years, unless killing's involved. They never give up then."

"Did you ever kill anyone?"

"Butch didn't hold with it, so I was always careful."

Tom spent the rest of the drive wondering if his question had been answered.

He stopped several times for the ex-convict to get out and urinate. Each time it took him the better part of a minute to finish up. Tom had never known a man to hold so much or need to relieve himself so often.

"It's this low altitude," Starling explained once. "Up in Idaho I could drink a gallon of coffee at sunup and go all day without pissing. Harvey Logan said when I kicked off he was fixing to cut out my bladder and make a saddlebag out of it. Also it ain't been the same since I picked up a dose from a Paiute whore in Reno. I don't recommend the cure. Croaker runs a silver rod up inside your dingus. Next time I believe I'll keep the clap."

Tom was only half listening. They had turned off the coast road, moving slowly as always over the ruts and potholes, and come to a stop before the white-washed gate, or where the gate had been. The splintered pieces that remained of it yawned inward on either side of a gap as wide as the path. There was no sign of the young security guard Buck had hired to replace Lester.

"Dogs," said Starling, gaping at the wreckage. "Just when I thought the West had settled down too far to suit me."

Chapter 20

T he drive up the battered path to the big barn on the hill seemed interminable. A black smudge of smoke stained the sky, and the road itself had a deserted air—more a feeling than anything he actually saw or heard—that placed a cold lump of dread in the pit of Tom's stomach.

They had just come within sight of the building when the car was hemmed in suddenly with horses. Tom had not seen them coming; they might have materialized from nothing, like one of the rude special effects in Buck's *Ghost Riders of Eldorado*. He was forced to brake to avoid hitting the one in front of the car. In the next instant he realized the horses were manned, and that each man had a pistol aimed at the Ford's occupants.

"Get your hands out where we can see 'em!" barked one of the riders.

Tom placed both hands on the steering wheel.

Starling rested his on the dashboard. "If this here don't just take the cake," he said. "One week out and I get stuck up by road agents."

"Shut up!"

The rider who had been snarling the orders was mounted on the driver's side. He leaned down from his saddle to peer through the window. His eyes, granite splinters in a narrow face burned by wind and sun, took in both the front and back seats and rested on Tom.

"You fellows have balls for brains," the man said. "Roll right on in without guns, bold as Maggie's nipples. Did you think your pards finished the job?"

Something about the man's neatly pressed twill shirt and flap holster struck a familiar chord. His gray Stetson was blocked tidily and free of stains, unlike those worn by Buck's cowboy extras; this was one of the security men the producer had hired to patrol the ranch.

"We work for the Rocky Mountain Moving Picture Association," Tom said. "I'm Tom Boston. This is J. W. Starling. He's a star."

"Yeah, I think I saw his pictures in the post office. Get the hell out of the car. Move slow or we'll drill you where you sit." He backed his horse away from the Ford.

They obeyed. Tom had just stepped down from the running board when something slid down over his head and shoulders, pinned his arms to his sides, and snatched him off his feet. He managed to turn sideways just in time to avoid scraping his face on the hard earth. As it was he struck on one shoulder and emptied his lungs with a grunt. He heard a similar noise from the other side of the car and realized the same thing had happened to Starling.

"Give 'em some slack!" snapped the man with the words.

Iron shoes scraped stony ground. When he found

his wind he was able to turn over onto his back. Stiff hemp encircled his arms and torso, cutting off circulation to his hands. His gaze followed the rope to the horn of the saddle of the security man who had lassoed him. He was younger than his superior and less weathered, but dressed the same and his eyes were as hard.

Then the young man was blocked from Tom's vision. The man in charge had dismounted and stepped between them to stand with his boots spread apart at Tom's feet. The bore of his sidearm looked as big as a phonograph record.

"You're first if Calvin doesn't pull through," the man said.

"Let him up."

This was a new voice, and a welcome one. Adele Varga, dressed for work in her voluminous gingham dress, appeared at the man's side.

"Let him up, I said. He's a friend."

The man hesitated long enough to register his reluctance to take instructions from a woman, or perhaps to take instructions at all. Then he nodded to the man in the saddle, who kneed his horse forward, unwound the rope from the horn, and gave it a flip. The ring through which the loop was drawn slipped, freeing Tom's hands to pull it over his head. He climbed to his feet.

"What about the other one?" asked the guard in charge.

"He's Starling," Tom told Adele.

She nodded at the guard, who signaled the horseman on the other side of the car to release the bandit. A moment later, Starling came around from that side, dusting himself off. His eyes with their reptilian lids remained on the head guard, but his words were directed to someone else. "Is he fixing to put up that iron, or does he want me to ram it up his ass and jerk the trigger?"

"Put it away, Quintana," Adele said.

The security chief's hesitation this time had a broader base. His gaze held Starling's, expressing something deeper and more basic than hostility. Then he lifted the flap on his holster and slid the big revolver into it. The others then holstered their weapons without being ordered.

"What happened?" Tom asked Adele.

"I haven't seen anything like it since Villa came through Tijuana with a thousand men, Tom. There must have been fifteen touring cars, all in a line. The man at the gate said they must have been doing forty when they hit it. He drew his gun, but they ran right over him."

"Is he alive?"

"Some grips carried him up to the barn after it was over. His legs are broken and I don't know what else inside. Buck sent Morrie to town in the Rambler to bring back a doctor."

"Calvin's one of my best men," Quintana said. "Nobody else would try to stop an army."

Adele said, "They had men in the backseats with rifles and shotguns. They just kept driving around and around the barn, shooting. There were bullets and pellets and pieces of wood from the boards flying all over inside. We all hit the ground and stayed there. It seemed like hours. Probably it was five minutes. One of the kliegs blew up and started a fire. It's out now. The generator's finished. No one was hit, thank God. I don't think they were aiming at people. When they were through they just left."

Tom saw then the bits of straw in her hair and on her dress. "Wheelock?"

"He's probably having lunch in Los Angeles with Judge Mortenson. Who else would have arranged it? None of Buck's creditors is mad enough at him to pull anything like this."

"Where were the rest of the guards while all this was going on?" Tom glared at Quintana, whose granite eyes didn't move.

"I've got ten men—nine, now—patrolling a thousand acres. We all rode in when the shooting started. First man got here just in time to fire at their dust."

"They did their best, Tom. Even Buck didn't think Wheelock would try something this bald."

"When did it happen?"

"It's been less than an hour. I'm surprised you didn't pass them on your way up the coast."

"He wouldn't if they were headed to Sacramento," said Quintana.

"Pinkertons."

Everyone looked at Starling, who had spoken. He moved a shoulder. "It's the way they done things in the old days when they worked for the railroad. All that's new is the automobiles."

Quintana said, "That outfit's been trying to put me out of business since I set up shop. This senator's just an excuse for them to turn loose the dogs. They figure I'm too big not to hurt business and too small to give a decent account of myself in a real fight."

"Do you agree with them?" Adele asked.

"I might have, if they didn't go and run over one of my men."

"Where's Buck?" Tom asked.

"He went to Jerry's shack to check on the film. I'm

sure it's all right. They were mostly interested in the barn."

Quintana said, "I'll put somebody on the gate. They might come back."

"I doubt it," Adele said. "They accomplished their purpose. If they'd wanted to do anything more than scare the hell out of us, they wouldn't have stopped at shooting up a building and an obsolete generator."

"They didn't," the security man reminded her.

"I'm sorry about your man. He'll get the best medical attention, even if paying for it means cutting Jerry Jarette into thinner slices than he's in now."

"I'll see to that myself. It's part of the job." He mounted.

Adele, Tom, and Starling started toward the barn on foot. She said, "Not that much is different here from Tijuana. Whenever the mayor or the local captain of *federales* thought the graft was too low, they hired yanquis from the mines to bust up the place with clubs until we agreed on a price. In California everything is done with cars and guns."

"I was saying something like that on the way up," Starling said.

She stopped to face him and stuck out her hand. "I'm pleased to meet you, Mr. Starling. I'm sorry the circumstances aren't more genteel."

He stared at the hand for a moment before taking it; Tom realized that at the time the former bandit had gone to prison, women didn't shake hands. As he did it, he showed his good teeth. "No sorrys about it, ma'am. Where I been we didn't tip our hats unless we wanted somebody to bend a stonehammer over our skulls."

"Please call me Adele. And I'll call you . . . J. W.?"

"Call me whatever tickles you, so long as it ain't

six-three-two-nine-four. That's what it's been for fifteen years and I've had my life's portion of it."

"J. W., then."

They resumed walking. Grips were already at work
outside the barn, picking up pieces of torn siding and
raking the grass for bits of shattered glass. Small round
holes peppered the walls and double doors in no particular pattern amid great gaping maws where fist-size
balls of shotgun pellets had punched out whole
sections. The smoke from an interior fire, dissipating
now, trailed out through the latter. The brimstone
stench of spent gunpowder overlay everything.

The cold spot in Tom's stomach had turned into a
knot. He had read of such things in Jack London and
Rex Beach, but they had merely thrilled him. The
skills of even the best writers were inadequate to convey the full emotion of planned destruction. "Has anyone called the sheriff?" he asked Adele.

"Mutt Peavey? He'd make a thorough job of counting all the holes and putting a dollar amount on the
damage, depend on him for that. He's a first-class
clerk. He might even arrest a couple of drunks from
the Watering Hole. He'd have no trouble getting a
conviction from the jury pool here; the natives have
had it in for us movies ever since Uncle Carl Laemmle
carried his first camera over the Rockies. If the Trust
gave the senator enough expense money to hire fifteen
cars full of Pinkertons, he had enough to buy Peavey
too. Anyway, they shot through the telephone line.
That's why Buck had to send Morrie for the doctor.
How is that poor guard?" she asked one of the grips
raking the grass. It was Andy, the pretend Indian.

"Still breathing last time I looked," he said. "I

wanted to give him a slug of whiskey for the pain, but one of them damn cowboys said no."

Starling said, "He was right. You don't give a man nothing to drink if he might have something tore loose inside."

"What're you, some kind of doctor?" Andy looked him over from stubbled chin to convict shoes.

"I patched up my share of holes, tenderheel. What about you?"

The grip fell silent and put his rake to use on the broken glass.

Adele said, "Let's go around back and talk to Buck. If I know him he's already got tomorrow's shooting schedule worked out in his head."

The long side of the barn was in even worse shape than the front, although it was clear from the height of the bullet holes that the shooters had adjusted their aim to avoid hitting anyone who'd had the good sense to prostrate himself on the floor. The holes made by the shotgun blasts were big enough to look through and see the laborers cleaning up the mess inside. Adele had been right about the generator; the belt pulleys were shot to pieces and the pungent odor of gasoline rose from a dark stain on the bare earth beneath the tank, which was riddled with holes. The wonder was it hadn't exploded—but then the men behind the guns had been skilled and careful. Tom decided it was the *order* of this particular chaos that chilled his blood.

The padlock dangled open on the door to Jerry Jarette's little shack. The electrical cord he had argued with Buck for so long to install lay on the ground, torn down or shot through, like the telephone line. Adele knocked and, when there was no answer from inside, tried the handle. When the door opened she raised her eyebrows. "Funny, they always shoot the bolt." She pushed the door open the rest of the way and stepped across the threshold.

"*Madre de dios.*" She crossed herself.

Tom had to crane his neck to see past her. Buck Bensinger was on his knees in front of Jarette's littered workbench, next to the wooden stool where the little Frenchman sat when he edited film, cradling Jarette's head against his chest. The cameraman's untidy hair was matted with something. A shaft of bright sunlight no bigger around than a broomstick canted in through a ragged hole in the clapboard wall above the bench. The producer was crying so softly Tom could only hear his broken gasps for breath.

Chapter 21

———

Clarence Peavey kept his office on the second floor of a wooden-framed brick building on Spring Street, at the end of a narrow hall with a rubber runner and framed sepia photographs of city founders with handlebar moustaches and stiff collars. One window looked out on a spacious boulevard widened recently to accommodate automobile traffic, another on a sun-slammed section of dog walk that might not have changed since men wore sabers. Well-kept wainscoting lined the walls at shoulder height, above which hung antique pictures of frontier Los Angeles on green-painted plaster. A fan nearly as old as the pictures swooped at a stately pace beneath the ceiling, far too high to have any effect upon the air at door level. The room smelled of fresh varnish and apple-scented pipe tobacco.

The pipe, a curved brier, drooped from a corner of the sheriff's mouth. He sat behind a square desk with a leather top. His bony elbows rested on the leather as he read through the typewritten report that had been handed him. Behind him hung a large-scale map of Los Angeles County, parchment-colored like a sixteenth-century mariner's chart of New Spain. Its shape reminded Tom vaguely of a can opener.

At length, Peavey laid down the last sheet and unhooked his reading glasses. "Coroner's report says ricochet," he said. "Bullet glanced off something, probably the generator, went through the wall of the shack, and struck Jarette. He died instantly. Death by misadventure."

"Horseshit." Buck sounded tired. Tom was pretty sure the producer hadn't slept since before the ambulance came to take Calvin, the injured guard, to the hospital and Jerry to the morgue. Now he was leaning against the frame of the window above the boulevard, looking out and probably not seeing anything. He hadn't changed his clothes in two days. His hair, normally unruly, was lank. He made no attempt to brush it back out of his eyes. "Wheelock's Pinkertons murdered him. He was the only thing I had that was worth the powder it took to blow the ranch to hell."

"I called the regional director in Sacramento," Peavey said. "He says he never heard of Alvin Wheelock and denies sending any agents there. Wheelock told Angel he was in San Diego day before yesterday, visiting an old friend. The friend confirms they were out on his boat all day. He was Grover Cleveland's postmaster general."

"He's probably telling the truth anyway. Wheelock wouldn't bend down to button his damn spats if he could hire someone to do it."

"Angel thinks the raid was planned by one of your competitors." The sheriff cracked his knuckles, one at a time. They were as large as crabapples.

"Angel's in bed with Wheelock."

"I hired him myself. He's a good man in a tight spot."

"He's a pimp."

Tom said, "Which one of Rocky's competitors does Angel think did it?"

"He's out interviewing them all. Some of them have pretty nasty records. Most of them left a string of lawsuits back East. They've all got drunks and horse thieves on their payrolls. Your own late star was a homosexual and a drug addict, and the man you hired to take his place is an ex-convict. Put yourself in my place. Who would *you* choose to investigate?"

Buck pushed himself away from the window. "Let's go, Tom. I told you this was a waste of time."

Tom kept his seat. "You're forgetting why we came. When are you releasing Jarette's body?" he asked Peavey.

"You can claim him anytime."

Buck said, "I cabled his sister in Paris. She's making arrangements to ship him back home to bury in the family plot. They wouldn't have anything to do with him all the time he was in pictures. I guess now that he's dead he's good enough to rot next to his ancestors."

The sheriff pointed the stem of his pipe at him. "If I was you, I'd keep a lid on that head of steam. You've got a printer's bill to pay by the end of the month. Otherwise we'll padlock what's left of that barn and your place here in town."

"Why wait till the end of the month? Without Jerry I don't have a thing worth locking." He went out, leaving the door open behind him.

Tom rose and looked down at Peavey. "Do you seriously believe this is all just a row between small-time moving picture makers?"

The sheriff's long, clerkly face was full of sags and pouches. "I'm a civil servant. When you take that test there's no blank to fill in saying what you believe."

Tom caught up with Buck at the top of the stairs down to the lobby. The producer had stopped to light a cigar.

"You're not giving up?"

He shook out the match and flipped it onto the runner. "It's not so hard when you've got nothing to give. Jerry was all I had."

"Don't you have anyone else who can work a camera?"

"There's the second unit, but there isn't a genius among them."

"Does every company have a genius?"

"Essanay doesn't. But they've got Broncho Billy Anderson."

"You've got J. W. Starling."

"I don't even know if Starling can act."

"You said Latimer couldn't act, but you made him famous."

"I was full of piss and vinegar then, and I had credit. Without Jerry for collateral, I won't be able to borrow so much as a match from any of the other companies."

"They're in this fight too."

"If they could fight they wouldn't have run out here in the first place. All they can do is stand around like scared hens hoping the fox will glut himself on the rest of the flock before he gets around to eating them. We thought we'd call the Trust's bluff by setting up shop outside its reach. Only it wasn't a bluff. Edison has longer arms than Jack Johnson. We gambled and lost, Tom. Even the muleheadedest player knows when it's time to throw in his hand."

"You're forgetting Rocky's greatest asset."

"Adele? She can balance a ledger in a blizzard, and she's got fight enough for all of us. But not enough for Wheelock's army of bullies."

"I was talking about Buck Bensinger."

This drew a spiritless smile that had not previously been part of the kaleidoscope that was Buck's face.

"I'm a hack, Tom. Everything I've done I cribbed from someone else who did it before and better. My first feature was a scene-for-scene reshoot of *The Great Train Robbery*. Adele's magazine subscriptions are my entire story department. You've seen the trademark that appears before the main title?"

"A buffalo on a penny."

"Essanay uses the Indian head on the other side. All I did was flip it. It costs the public a nickel to see a Rocky Mountain moving picture and I ought to be arrested for petty larceny. I'm no asset."

"You're the soul of this business," Tom said.

Buck dragged on the cigar, inhaling the smoke. Then he took it out of his mouth and looked at the glowing tip. "You might be closer to the truth than you think. Anyway it's time for this soul to leave its body. I'm going home and getting drunk. Tell Adele and the others they're free to do the same. They'll all be safe enough when Wheelock sees he's won."

"I never saw you for a coward."

"Cowards are the smart ones. I tried being a hero and it got Jerry killed."

"You didn't kill him."

"I loved that little frog. My old man died when I was little. The only reason my uncle raised me was for the free help in the store. Jerry was the only real family I ever had. I wish I'd told him that. Film was all we ever talked about, as if that was the only important thing in the world."

"It was to him. If you turn your back on Rocky now, he'll have died for no reason."

"He already did. Nothing's worth giving up your life."

"He didn't feel that way. He proved that in China and Mexico."

"What do you know about it? This is just a hobby for you. You can always run back north and work for your old man."

Tom looked at him, a pudgy little man in wrinkled clothes. "Go home and get drunk," he said. "Your job's done. You just managed to kill Jerry all over again." He went downstairs, leaving Buck smoking his cigar at the top.

That afternoon Adele Varga convened a council of war at the Rocky office on Yucca Avenue. Tom attended along with Yuri, Ray Quintana the security man, Morrie the grip, and J. W. Starling. In the absence of sufficient chairs, packing crates and pieces of scenery had been brought in from the outer office, and these were occupied by all but Quintana, who preferred to stand at parade rest with his feet spread and his hands folded behind him, and Adele, who sat behind the desk in her daily uniform of white blouse and dark skirt. She had cleared the desk of clutter and spread out a survey map of the ranch, upon which she had drawn rectangles to represent the barn and outbuildings and an X on the hill where Buck's Civil War cannon stood.

"What's the story on that?" she asked Morrie, tapping the X with a scarlet-nailed forefinger. "Is it in working order or just decoration?"

"The barrel ain't plugged, I checked on that," he said. "I can give it a cleaning and get the powder and shot, if I can find somebody with the guts to test fire it. I wouldn't do it myself without twelve feet of fuse and a clear run to a deep ditch."

"Get it ready. I'll test fire it myself. I want it aimed at the road up from the gate and primed to fire at all times."

Tom said, "Do you really think they'll try the same thing twice?"

"I plan to make them." She looked at Quintana. "How many men can you spare from other jobs?"

"I've got a man in Our Lady of Mercy with both legs in casts and no spleen. There aren't any other jobs. I have fifteen experienced field agents I can count on, including two independents I use part time. They all know Calvin. They'll report for duty."

"We'll find work for them when the time comes. Until then they're on full retainer."

Tom said, "Can we afford that?"

Her smile was grim. "We can if enough employees agree to suspend wages until this thing is over. I can get Ince and Griffith and Uncle Carl and the rest of the studios to pass the hat. It's cheaper than fighting the battle themselves."

Starling said, "I like a good fight. I ain't had one to speak of since a China boy tried to knife me in the jute mill in '99."

"You're *hors de combat*," Adele said. "That means no fighting for you. If you violate your parole we lose our only real asset. Wheelock would get his way without having to fire another shot."

"I reckon I'll fight when I'm fought."

"We'll see you won't have to. Tom, I'm putting you in charge of J. W. What happened to Jerry might have been an accident, and he might have been targeted because they knew how important he was to Rocky. That puts our Yukon Jack at the top of the list. That may mean your moving in with him and Buck. Lock him in his room if you have to."

"Buck's bungalow isn't exactly San Quentin," Tom said. "It'll take at least two people to watch him around the clock, and Buck isn't in shape for it."

"I'll help."

Everyone looked at Yuri. The big Ukrainian hadn't spoken since he came in.

"Move him to our place," he said. "He can have my room. I'll sleep in a chair with the door open."

Starling said, "Makes me no never mind where I bunk. I'd admire to see just how big this here Rooshian is when I get restless." He smiled at Yuri, whose face remained stony.

"San Fernando might be a good place for him," said Adele. "It's out of the crossfire."

"Can't Quintana assign a couple of men to look after him?" Tom asked.

The security man shook his head. "I don't have near enough men to ride the fence at the ranch."

"You're it, Tom." Adele smiled. "It should give you a chance to finish that scenario."

He said nothing. He wanted to point out that when he came to work there he hadn't signed on as a jail-keeper and bodyguard, but he was still smarting from the dressing-down Buck had given him a few days earlier. He had a suspicion he was being put out of harm's way.

Morrie said, "I guess we're shutting down production till this blows over."

It was Adele's turn to shake her head. "We make moving pictures. If we stop doing that we might as well hand over the keys to the barn to the Trust. We've got two more days' shooting on *Sioux Massacre* and then we'll set up for the Alaska picture. If Buck doesn't want to see it through, I'll take over. If Broncho Billy can direct himself, there's no reason I can't do the same."

"There's one," Morrie said. "You're a woman."

"And you're a son of a bitch. But that won't get in the way of your putting that cannon into working order."

He retreated before the heat in her eyes. "I got no problem with your being a woman, it's the cowboys from the Watering Hole I'm worried about. Most of them will only take orders from pants."

"I think I have a pair lying around. What are you doing about the generator?"

"It's scrap. Andy took the train to Frisco to look at a used one some construction company's got up for sale. It'll run us a couple of hundred."

"We'll wire it. Meanwhile we'll shoot outside, the interiors too. Just like we did before kliegs."

Morrie said, "You're counting an awful lot on the competition coming through with enough cash to fight a war *and* stay in business."

"He's right," Tom said. "Five years ago when our cutters went on strike, the other ice companies lent my father money to pay his bills, but not enough to hire replacements. Meanwhile they pirated away several of our best customers."

Adele tapped her nails on the desk. "I'll sell the Rambler. That should keep us going through the end of the month. By then we'll be getting checks from distributors for the rental fees on *Sioux Massacre*."

"You forgot the printer's bill," said Morrie. "The fees won't cover it by the end of the month, and that's when the note comes due, along with Peavey and his padlocks."

There was a silence during which not even Adele's nails were heard. Yuri broke this one too. He rose to his full impressive height, unwound the string of gold coins from his neck, and dropped it on the desk. They made a pile of tiny suns in the afternoon light coming through the window.

Chapter 22

That was a reckless thing to do," Tom said.

Yuri, riding on the passenger's side of the Model T's front seat, grinned at the windshield. The Ukrainian seldom smiled—never in Tom's presence since shaving off the beard—possibly because he was ashamed of his teeth; they were stained a uniform shade of amber from the coarse Turkish tobacco he burned in his pipe. Starling rode in back and took no part in the conversation. He hadn't spoken since leaving the office.

"It was getting heavy," Yuri said. "Like wearing a belt chain around my neck."

"It's your legacy. What if it gets spent and the company goes out of business anyway?"

"Then I'll get another one."

"What are you so happy about? Have you got so much Tartar blood you *like* the idea of going to war?"

"I saw a whale."

"What?"

"This morning, at dawn. I hired a boat and we went out a mile. I saw it through the glass as clear as I'm seeing you. It broke up out of the water like somebody threw something big through a window, and it just kept going up and up and just when you thought nothing would stop it from going up, it stopped itself and just hung there. It seemed like it hung there for five minutes. Then it turned all the way over and started back down. It didn't even make a splash going back into the water; you'd have thought there was a slit of some kind and it just slid through. It was blue on top and white on the bottom, like a new boat, with a big jaw and teeth like harrows. The man who ran the boat said it was a blue whale."

"How big was it?"

"Tom, it wouldn't fit in the lake."

Tom drove in silence for several blocks, working up courage to ask the next question.

"I suppose you'll be going home now that you've seen one finally."

"I can't go home after seeing that. At least not until I've seen so many I get tired of it."

"Judging by how long it took you to see just one, that might take you the rest of your life."

"It probably will. That's why I gave Adele the necklace. I'll need a job if I'm going to be here that long."

The door to Buck's bungalow wasn't latched. It drifted around on its hinges when Tom rapped his knuckles on it. Buck was sitting on the camelback sofa in his creased and wrinkled clothes with a glass in his hand. The tequila bottle on the table was almost empty. He didn't look up as Tom told him Starling was moving out and filled him in on the other details of the meeting in Buck's office. Yuri stood on the threshold while the ex-convict went into his bedroom to collect his belongings. The producer didn't say a word until he came out with his blanket roll slung over one shoulder by its rope.

"You can't win."

Tom watched him refill his glass, draining the bottle of the rest of its contents. "Adele says the Trust is only interested in making money. If we can hold out long enough to make winning not worth the outlay, Wheelock's employers will recall him and let us alone."

"They're robber barons. You don't get to be one of those by stopping short of destroying your enemies. They can afford to carry red ink on the books for a year. That's six months longer than all of the independent studios combined can hold out. They'll drop out one by one, agree to pay the damn licensing fee, and hang us out with the wash."

"Maybe they will," Tom said. "But at least they'll have put up a fight."

Buck looked up then. The whites of his eyes were as red as his hair.

"Ask Griffith about that. Ask if he'll think the fight's worth it when he loses Billy Bitzer."

Tom said, "What happened to Jerry wasn't your fault."

"What if your little coalition holds out for a year, or ten? That isn't a pimple on the ass of how long the ones that die will be dead. All I wanted to do was make pictures. That's all Jerry wanted, and they killed him. Did you know Edison didn't invent the light bulb? He stole that, just like he stole the phonograph and moving pictures. He didn't invent the dirty deal either, but he sure improved on it. The Lizard of Menlo Park." He drank.

Starling said, "Let's get going before this yellow son of a bitch pees his pants."

Buck seemed to awaken. His eyes came into focus and he leaned forward and set down his glass with a loud thump. "I did my homework on you, Mr. Big-time Highwayman. The technical advisor on my first feature worked undercover for Wells Fargo for twenty years. He's eighty-seven, living in a retirement home in Riverside. A lot of desperadoes went to prison and some to the scaffold, never knowing their old pard Zeke Flood was the one who gathered all the evidence against them. Do you recall the name?"

The former bandit shifted his blanket roll to the other shoulder. "Butch used to sell stolen paper securities to an old storekeep name of Flood. We all called him Pop."

"He knew more about you than you did about him. He listened to everything you boys talked about, from Harry Longabaugh's piles to the women's lingerie advertisements Kid Curry tore out of the Monkey Ward catalogue and carried in his saddlebags. Do you remember what name they all knew you by in those days?"

"I always been Starling. Longabaugh always went around trying to get folks to call him the Sundance Kid, and Ben Kilpatrick favored the Tall Texan, but I never had any truck with that."

"I don't blame you. I'd feel the same way if everyone who knew me called me Shit-beetle."

Starling lunged, swinging around the end of the blanket roll, which was stiff and moved as if it were heavy. Yuri moved faster. He caught the end of the roll in one hand and pulled, throwing off the ex-convict's balance; as he stumbled, the rope slid off his shoulder and the bundle fell to the floor with a clank.

Buck hadn't moved, even to duck the blow that had been intended for him. He was looking at Tom, for whom events had moved too swiftly to react. "Starling was lucky," the producer said. "The newspapers ate up those nicknames like candy. But they couldn't print Shit-beetle, so it didn't get to be famous, like Billy the Kid or Mysterious Dave Mather."

"You're a damn liar." But Starling was preoccupied. The brittle old blanket had split open when it struck and he knelt to rearrange the folds. Tom caught a glimpse of gunmetal, quite a bit of it. He knew now where the old bandit had gotten the pistol he slept with. He wondered what condition the rest of the contents were in after lying under a porch in San Francisco for fifteen years.

Buck went on. "Flood said I was lucky, too; most of the people who knew Starling in the old days are dead or in prison for life. He wouldn't be much of a draw if it got out the only reason Butch Cassidy and the others kept him around was to clean up after the horses. The one time he tried holding up a train he fell out of his saddle and knocked himself cold on the cowcatcher. He woke up in manacles."

"Horseshit. I got shot in the back of the head as I was riding away with the money. A yellow fireman had a pistol hid out in the box."

Tom watched Starling tucking in the ends of the blanket, taking time to make them just so instead of looking at Buck and the others, and he knew the producer's story was true. He felt sorry for the ex-convict then.

"Everybody's clumsy one time or another," Tom said. "Anyone can fall off his horse or trip over a bucket of washers in a hardware store."

Buck made no response other than to retrieve his glass and resume drinking. Starling finished lashing his bundle and led the way out.

They made the trip to San Fernando through a rain so light it nearly qualified as vapor. The residents of Ingot would have gone about their business in such weather bareheaded, but in suburban Los Angeles, pedestrians gathered under shop awnings waiting for it to change or dashed to the shelter of their vehicles using newspapers as umbrellas. Tom wondered if the January thaw had set in back home or if the lake was still making ice. There was no conversation to distract him from this reverie. Yuri's detached expression said he was thinking about his whale, and Starling rode with his blanket roll across his lap, staring silently at the floor of the backseat. They were nearly through town when he looked up.

"Spies are professional liars, you know," he said. "There wasn't a one of them Wells Fargo boys would stand up and face you like a man."

Tom said, "You can't trust the stories people tell. Henry Ford says history is bunk."

"Well, he's a smart fellow. Whoever he is." The ex-convict showed renewed interest in the scenery. "Can't tell a saloon from a ladies' millinery," he murmured.

They turned in at the sign reading BUNGALOWS FOR RENT BY WEEK OR MONTH. It reminded Tom of his plans to switch to the monthly rate. The charmless little place had begun to feel like home.

Driving around to the bungalows in back, he braked suddenly, forcing Yuri to brace himself against the dashboard and tearing a violent curse from Starling. The bottle-green Chevrolet touring car owned by Tom's uncle was parked in front of their door. His father stood alongside it smoking his pipe.

Chapter 23

Andrei Ivanovitch Pulski looked smaller than his son remembered; but that might have been an illusion created by the car, which was longer and higher than the Ford. His heavy tweeds and tall boots, so appropriate for the snowy terrain surrounding Mount Shasta, looked ludicrously out of place in southern California, and Tom felt the little death that comes when the stature of one's father is suddenly diminished. There was, too, an Old World quality about his neat goatee and carefully brushed hair that made Tom think of the antiquated photographic portraits lining the corridor to Sheriff Peavey's office. His pipe, an elegant rosewood with an amber stem, appeared fussily Victorian in that casual venue and effeminate when compared to Buck Bensinger's cigars. His son, at that time but dimly aware of the perspective-altering atmosphere of Los Angeles, concealed his chagrin behind a glad face that he knew looked as false as it felt. "Father! This is a surprise."

The elder Pulski knocked out his pipe against the Chevrolet's spare tire by way of acknowledging his son's greeting. "They told me at the moving picture office you were staying here. I had to introduce myself as your father before the woman I spoke to knew who I was asking for. She had never heard of Dmitri Andreivitch Pulski."

"Here they know me as Tom Boston. In this part of the country people have trouble remembering and pronouncing Russian names." He hated himself for feeling the need to explain his decision, especially in front of others. "This is J. W. Starling. He's with the company."

"Pleased to meet you. You got a fine boy, polite to his elders." The former bandit shifted his blanket roll to offer his hand. Tom shrank inwardly at his father's hesitation, but at length he grasped the hand briefly and let go.

"His mother taught him most of his good manners. Unfortunately, answering wires and letters wasn't among them."

"I was going to write you this week. A lot has been happening." He pleaded with his eyes for a postponement of this discussion. But by then Andrei was looking at Yuri.

"You shaved your beard. Is it that warm here?"

"It's warm," said the Ukrainian. For once Tom envied him his taciturnity.

"We've missed your strong arm. We've harvested two more tons of ice since you left."

"I hope whoever's been using my saw is remembering to sharpen it."

"I only hire capable men." He looked at Tom. "Is there a place where we can talk?"

Tom led the way to the bungalow door and unlocked it. "Yuri, can you show Mr. Starling where he'll sleep?"

The big man, who took such requests literally, pointed out the door to his room. "Put your things anywhere. I'll be in to get mine later."

The ex-convict went into the bedroom and shut the door behind him. Immediately there was a wheezing of springs as of something heavy flung on the bed. Within thirty seconds he was snoring.

"I'll go out and have a pipe," Yuri said.

"Use my tobacco." Andrei produced a pebbled leather pouch with his initials stamped on it in gold, redolent of the fine English blend he had made to his order in San Francisco.

"I'm used to my Turkish." Yuri went out.

Alone in the little sitting room with his father, Tom was conscious of its shabbiness. The two horsehair chairs might have been bought in separate hemispheres, the sofa's tapestry covering was worn shiny from contact with a hundred transient pairs of buttocks and grubby on the arms, and the landscape on the wall was a cheap print made with smeared plates from a painting that had not been good to begin with.

"This is how you live?"

"It's where I sleep and sometimes write. I spend most of my time at the studio. That's what I was going to write you about. I'm leaving the ice company."

"To aet in moving pictures?"

"To write for them. Buck Bensinger's offered me a chance I haven't gotten from the magazines. I have to try it."

"I wasn't aware they were written. The few I've seen appeared to have been made up as they went along." After conducting a visual comparison between the chairs, Andrei sat in the one to the right.

Tom remained standing. "It's a new business. Nothing's standardized."

"There's a matter of three hundred dollars I gave you for the trip down and your stay. Have you spent it?"

His son was wearing the light cotton jacket he'd bought in Los Angeles to wear mornings and in the late afternoons when the air grew cool. From an inside pocket he drew the envelope his father had given him the morning he left home and held it out. "That's just over half, more than you expected back. I've been living on what Buck pays me."

Andrei took the envelope and pocketed it inside his coat without counting the bills. "There's a matter of the automobile I lent you."

"I thought I'd send it back with the trucks after the ice was delivered. I'm sorry for the hardship. It's impossible to get around here without your own transportation. The trolleys don't go everywhere."

"It hasn't been so inconvenient. Your Uncle Paul is generous with his automobile." Only Andrei's son knew the effort it cost him to say anything favorable about his wife's brother. "They are paying you well? They are not taking advantage of your youth and inexperience?"

"Well enough, Yuri too. You'd approve of the way I negotiated for him. He's the star of the picture we're shooting. That's why he shaved his beard."

"He looks ridiculous without it."

Tom had nothing to counter that. In the silence his father produced his pipe from a vest pocket, but after fingering it for a moment he returned it. He looked up at his son.

"Come home with me, Dmitri. This is no work for you."

"That was true of the ice business. My heart was never in it; you must have suspected that. It was Yuri who kept the sawyers from brawling with each other and made sure Esaul didn't fall asleep at the plow. I spent most of my time at the lake inside the shack, writing. I felt guilty about it there. Here it's my work."

He'd had the words ready for a week, to put in the letter he'd been working up the courage to start. He couldn't tell if they had any effect. He wondered if his father was listening at all or just waiting for him to finish.

"The ice business is stable. Moving pictures are a novelty. They won't prevent food from spoiling or provide you with a cool drink when the sun is hot. If you wanted to work at something so frivolous, you might at least have chosen a firm that pays its bills. I've been making calls since you left, asking questions. This Rocky Mountain company owes more than it made last year. The local sheriff is ready to foreclose, and according to some of the people I spoke to, there's a question about whether what it does is even legal. I got the distinct impression from the woman at the office that the place is under some kind of siege. Are you prepared to go to jail? Are you prepared to die?"

"They've already killed one of us," Tom said. "A harmless little man who only wanted to make good pictures. They claim the law is on their side and they shot him in cold blood."

"That decides the issue. You're coming home with me." Andrei stood.

"Your great-grandfather was a soldier of Russia. Your grandfather fought Indians for the right to hunt and trap in the Sierra Nevadas. You saw men drowned and killed by runaway plows when you cut ice as a boy; that could just as easily have happened to you, but you stuck with it until you owned the

company. I don't see how I could do less and remain
a Pulski."

"But you are not a Pulski. Your name is Tom Boston."

The statement, delivered in a tone as cold and
sharp as a sawyer's blade, divided father and son as
cleanly as two cakes of ice.

Tom said, "You put on heavy clothes to harvest
the lake. Now you put on suits to sell what you harvested. Down here we put on new names to make
pictures: Buck instead of Arthur, Wild Bill instead of
William David Garrick Latimer, Tom Boston instead
of Dmitri Andreivitch Pulski." *J. W. Starling instead
of Shit-beetle*, he thought. "You're still the same man
under the suit that you were under scratchy wool, and
I'm still your son no matter what I call myself."

Starling's snores spluttered through a long silence.
Then Andrei tugged down the hem of his coat. It had
been tailored especially for him in San Francisco and
needed no tugging.

"You've made up your mind, then," he said.

"I have."

"I owe you three weeks' wages. Keep the Ford as
payment. I've been considering buying an automobile
more in keeping with a man in my position anyway.
It won't be a Chevrolet," he added; and for the first
time since their reunion, Tom felt like laughing. He
watched his father walk to the door, then pause with
his hand on the knob to look him over from head to
foot. "You're thin. I'd like to be able to tell your
mother you're eating properly."

"I am, Father. I'm on my feet a lot."

"Odd. I thought writing was a sedentary profession."

"Not down here. Everything's different in southern California."

"I can see that."

Still he hesitated, long enough for Tom to wonder if he should embrace his father or at least shake his hand. But he remained rooted in the center of the room.

"The ice will be delivered tomorrow," Andrei said. "I made better time than the trucks." He let himself out.

Chapter 24

―――――

Adele Varga, directing operations like a field general from behind Buck's desk in the office he rarely visited, balanced the upright telephone in one hand, holding the tin-cup receiver to her ear and supporting the standard by its brass hook with her little finger, while she rolled cigarettes with her other hand and plotted out a shooting schedule in grids on a sheet of typewriter paper. Tom, there ostensibly to take part in a story conference but actually to help out with legwork, listened to the conversation on her end with a sense of wonderment approaching awe.

"Ince, honey, we're in a tight. I know that building's not part of the lease, but you know what shape the barn's in right now; we can't keep birds out, let alone cold in. Well, we've got ten tons of ice coming today and no place to store it. We could throw a champagne party, but Buck doesn't have that many friends. How long?" She consulted the gridded sheet. "Four weeks, if we move up all the studio exterior footage. Tommy, sweetie, you've got more buildings than Pasadena, why don't you send Bill Hart and his company to one of the others? Well, hell, I didn't know he was such an old woman. Three weeks, then, but it means we lose the dogsled chase. No, we're not interested in buying stock footage. All right, darling. Thanks." She hung up. "Tommy Ince is an easy trick. I'd have settled for two weeks. The dogsleds are back in, and see if you can work in a gunfight in a blizzard. The suckers will be on the edge of their seats wondering who shot who."

"Buck says snow scenes are hard to shoot," Tom said.

"Not if you backlight them. Our second unit cameraman, Phil Weed, isn't too proud to let the gaffers carry their weight. He isn't a genius."

"I'll have to shorten the saloon scenes to make room for the chase and a gunfight. We're into three reels now."

"The saloon scenes are my scenes. Shorten them and I'll shorten your dick." She smiled radiantly and lit a cigarette.

"I thought two reels was Rocky's limit."

"Two reels is Buck's limit. You might have noticed I'm not Buck. Film is two cents a foot. J. W. Starling's first starring feature is worth the extra five bucks. We'll go four reels if the story's strong enough. That's your department."

He hesitated. "Did Buck tell you what he found out about Starling?"

"He told me. So he's a four-flusher. He came to the one place where he can lose himself in the crowd."

"What if people find out he wasn't a cross between Jesse James and John Wesley Hardin?"

"What if they find out your real name is Dmitri Pulski?"

Tom said nothing. It was the first time the subject

of his father's visit to the office had come up.

She sat back, smoking. "Don't worry, your secret's safe. Not that it would make a difference if we ran it under the *Yukon Jack* opening title. I was a whore. Now I'm a producer as well as an actress. We won't even count secretary and bookkeeper. Buck used to write prices on pipe couplings, then he made pictures, now he drinks and feels sorry for himself. Tomorrow he may run for governor of California and win. Jerry Jarette's father was a marquis. He probably told you something else, just like he lied to Buck about being a baker. It's the same at the other studios. Tommy Ince was a theatrical booking agent, Griffith a cash boy in a dry goods store. We've got candy sellers and junkmen. There's a fellow producing comedy shorts in Oxnard who used to be an undertaker; when the box office is light he still dresses corpses on the slab where he cuts film. Those are the legits. If you weeded out all the con men and pederasts, there wouldn't be enough competition out here to stir the Trust's feathers.

"Twenty years ago they closed the frontier," she said. "As soon as they did, it busted wide open here. Hollywood's the latest in a long line of western boomtowns, a place where no matter what you're guilty of or how many failures you've had, you can start all over again with clean sheets. We really ought to slap people like Starling on the ass the minute they cross Highland Avenue. That's what they do the first time you're born, and it'd serve as well for the second. Why do you think people go to see westerns? Not for the shooting and horseplay. They want to go back to the border for a fresh start."

"Then our job's to forgive them their transgressions?"

"That's God's job. Ours is to wipe them out. They never happened. Would you like to see the biography I put together for Starling? I knocked it out this morning at four o'clock." She drew a sheet from the belly drawer of Buck's desk and passed it across the top.

It was single-spaced, typed on the Remington in the outer office. He read it swiftly. "Isn't he a little young to have ridden with the Jameses and Youngers?"

"It doesn't matter. The audiences who come to see *Yukon Jack* will want to believe he did, so they won't bother to do the arithmetic. That's marketing: Tell people what they want before they know themselves, then sell it to them."

"Why not just say he rode with Butch Cassidy and the Wild Bunch? It's easier to defend."

"You're not listening. As long as they like what we're saying, it won't need defending. All the truth in the world won't stand up if people don't like it. Anyway, not that many people have heard of Cassidy, but kids are born knowing all about Jesse James. You have to play to the balcony."

"Buck taught you that?"

"Just the balcony part. Everything else I learned in Tijuana. Here, there, the work's the same. The only difference now is, when I go to bed, I'm done for the day."

He returned the sheet. "What if your star objects to his new history?"

"He won't, as long as the name Shit-beetle doesn't appear. In any case it isn't his history. It belongs to the Rocky Mountain Moving Picture Association publicity department. That's me."

"How can such a small head wear so many hats?" He smiled.

"I've been everything from Little Bo-peep to Marie

Antoinette," she said, "and that was before I came north. If I did twice as much it would still be a vacation. How did Buck look when you saw him yesterday?"

She had pulled off the change of subject while returning the biography to the drawer, not looking up, sounding as if she were asking just to be polite. He answered in the same tone.

"He looked like someone who's made up his mind to drink himself to death."

She met his gaze. Then she tipped cigarette ash into the heavy bronze tray on the desk and sat back again. "And I suppose you know what that looks like."

"My father offers work to runaway serfs, Imperial Army deserters, and Cossacks who took part in rebellions against St. Petersburg. Most of them can never go back home. At the end of the harvest they get together and hold contests to find out who can drink the greatest amount of vodka in the shortest amount of time. One or two die each year from the shock. Others go to their houses and do the same thing more slowly. I grew up among them. After a while you get so you can tell from their faces which ones won't be back next year. I saw that in Buck's face yesterday."

She smoked in silence for a minute. Then she leaned forward and squashed out the cigarette. "Well, we can't have that." She rose and smoothed her dark skirts.

"Do you want me to drive you?"

"I'll go alone in the Rambler. I've decided not to sell it. I'm negotiating with a rare coin dealer downtown for a price on those gold coins. Judging by how much he's stalling, that necklace should keep us in business through December. Your friend Yuri just bought himself in for ten percent."

Tom stood. "I thought gold was only thirty-five dollars an ounce."

"Gold, yes. Uncirculated Russian gold coins issued under Czar Alexander,II are a whole different story, apparently. Collectors are crazy, even for southern California. You know him better than anyone. Do you think he knows what he's doing?"

"Nobody knows Yuri."

She opened another drawer in the desk and gathered her cigarette makings. When she had them in her purse, an old-fashioned drawstring reticule that had probably come from the prop department, she gave Tom a long look. "You haven't said how things went with your father."

"They went all right. He's letting me keep the Ford."

"Did he give you his blessing?"

"No, just the Ford."

"I'm sorry."

He shrugged, feeling uncomfortable. "I need the car to get around."

"Use it, Tom. Keep moving. Nobody dies at full gallop." She glanced down at the tiny silver watch pinned to her blouse. "Yuri's due at the barn in an hour for close-ups. A car's on its way with two of Ray Quintana's men in it, just in case Wheelock's Pinkertons find their backbone and try something on the street. Why don't you go back to San Fernando and spell him? You can write some more on the scenario and bring Starling at four o'clock. That's when the ice is coming. He can take a look at the building where we'll be shooting the gunfight and the dogsled chase. I'm glad he's got a good imagination. Until the carpenters and painters are finished with it, it's going to look like an ice house."

"Where will you be?"

"I'll meet you there. No, wait. Leave the Ford here and take the Rambler. Drop me off at Buck's and pick me up on your way to the ranch. We'll need the room if I can talk Buck into going along and postponing his appointment with the Grim Reaper and a case of tequila."

"Think you can do it?"

"I'm not sure. You know Buck. It's a hell of a scenario to pass up."

Chapter 25

In front of Buck's bungalow, Tom asked Adele if she was sure she didn't want him to go in with her. "He was a grim enough sight yesterday," he said. "I doubt twenty-four hours have improved him."

She laughed, a beautiful sinister huskiness, and he thought what a tragedy it was the people who saw her pictures didn't get to hear it. "Dear boy, I hope you never have to help a Chihuahua horse thief out of clothes he's been sleeping in for six weeks." She pushed shut the door on the passenger's side.

"He might become violent."

"If he doesn't, I will."

"I'm serious."

"Do you think I'm not?" There was no trace of laughter now in her face. She wound the purse strings around her wrist and started up the walk.

Even so he waited for five minutes after she knocked, then let herself in the front door, listening for raised voices and breaking glass, before he pulled away. He wondered as he did so if he were more concerned for Adele or Buck.

It was another sunny day, the light at midmorning of that deceptive burnished-bronze quality he associated with late afternoon in northern California. His internal clock had yet to adjust. It occurred to him that that might never happen. He wondered if a chronic state of disorientation might not be responsible for the unique world perspective of the natives. Add to that a point of view framed by the eyepiece of a camera, by the rectangular boundaries of a moving picture screen, and the result was a kind of false clarity of vision, like the philosophy that came from a bottle of vodka. Certainly that would explain the conviction of everyone at Rocky that the Trust could be defeated by a company that depended for its survival upon how much it could get for an heirloom donated by an unlettered ice cutter.

It was just possible that Buck Bensinger suspected this as well. Jolted by Jerry Jarette's death into an unwelcome reality, he had taken to drinking, not to escape, but to reach a condition in which he could share in the cockeyed optimism.

The trouble was, now that his father was on his way back north, Tom couldn't think of a single person who wasn't too deep under the spell of the area to appreciate this confidence. Even Yuri had become seduced by a three-thousand-pound mammal.

Rolling along quiet Mulholland, the grumbling of the Rambler's motor and the swish of its tires on macadam the only sounds, he considered the weeks he had spent south of Ingot and home—a place already fading into a chiaroscuro effect, as when poor Jerry Jarette had smeared Vaseline on his lens in order to simulate a mirage in the desert. Memories of people and events less than a month in the past fluttered by like an undercranked street scene, the figures darting in and out of doorways in comic anonymity. He could actually feel the bewitchment consuming him; in a month, two weeks, perhaps, he might no longer be capable of his present rationality. He suspected it was this way for someone aware of his own increasing senility. And he embraced the warm immersion, the renunciation of cares, as much as he feared it.

Preoccupied as he approached Sepulveda, he had just time enough to wonder about the all-black Cadillac touring car standing against the right curb a hundred feet in front of him, and why whoever owned it had gone to the trouble to paint over all the nickel and brasswork, even the radiator, when it suddenly swung out broadside, blocking his lane. He jammed down the brake. The sudden friction was too much for the right front tire; it blew with a report like a gunshot and the car listed, throwing him sideways against the shifting cane. He struck the hard rubber knob with the force of a fist in his ribs. For several seconds he couldn't get air into his lungs, and in his pain and shock he was sure a rib had broken and gone into one of them, collapsing it like a balloon. When at last they began to inflate, his vision cleared, and he saw that he was surrounded by men, men who had piled out of the Cadillac in black bowler hats as hard and shiny as beetles' backs and long overcoats too heavy for the California climate, pointing at him; but not with fingers. They held short, ugly revolvers and twin-barreled shotguns blunted back to the wooden stocks.

"Shit!" barked the one nearest him, a flat-faced Irishman with carroty orange hair that stuck out under his bowler and freckles spilling down inside his boiled collar and out of his cuffs onto the backs of his hands—bestial hands, more like paws, stubby short with shining calluses on the knuckles. "Where's that Mexican whore?"

It did not occur to him to ask who they were until they were on the road, by which time it was no longer necessary to ask.

Still dazed from the suddenness of it all, in pain every time he gulped air (one rib at least was cracked, that much was certain, for it pinched him sharply unless he remembered to take only shallow breaths), he had been manhandled out of the Rambler, groped all over for hidden weapons, and flung across the rear seat of the Cadillac. He barely had faculties enough to make sense of the conversation that took place in snatches among his captors.

"Sure this is the right car?"

"If it ain't, it's the right model rolling around with the same plates."

"Well, where the hell's the *puta*?"

"You're asking me?" The Irishman leaned in and lifted Tom by his collar. The splintery pain in his side forced him to draw his knees into his stomach. "Where's the woman?" The man's breath smelled of gin.

"What woman?"

A backhanded slap stung the left side of his face. The man let go of his collar and he fell back. That hurt even more.

"He's lying," someone else said. "Why give him a break?"

"He's busted up inside already. I don't want to drive around all day with a fucking corpse."

"Dump him in La Brea."

"Out of our way. Anyway, we don't know who he

is. Our orders was to stop the Rambler and grab the woman. It ain't our fault she wasn't in it."

"Well, what do we do with him?"

"Take him on up and wait for the senator. If he don't know what to do with him, that's his potato."

"That's kidnapping." This was a younger voice than the others.

"That's what it was before, boyo," said the Irishman. "Just 'cause it's a different passenger don't change things. You had a problem with that, you should of took it up with Mr. Pinkerton yesterday."

The door on the other side in back opened and someone began to push Tom into a sitting position. To avoid further discomfort he helped, holding his right side as he placed his feet on the floor and struggled upright. The man sat next to him and another one got in on the other side, forming bookends with Tom in the middle. Two more climbed into the front next to the driver, a young man close to Tom's age, who shot a worried glance back at him. This was the fellow who didn't care for kidnapping.

"What about the Rambler?" he asked.

"Let the cops find it and talk to Bensinger. The senator said he wanted him to sweat." The Irishman, sitting on the far side in front, produced a flat pint bottle from inside his coat, uncorked it, and tipped it up. Tom smelled again the odor of fermented junipers.

The young man engaged the clutch and they swung back parallel with the curb and started rolling in the direction Tom had been heading before. The Cadillac smelled of various kinds of liquor and perspiration; the men were sweating in their overcoats, which Tom suspected they wore to cover their guns. The men flanking him rode with their sawed-off shotguns drooping between their legs like spent phalluses.

They turned onto Sepulveda and then down a succession of side streets lined with palms, one-story bungalows, and the occasional complicated Victorian house that had been built when the railroad came and before the streets were paved. Tom soon became confused by the turns and the Spanish street names. It was plain the driver was trying to discourage anyone from following.

"Bottle that," the Irishman said finally. "If there was anybody to lose and we ain't lost them by now, we ain't likely to. That's what the scatterguns are for."

In a little while Tom smelled mountains. They were ascending into the foothills.

"We aren't going to Sacramento?" he asked.

The Irishman turned his flat face around. His nose had been pushed in, not by nature, and his bristly red eyebrows grew sparsely through old scar tissue. "What made you think we was going to Sacramento, boyo?" He smiled with a bottom row of teeth worn round around the edges like headstones.

Tom met his watery blue gaze. "Because that's where your headquarters is."

"Ain't you the brainy one. You must have a drop of the old sod in you. Here's some more smarts, boyo. A Pinkerton's headquarters is in his hat."

"Yours looks like a piss-pot."

The Irishman's eyes flicked toward the man seated on Tom's right, who sent his elbow into his ribs. A shard of white-hot pain went up his side. He doubled over to keep from fainting.

"I was wrong about you, boyo. You ain't got brains enough to be an Englishman."

The man seated in the middle in front laughed.

They continued to climb. At last they turned into

a drive paved with limestone that graded upward thirty degrees and stopped before a gate in a six-strand barbed-wire fence. A metal sign on the gate read:

PROPERTY OF THE COUNTY OF LOS ANGELES

KEEP OUT

A man wearing a tan uniform and white Stetson stepped out of a square shack made of new yellow plywood and approached the driver. He had a five-pointed star on his chest, and the polished walnut handle of a revolver stuck out of a holster strapped around his waist.

"This here's county property," he said. "I'm going to have to ask you fellows to turn around and go back the way you came."

The Irishman leaned over from the passenger's side. "We work for Senator Wheelock."

"Well, I don't know who he is, but unless he's with the county I'd tell him the same thing."

"This one's too big for you, Junior. There anybody here in long pants we can talk to?"

The guard was only a year or two older than the driver, but he had stony eyes that grew harder when he looked at the Irishman. After a moment he turned his head toward the shack. "You want to come out and talk to these fellows? Maybe they need to hear it in Mexican."

There was a long pause, and Tom began to wonder if there was anyone inside when a shadow stirred and another man in uniform came out. He was smaller than the other but built more powerfully, with a thick chest and muscular thighs that strained the seams of his tan trousers. He had hot eyes and long dark lashes like a woman's. His coloring was Latin.

Angel, Mutt Peavey's deputy, stopped halfway to the car. "Where's the woman?" His voice was harsh.

"We didn't find her," said the Irishman. "This fellow was driving the Rambler. The senator didn't say what to do in a case like that, so we brung him along."

The deputy spat a stream of violent Spanish. The men in the car shrank, as before a blistering wind. The stench of perspiration increased.

When it was over, Angel strode up to the car on the passenger's side and stared at the captive. After a moment he nodded. Tom was impressed despite himself. This was only his third sighting of the deputy, and Angel had not spotted him the second time. They had never spoken.

"I've seen him with Bensinger," he said. To the guard: "Open the goddamn gate."

Chapter 26

Inside the fence, the limestone drive bisected a band of sparse grass, then deteriorated into a pair of ruts in a field of marbled clay. Bulldozers and steam shovels had planed the top off the hill for four square miles, in the center of which lay a dazzling white bowl of fresh concrete, big enough to submerge all of the town of Ingot in the water that filled it to within a few feet of the top. The surface was as smooth as plate glass and sapphire blue beneath a cloudless sky. As they drove along the edge, a wind came up and pushed a creamy ridge across the surface, as straight and precise as a crumb scraper smoothing a linen tablecloth. White gulls, deceived into thinking they had reached the ocean, swooped at the traveling wave and hopped along the concrete lip, searching for mollusks as on a beach.

This, Tom realized, was the great new reservoir everyone was talking about, designed to bring water to the desert town of Los Angeles and attract residents from all over the country. The smell of the water was strong and clean and reminded him of the lake near

Shasta when the spring breakup came early. The memory brought a pang as sharp as the one in his side; had he stayed there, he would not be here.

They stopped before the only aboveground structure inside the fence, a blockhouse built of white masonry with a flat roof and a plank door set deep, like a mausoleum. It resembled one of the Spanish Army strongholds he had seen in photographs taken of the San Juan Heights during the war in Cuba. It made him uncomfortable to think that they had been built to withstand a siege. Theodore Roosevelt was in Brazil, too far away to reconvene the Rough Riders.

The Pinkerton detective seated to Tom's right opened the door and got out. The one on the other side nudged him and he slid over and stepped down from the running board, holding himself. Here the sun hammered, as if the difference of a few hundred yards from the valley floor were enough to increase its heat. The clay beneath his feet, exposed only recently, had baked as hard as ceramic, preserving the tracks of vehicles that had sunk to their hubs in the slippery ooze. Thousands of hairline cracks made the yellow-brown surface look as ancient as the road to Rome. The polite *slap-slap* of the water against the side of the reservoir tantalized him; he was suddenly almost unbearably thirsty.

Angel caught up with them on foot, selected a key from a ring attached to his belt by a brass chain, and unlocked the door. He stood aside and one of the Pinkertons behind Tom gave him a shove. He stumbled across the threshold, but caught himself against the wall opposite; the room was less than eight feet deep. A single recessed square window near the ceiling let in light and air, and there was a painted wooden table with an upright telephone on it, two straight chairs, and a calendar on one wall featuring a Gibson girl in furs. The presence on the table of a deck of cards and a tin ashtray containing several cigarette butts told him it was a place for a caretaker to rest and pass the time. The back wall was whitewashed plaster with a door in it that would lead to a water closet.

The blocks were eighteen inches thick, providing insulation against the sun's heat; but it was a clammy sort of coolness that made him perspire all the more freely. It would have been in just such an environment that J. W. Starling had spent fifteen years of his life in San Quentin. Tom found it uncomfortably claustrophobic after just thirty seconds.

The room wasn't large enough to contain the entire group. The Irishman stepped inside and turned to face Angel, who remained framed in the doorway. "I'll call for instructions," he said. "If he says to stay put I'm going to order more men. You might tell your boy at the gate to put on coffee."

"He doesn't have a stove."

"It's a joke, boyo. You need to get to town more often." He shut the door and shot the inside bolt. "What's your name?" he asked Tom.

"Tom Boston."

"You from Boston?"

"No."

"I got a cousin there. He's deputy street railroad commissioner. Good graft." He hooked one of the chairs by its rung with a foot and pivoted it away from the table. "Take a load off."

"Could I have a drink of water?"

The Irishman's scowl increased his resemblance to a bulldog. He stepped over, opened the door to the water closet, and looked inside. Then he moved back out of the way. "Help yourself. There's a tap."

Tom went in and closed the door behind him. This room was so narrow he could touch the wall on either side without straightening his arms. It contained a toilet with a tank mounted on the wall and a pull chain and a round sink with white porcelain handles, nothing else. There was no window. He turned on the coldwater tap, made a cup with his hands, and drank the sweet fresh water. He splashed more on his face, looked around for a towel, found none, and wiped himself with a sleeve. He felt refreshed, and a little less light-headed.

When he came out, the Irishman was seated at the table with one hand wrapped around the telephone standard and the other holding the receiver to his ear. He'd shed his overcoat and a brown tweed suitcoat and hung them over the back of his chair, but had left on his bowler. He wore a white shirt with broad red stripes and a detachable collar, a red tie knotted into a crooked bow, and a shoulder holster over his vest, the brown leather rubbed as shiny as old mahogany from use. The black rubber butt of his revolver was twisted forward, showing the unblinking cyclops eye of the Pinkerton National Detective Agency engraved into the brass backstrap. He jerked his chin toward the other chair. Tom sat down.

"Yeah, Operator, I'm still waiting on that call to the Valley. It's only six miles away, I could of pedaled there quicker than this on a bicycle." He paused. "Hello, Caesar, he in? This is Riordan, if it's any business of yours. Yeah, why don't you go and do that little thing? Uppity black bastard," he told Tom. A minute passed, then another voice came on the line. Riordan sat up a little straighter. "Yes, sir, it's me. No, there was a hitch. The woman wasn't in the car.

We got somebody else." He flinched away from the harsh sound in the earpiece. "You said stop the car. I didn't know what else to do. He says his name's Tom Boston." His pale blue gaze traveled over Tom. "Oh, nineteen or twenty, five-ten, hundred and sixty, curly black hair, brown eyes. Angel says he belongs to Bensinger. Yeah. Okay, we'll hang on to him. When?" He let go of the standard, pulled a watch out of his vest pocket by its rabbit's-foot fob, glanced at the face, and put it back. "We'll be here, Senator." Tom heard the hollow *plop* of the telephone being hung up on the other end.

Riordan rattled the riser. "Long distance." He winked at Tom. "He says he remembers you from that nancy Latimer's funeral."

"Wheelock? He barely looked at me."

"Politicians. They remember names and faces. It's promises they forget. My cousin said he'd get me into the treasurer's office in Boston. That was two years ago, and here I am still in the fucking desert. Hello, long distance? Give me Sacramento. Fulton six-two-seven-oh. Make it today, sugar. If you girls was race horses you'd all be shot." He pegged the receiver.

He reached behind him and scooped the pint of gin out of his coat, but the telephone rang before he could pull the cork. He winked again. "See? Just like horses. You got to give 'em a bit of the quirt." He answered, thanked the operator curtly, and waited a beat. "Halloran? Riordan. I need twenty more men here at the reservoir. No, I ain't expecting trouble, just trying to prevent it. Well, shake some loose. You don't need fifty men to bust up a strike. In the old days we did it with ten. Ball bats, what you think? Okay, see if you can get them here by midnight." He rolled his eyes. "Put 'em on the train, for chrissake.

They can hire cars in Los Angeles. Sure, the client's good for it; he's got bales. He didn't kick last time, did he?" He hung up and unstopped the bottle. "Prick."

Tom watched him drink. " 'Last time' was when you attacked the ranch, wasn't it?"

The Irishman swallowed and looked at him without lowering the pint. "I heard you had a fracas up there. Some little frog wandered into a bullet."

"I read a book about the Pinkertons once. It didn't say anything about murder."

"Slugs don't keep the Commandments. They go where they go, and if you forget to duck it ain't murder. Anyway, your boss is a crook. The Pinkertons only side with the law."

"Even if it involves kidnapping?"

"It's that little numb-nuts Pollard put that word in your head back on Mulholland. He's studying for the Bar, and I bet he passes. He sure ain't got the tools for this work." He took a swig.

"What are you planning to do with me?"

"That's up to the senator."

"You must have had a plan for Adele Varga."

"That's the slut's name? Well, what I had in mind for her don't work for you." He showed his bottom teeth.

"That's not what the senator had in mind."

"Know how he thinks, do you?" He drank again and thumped down the bottle.

That was the end of that conversation. Riordan picked up the deck of cards, shuffled, and asked Tom if he were interested in a hand of poker. When Tom declined, he shrugged and laid out a game of solitaire. He cheated openly. Tom, who had known some ice cutters who tipped the edge when they played against themselves, had never seen one quite so blatant about it. He tried a few times to reopen the subject of his own fate, but it seemed the more Riordan drank, the less informative he became.

At the end of half an hour, the rumble of a powerful exhaust reached their ears simultaneously. It grew louder until the vibration shook the plank door in its frame, then cut off.

"That'll be him. You can hear that bus of his clear up in Sausalito." Riordan slid the cards back into the deck and got up to throw back the bolt.

Alvin Wheelock strode in on his short legs, his chest thrust forward and his large, white-maned head tilted back, as if he were marching at the head of a parade. He had on his gray homburg, pinch-nez, morning coat, and striped trousers, and the cigarette holder with its smoldering burden slanted up at an arrogant angle from between his clamped teeth. He stopped when he saw Tom, removed his glasses, squinted, and returned them to the bridge of his nose with a short nod.

"That's the fellow," he said. "He and Bensinger must be close if they attend funerals together."

"Then it's okay we grabbed him instead of the woman." The Irishman gnawed at his upper lip.

"You bungled that and there's no sense putting a bright patch over it. But we may snatch something out of this yet. Yes, I believe we may." Wheelock unbuttoned a pair of dove gray gloves that matched his hat and spats and peeled them off. "Is that telephone operating?"

"I used it to call you."

"Do you have Bensinger's home number? That's where he spends most of his time now."

Riordan's hand went to his breast before he remembered he wasn't wearing his suitcoat. He leaned over his chair, groped in an inside pocket, and brought out a small leatherbound notebook. He paged through it, said, "Got it," and scooped up the telephone while Wheelock sat down in his chair and placed the homburg on the table. He hummed a sprightly tune and paid Tom no more attention than the calendar on the wall.

"It's ringing." The Irishman held out the telephone.

Wheelock propped his cigarette in its holder on the edge of the tin ashtray and took the standard and receiver. "Bensinger, is that you? Oh, pardon me, this must be Miss Varga. This is Alvin Wheelock. Is Mr. Bensinger available? He isn't. Well, I shouldn't wonder, the amount he's been imbibing lately. I think you'll agree it really doesn't matter how I happen to know that. Please tell Mr. Bensinger we have his friend, Mr.—?" He lifted his brows in Tom's direction. Tom said nothing.

"Tom Boston," Riordan said.

Evidently Adele had overheard. Wheelock listened, then held out the telephone. "I don't suppose you'd care to identify yourself to Miss Varga."

Tom took it. "Adele, it's me. I'm at—"

The Irishman's reflexes were impressive, given the amount he'd drunk. He snatched away the instrument and returned it to the senator.

"No, he's in good health," Wheelock said. "I must say he's not good company. We'll be happy to see him take his leave, just as soon as Mr. Bensinger surrenders any moving picture equipment he owns and every reel of every film he has shot that he has not yet released, including the negatives and master prints. In addition he will turn over his account books so we can determine nothing was missed. On the contrary, Miss Varga, I think it's quite generous. The gentlemen I represent would be within their rights to compel him to recall all the prints currently in distribution at his own expense and surrender those as well. We are offering to assume that responsibility, provided he acts swiftly. This offer expires at noon tomorrow. If he fails to meet that deadline, I will swear out a warrant for Mr. Bensinger's arrest on seventy-two counts of patent infringement and piracy." When he looked at Tom, the sunlight coming through the high window struck the lenses of his glasses, making them as opaque as two circles of white cardboard. "I nearly forgot the rest. In the event of failure, neither of you will ever see young Mr. Boston again. No, please, I insist upon being the one who calls you."

He handed Riordan the standard and receiver to hang up, then retrieved his cigarette and holder from the ashtray. "I must say, this frontier life agrees with me. Things are so much more direct out here."

Chapter 27

T ell me something *hombre a hombre*," Angel said. "Man to man. Does Adele take on you moving picture boys one at a time or all in a pile?"

Tom said, "If you're trying to provoke me into fighting, your boss won't approve. I'm sure he wants to deliver me in good condition."

"Wheelock isn't my boss."

"Sheriff Peavey, then. He's part of this, isn't he?"

"Peavey's *finito*. With what I'm being paid for this, I'll run against him next election and send him back to the clerk's office where he belongs. Mexicans out-number the gringos in this county four to one. All I have to do is get them to the polls."

"How many times?"

"As many as it takes until the vote comes out right. Just like in Tijuana."

"That's your goal? To be elected sheriff?"

"It don't look like much now, but come back in a year. The sun is warm, the palms are pretty, it never snows. Up until now the only thing keeping people away is no water. As soon as they open them sluices,

all the real estate salesman you see standing in their
doorways will be too busy answering the phone and
writing up land contracts to piss. There'll be construction everywhere you look: roads, office buildings,
apartments, houses. People coming in by the busload,
all with money. They'll be spending most of it in gam-
bling dens and whorehouses. You can't operate them
places without protection. The weekly pickup alone
would keep me in cornmeal and tequila for a year in
Mexico. Only Angel isn't going back there. He's staying here and becoming a millionaire."

"Then Peavey doesn't know you're doing this."

"*Es no muy difícil.* He's like you say, a mutt."

"Are you really going to kill me if Buck doesn't
agree to Wheelock's deal?"

"It's a fight, isn't it? A fight don't end until somebody gives up or dies."

"Who does the killing? You?"

Angel made no answer other than to grin, teeth
pithy white against the even brown of his skin.

Alvin Wheelock hadn't stayed long enough to finish
his cigarette. Once he'd placed his call, he'd put on
his gloves and buttoned them, placed his hat on his
head, popped the crown, and left, instructing Riordan
to call him at home if anything came up. The Irishman had played several more illegitimate games of
solitaire and drunk off most of the gin before Pollard,
the young detective who had expressed reservations
about kidnapping, arrived with a paper sack containing sandwiches and a quart of milk. Tom had realized
then that he hadn't eaten all day. He ate two ham-
and-cheese sandwiches and drank all the milk, Riordan having pushed it across to him with a grimace.

After eating, the Irishman had grown sleepy. Angel
came in to take his place while he went back to his

hotel in town to sleep off the effects of the alcohol.

Angel was boring company when he wasn't needling his captive or discussing his plans for the future. He amused himself by sitting back in the straight chair and performing tricks with his sidearm. It was a Model 1911 Colt Army semiautomatic pistol, gas-fed from a magazine loaded with .45-caliber cartridges inserted in the handle, the first Tom had ever seen; square and heavy looking, blue-black, with checked walnut grips, it spun smoothly on Angel's forefinger in the trigger guard—backward, forward, sideways in a blur, finally executing a somersault and ending up neatly in its holster. Soon the novelty wore off and Tom dozed.

He didn't sleep comfortably, and not just because of concern for his fate. The wooden chair was hard and old, worn to a slick patina on the seat, and whenever he managed to find a position that didn't make his back ache or aggravate his injured rib, as soon as he lost consciousness he began to slip. Several times he awoke just in time to keep from sliding off. He'd gladly have stretched out on the floor, except it was a poured concrete slab and as hard as stone.

As night fell and Angel lit a kerosene lantern that spent the daylight hours on the floor beneath the table, the room grew cold, a desert phenomenon to which Tom, who sweated when he worked hard on the surface of a frozen lake, had yet to become accustomed; he hugged his arms and slid his chair closer to the table and the burning wick. Hours later—it must have been past midnight—the vibration of motors and crunching of tires on limestone outside announced that the reinforcements Riordan had ordered from Sacramento had arrived. Angel went out to greet them, locking the door behind him from the outside.

When after a few minutes the lock rattled again and the door opened, it was the Irishman who came through it. He looked refreshed. When he shrugged out of his overcoat and suitcoat, Tom noticed that he'd changed collars and cuffs, but wore the same red-and-white-striped shirt. He stood a flat pint of gin on the table. It was already missing an inch or two off the top of its contents, but then it was six miles to town.

"You look blue as Dublin harbor," he observed. "Better take a pull and warm up your biscuits."

Tom said, "I'm not much of a drinker."

"Who asked you? Milk's jake for cows, but they all come with leather coats. Go ahead, suck some down. Maybe God ain't looking." Chuckling, he jerked out the cork and thumped the bottle down on Tom's side of the table.

Tom sniffed at it, smelling junipers, then wiped the neck with his sleeve and sipped. The liquor brought a flush to his face as soon as he swallowed. He took another drink, slightly larger. He heard his pulse beating in his ears.

The pounding grew sharp. It was only when Riordan transferred the lantern from the table to a nail in the plaster wall and drew his ugly, short-barreled revolver from his underarm holster that Tom realized the noise was coming from outside. The Irishman lunged for the sliding bolt just as the door exploded off its hinges. It struck the Pinkerton man, pushing him back and flinging his gun arm to the side. Tom was getting up from his chair when the table went over. Riordan untangled his legs from those of the table and dove for the revolver where it had come to rest against a block wall. He scooped it up, but by then the giant who had broken through the door was inside and kicked it out of his hand. It was Yuri, huge and foreign in the woolen shirt, heavy canvas trousers, and knee-length lace-up boots he wore when he cut ice.

Propelled by the momentum of his kick, the big Ukrainian straddled the man on the floor, lifted him by the front of his shirt and shifted his grip, bending his left arm behind Riordan's neck and crossing his throat with the left. As he applied pressure, the Irishman's freckles disappeared into a red discoloration that quickly turned purple as he struggled to breathe, his fingers digging into Yuri's forearm. It was a maneuver Tom had witnessed before, when a fight erupted between sawyers; men from the Caucasus had employed it for centuries to kill their enemies in hand-to-hand combat.

"Yuri, stop!" Tom grabbed his friend's shoulders and pulled. He didn't budge. He was rooted to the spot, as immobile as a redwood.

The Irishman's strength was failing. His fingers had begun to slip. Only the whites of his eyes showed. His face was turning black.

"Yuri, it's Tom! I'm all right!" He tugged at Yuri's right arm with both hands.

Riordan's body went limp. The big man didn't relent.

"It's Dmitri! Dmitri, Yuri! I'm all right. I'm not hurt. Let go! Yuri, it's Dmitri!"

"Dmitri?"

The big man appeared to awaken from a troubling dream. He relaxed his grip. Riordan slid into a heap on the concrete floor.

Tom bent over him. He couldn't tell if the Pinkerton was breathing. He looked around. The room stank of gin; the bottle had smashed to the floor when the table fell. He spotted the cork lying in a puddle, picked it up, and held it beneath Riordan's nose, cradling his head with his other hand.

"Dmitri, are you really all right?"

He ignored Yuri. He slapped the Irishman's cheek once, twice, waved the cork under his nose again. Riordan's nostrils twitched. He grunted. "Better take a pull and warm up your biscuits," he muttered. "Maybe God ain't looking."

Tom dragged the Pinkerton's coat off his chair and bunched it behind his head to form a pillow. The man broke up strikes with ball bats and worried when his kidnap victim caught a chill.

As Tom rose, he heard more gunshots outside, men shouting, hoofbeats. It sounded like a Rocky shoot.

"What happened?" he asked Yuri. "How'd you find me?"

"I came with Quintana. He picked up Starling and me on the way."

"Quintana's here?"

"They're all here: Buck and Adele and the cowboys from the Watering Hole. You're sure you're not hurt?"

"I'm fine." Tom was barely listening. He was staring at the doorway and the bald old man standing outside it, the tips of his huge white moustaches extending beyond the frame. It was Esaul the Cossack, the oldest member of his father's crew of ice harvesters. He was holding a cant dog in both hands like a club.

"I forgot to mention your father's men," Yuri said. "They're here too. They were delivering ice at the ranch when Adele called."

"I still don't know how you found out this was where they were holding me."

"He didn't. Quintana did." It wasn't Yuri speaking.

Esaul was gone, out looking for someone upon whom to use his cant dog. Buck Bensinger came in. He was dressed as Tom had seen him last, in his dirty shirt and wrinkled whipcord trousers. His beard had grown out and his red hair was in tangles; but he was clear-eyed. His right fist was wrapped around the antique pistol he used to signal action when shooting outdoors.

"Quintana had a man following Wheelock," he said. "When that colored driver of his took him up here, he figured something was on and reported to his boss. Quintana wasn't sure what to do with it until Adele called the ranch and told him what Wheelock had told her. When we heard about the reservoir, Adele and I walked to the office and borrowed your Ford. It was a three-mile walk; it sobered me up. We caught up with the rest of the crew at the bottom of the hill. It was Quintana's bright idea to lie low and wait until late and the guards were sleepy before we raided. When the rest of the Pinkertons showed, we had to move fast, before they got settled in. You ought to have seen it, Tom. I couldn't have shot a better scene. I'm going to cast every one of those drunken cowboys and your father's icemen in one big feature. I want you to write it."

"What about Angel?" Tom asked.

The kaleidoscopic face went blank. "Angel's here?"

"He was guarding me most of the day. He must have slipped over the fence when you came through it."

"Through it is right. Those big ice trucks never saw the gate that could stand up to them. Let's get going, but keep your head down. We're still cleaning up."

The cool air smelled sweet after the kerosene atmosphere of the blockhouse. A three-quarter moon lit the hill as bright as morning. The surface of the reservoir gleamed like metal. The shooting had moved farther down the hill; it sounded like ice cracking. The blunt snouts and canvas-covered boxes of the trucks angled off in every direction, patiently awaiting the return of their drivers. Some of the motors were still running.

The truck Jerry Jarette had used to film the Fetterman chase had slued to a stop across the limestone drive. Buck's Civil War cannon stood in the box, its great barrel tilted down over the sideboards, aimed at the Cadillac touring car that had brought Tom there. Just as he spotted it, Ray Quintana and three of his men surrounded the car with guns and ordered the four men seated inside to come out with their hands up. When they obeyed, Tom recognized young Pollard and the rest of his kidnappers.

"It was Adele's idea to bring the big gun," Buck said. "We never did get the damn thing to work, but the Pinks didn't know that. Some detectives."

"Look out." Yuri threw an arm to stop Tom just as a lean cowboy in a shapeless Stetson galloped his horse past within a half-dozen yards, hanging off one side and firing a pistol under its belly. It was Chickamaw.

"Where *is* Adele?" Tom asked. "She shouldn't be here."

Buck laughed. "Who was going to stop her? I talked her into staying in the car."

"No, you didn't," Yuri said.

The Ukrainian had sharp eyes. Tom followed his gaze. He spotted Adele's starched white blouse in the moonlight near one of the trucks and opened his mouth to call out her name. He closed it when he saw Angel standing close behind her. The front of her body was stretched unnaturally taut, like a bow. She had one arm twisted behind her back.

"Buck!" The cry ended in a gasp. Angel had twisted harder.

"Shed the pistol, amigo," the deputy said. "I got a forty-five in the *puta*'s back and it don't like company."

Buck said, "It's over, Angel. *Finito*. Let her go."

"Like I told your boy, a fight don't end until somebody gives up or dies. Shed the pistol." A hammer clicked.

Buck dropped the revolver.

"This place is crawling with my men," he said. "If I had a camera I could shoot a picture. There's no place to go."

"There is once we climb up in this truck. We're going out the way you came in. It's up to you whether I turn your whore loose down the hill or fill her full of moonlight right here."

Yuri took a step forward. This time it was Tom who threw an arm in front of his friend. "He's serious."

"You're right about that, ice boy. I'm a serious man. *Muy sincero*." Angel backed toward the open cab of the truck, bringing Adele with him. Its motor drummed, idling.

Buck raised his voice. "You'd better hope so. If you get away from here and you don't turn her loose in one piece, there won't be a village in Mexico where you can hide from me."

"That's pretty good, amigo. You ought to save it for a title card." He stepped up onto the running board and bent his legs to hoist the woman. Adele twisted out of his grip, reached through the slit in her riding skirt, and came up with something that flashed in the cold light. As she swung it around, Angel screamed something in Spanish, grabbed at the arm holding the gun, and aimed it down at her.

A spot appeared on his shirt two inches to the left of his deputy's badge, black under the white moon. His feet slid forward and he sat down on the floor of the cab. Adele ran toward Buck, throwing away the knife.

Tom hadn't heard the crack of the rifle, only its echo as it rattled around among the foothills. He saw J. W. Starling when the others did, standing fifty yards away near the smashed gate, smoke twining from the muzzle of the lever-action carbine in his hands.

"Tin stars," he said, and spat a stream of tobacco at the white concrete of the reservoir. "Ain't nothing changed in this country since '98."

1948

End Title

Y ou couldn't pay me to live here," the cab driver said.

His passenger looked out his window at the medium-size houses lining Laurel Canyon Drive, the fluted cliffs rising protectively behind them with sprays of flowering bushes caught in the crevices. The lawns were neatly tended, and with the afternoon sun of a smog-free day buttery on the asphalt, the neighborhood looked as pleasant as the Andy Hardy set at MGM.

"What's wrong with it?" he asked.

"Rain, then not enough rain. When it comes down heavy in the spring, them bushes grow like jungle. Then the summer drought comes and they dry up like old straw. One spark and the whole damn canyon goes up. Every couple of years they get burned out, then they come right back and rebuild. Crazy."

"Fortunately, they're living in the one place where reason is a liability."

"That's for sure. Give me East L.A. anytime. I can protect myself from them spicks in their zoot suits. It don't help to cross the street when you see a firestorm coming."

He tipped the driver for the conversation and got out in front of a cheerful yellow house with blue shutters. The doorbell made a sunny kind of sound and a voice from inside told him to come in. He opened the screen door and stood for a moment in the cool dim of a living room done in Mexican rugs and white-painted furniture, waiting for his eyes to adjust.

"That you, Tom?" The voice came from a bright patch of arched doorway on the other side of a kiva-style fireplace. Someone had gone to some trouble to convert the interior from California Modern to the Old Southwest. It might have been a previous tenant.

"Dmitri," he corrected.

"Fuck that. I got enough trouble remembering the names that didn't change. I'm in the solarium."

The room ran the depth of the house, with crank-out windows over new nylon screens. Most of them were open, allowing a breeze to stir the flowering hydrangeae growing in terra-cotta jars and hanging baskets. There was a rattan sofa and a matching armchair and rocker covered in chintz, but they were unoccupied. His host sat in an old-fashioned wicker wheelchair in an out-at-the-elbows red dressing gown with a Mexican blanket drawn over his lap.

"Pipe that, solarium," said the man in the wheelchair. "Back in Jersey we called this a porch. I'm acclimating. Give me another thirty-six years and I'll pass as a native. How the hell are you, Tom?" He didn't extend his hand. The right half of his face remained immobile when he smiled. That eye drooped and he leaned a little in that direction, as if to free up his unaffected left side for action. The wild shock of hair had thinned on either side of the widow's peak and gone mostly white, but traces of faded red showed at the temples.

"I'm fine, Buck. How are you feeling?"

"Better, when you call me Buck. You're one of only two who call me that any more. Even the nurse calls me Arthur, in that shitty voice you use when you're talking to a little kid. Take a load off. What do you think of the place?"

"Very nice." He sat on the sofa.

"It's okay for a rental. I'd stay if I could. Rate goes up next month, after that I move to Tarzana. Third hike in two years. This keeps up there won't be nobody left living here but Arab oil sheiks and five-hundred-buck-a-day hookers."

"I wish you'd let me lend you some money."

"I'm okay, just pissing. You get to do that after fifty. That German bayonet at Chateau-Thierry pays the bills." He pushed back his hair. "Jesus, Tom, I'm glad you called. How long are you in town?"

"Just till tonight. I'm flying to Honolulu and then Tokyo. I'm looking at three blocks on the Ginza."

"Buying up all of California ain't enough for you, that it? You want Japan too." There was no animosity in his tone; rather, it was that of a proud father.

"I've sold off most of what I owned here. I'm still hanging on to that piece of the ranch I bought with what Yuri left me. Someone wants to put in a retirement resort."

"You made a nice piece of change when Famous Players bought Rocky. I should've hung on to what I had. I sold out all my shares to make that turkey *William the Conqueror*. I should've stuck to westerns. I would have if I hadn't caught the Griffith bug. I never could sit through *The Birth of a Nation*. Every three or four hours I have to get up and take a piss."

"I only held on to it out of respect for Yuri. I never thought it would be worth anything."

"Neither did he. If he was money smart he wouldn't have invested that string of coins in an outlaw operation."

"He knew how much it meant to me."

Yuri Yaroslavl had died while filming *Radcliffe of the Royal Mounted* in 1915. A misplaced tripwire, intended to throw a stunt rider's horse to the ground for a dramatic effect, had led to a fall that broke the Ukrainian's neck, killing him instantly. A week had passed before Tom learned his friend had made him the sole beneficiary of his will. Two months later, his investment in the Rocky Mountain Moving Picture Association tripled in value when a federal court ruled that no one man or group owned the patent to the moving picture process. The Trust was disbanded. Thomas Edison died in 1931, possibly unaware of the importance of his invention or the means that had been employed to protect it.

"Big Russian went through that door like a rockslide," Buck said. "I didn't figure him for that kind of fire."

"It was there, just well banked. The only other time it flared up, he had to leave Russia. You never know what's in a man. Remember Sheriff Peavey?"

"I'll never forget the look on your face when he drove that big Packard of his through the reservoir gate with Alvin Wheelock handcuffed to the door handle. I guess I had the same look on mine. Old Mutt. He lost his job when that Harding crowd got in. Last I heard he was company comptroller for a mining outfit in Butte." He fished a cigar and a steel lighter out of a pocket in his dressing gown.

"Does your doctor know you're still smoking?"

"He weighs three hundred pounds and married a woman half his age. He's busy keeping himself alive." He thumbed the wheel, but failed to get a spark. "Shit. If I'd known I was going to have a stroke I would've been left-handed."

"Let me." He leaned forward from the sofa, took the lighter, and struck a flame. He held it under the cigar.

Buck nodded his thanks and sat back, puffing blue clouds. "You hear about the Supreme Court? They're taking away the theaters from the studios. No more block booking. That's the end of the system."

"I suppose it was unfair to the independents."

"Fuck the indies. All they did was whine for the government to bail them out. We never waited for that. We fought the fuckers until they hollered uncle. We had them beat long before the courts came in on our side. Anyway, some things are worth a little monopoly, like comfortable seats. You hear what they're talking about now? Drive-in theaters. Pile the kiddies into the back of the station wagon in their jammies and roll on in and hang a tin speaker on your window. All the thrill of stopping for gas."

"They have to compete with television."

Buck flicked ashes at the tile floor. "I'm talking to some television guys, did I tell you that? They want to buy out my inventory."

"Do you have one?"

"I got fifteen cans in a refrigerator in the basement." He smiled with one-half of his face, the kaleidoscope partially intact. "Sorry. Guess I shouldn't mention refrigerators. They put your old man out of business."

"He didn't live to see it. I sold the last of the equipment to a museum last year. They want to set up a working exhibit while there are still some people around who know how to operate it. What's the program?"

"Something called *Snicker Flickers*. It runs Sundays. I don't have a set, so I haven't seen it."

"I have. They speed up the film and dub in cartoon voices. They play it for laughs."

Buck didn't seem to be listening. "I hope that silver nitrate held up all right in the fridge. It rots, you know. Ninety percent of all the stuff shot before 1930 is gone forever. You know why I liked westerns?"

"Adele said it was because the prospect of being able to start all over in a new place was so appealing."

"That's why people paid to see westerns, not why I made them. I did it for those old pioneers who had the good sense to carve their names into the sides of mountains. If they wanted to be remembered badly enough to take the time, I thought I ought to help. That's the problem with silver nitrate, with being the wrong kind of pioneer. No mountains."

The visitor looked at his wristwatch for the first time. The talk was beginning to depress him, not what he had wanted when he'd decided to look in on an old friend. "I read in *Variety* that Republic is making a picture about J. W. Starling. They cast Sterling Hayden."

"They never would've heard of him if I hadn't dug him up in the first place. Those sons of bitches on the parole board shot us in the ass. If we'd hung on to him, he'd be bigger than Tom Mix and Rocky would have survived *William the Conqueror*."

"Technically, gunning down Angel *was* a violation. They could have locked him up just for holding on to that Winchester all those years. *Yukon Jack* was still a good film with Yuri in the lead."

He didn't know how he felt about Starling's fate. Returned to San Quentin for an additional five years, the old bandit had died in the prison infirmary of influenza in 1917. At that time the walls of his cell were pasted over with clippings from newspapers as far away as New York City about the old-time desperado's last gunfight. He may have gone in as Shitbeetle in 1898, but a historical fraternal organization called the Sons of the Border paid to ship his body to a cemetery near McAlvoy, California, the scene of the Sacramento Northern holdup, and buried him in outlaw state under a red granite headstone identifying him as the last of the great badmen. Wyatt Earp had served as a pallbearer.

"You writing these days?" Buck asked.

He considered the question. "I keep a journal, but that's all. Someone may want to publish it after I'm dead, as a memento of the early days in Hollywood. It's the only absolutely original thing I ever wrote."

"They won't. Nobody cares about those days. Ask Griffith, chasing blondes and drinking a hole through his liver in that room of his at the Knickerbocker. He hasn't worked since '31. As far as the world's concerned, this business started with Valentino. I shot a dozen westerns before the little guinea left Italy to bus tables in California."

"I went to see Jerry last time I was in Paris. He's in a family crypt with a coat-of-arms above the door. There's nothing to indicate he worked in pictures."

"He's not buried there. He's buried in the Westinghouse in my basement."

They sat in silence for a while. Cars swished past, heading home from work. Tom rose.

"I have to go. There's not another plane out until tomorrow."

"You'd better catch it." Buck's cigar had gone out between his fingers, but he didn't appear to have noticed.

"I'll stop by on my way back."

"Thanks for coming, Tom. Dmitri," he corrected himself.

"Tom's okay."

A plump woman came in the front door as he was heading that way. He strode forward to help her with her sacks of groceries.

"Hello, Tom," Adele said. "I had a hunch Buck told me the wrong time. I think he wanted you all to himself."

"I didn't know you were living here." As soon as he said it he wished he could take it back. He didn't want to get Buck in trouble for failing to mention her.

"I'm not. Well, not yet. I just help out on days when the nurse is off." She led the way into the kitchen, a bright room with walls textured like pink adobe and blue-and-white Mexican tiles on the floor. He didn't know how he'd failed to detect Adele's hand in the decorating. When they put the sacks on a butcher-block counter, she turned to face him. "Stand back and let me see you. You look older."

"You don't," he said; and she didn't, though she'd put on weight and he suspected she colored her hair. She wore it shorter than she used to, no need to put it up with combs to keep it from throwing off halos under the kliegs. Her simple white frock, not as dressy as the starched blouses of old but just as becoming, showed off the smooth brown of her skin. She still painted her lips and nails bright red. The color was back in fashion but he had a hunch she'd never abandoned it.

"I saw a picture of you with Barbara Hutton in

Time magazine," she said. "Was that serious?"

"I was out with friends."

"You ought to get married, Tom. People talk otherwise."

"That's a small price to pay for freedom."

"You're not free." She lifted the cover off a pottery jar, took out makings, and built a cigarette. Without looking up she said, "We're going to try it again, Tom. Buck and me."

"I'm glad. Congratulations."

"I couldn't take it before. He was so bitter about being abandoned by the business. It abandoned me too, but he didn't think of that." She picked up a book of matches and lit the cigarette. "No, that's cruel. They never meant to me what they did to him. For a while I thought that if we could move away from California it wouldn't be so bad. But the movies are everywhere. I read where they even show them at the North Pole, to keep the men stationed there from going crazy."

"I read that too."

"I had to go. It didn't mean I didn't love him."

"I'm sure no one thought that."

"But things are different now," she said. "Back then he could take care of himself. He needs me, Tom. Just like before."

"Will you invite me to the wedding?"

"If you'll tell me where to send the invitation. You move around so much."

He had an idea. "Do you remember the address of Rocky's office downtown?"

"Of course. But they tore down the building years ago. There's a skyscraper there now, forty stories."

"I own it. Send the invitation there. It will reach me."

She came forward and tilted her face up to be kissed. He obliged. She smelled of exotic blossoms of which his mother, still living in the Queen Anne house in Ingot, would no doubt disapprove. After all these years she was still wearing the same perfume.

"Funny, isn't it? About the movies," she said.

"Everything about the movies is funny. Even the unfunny parts."

"I don't mean that. I mean my thinking we could escape them just by leaving California. You can't get away from the movies."

"That's our mountain," he said.